The Thrall of Leif the Lucky

Ottilie A. Liljencrantz

Table of Contents

The Thrall of Leif the Lucky

Ottilie A. Liljencrantz

Kessinger Publishing reprints thousands of hard–to–find books!

Visit us at http://www.kessinger.net

THE THRALL OF LEIF THE LUCKY

A Story of Viking Days

FOREWORD

THE Anglo–Saxon race was in its boyhood in the days when the Vikings lived. Youth's fresh fires burned in men's blood; the unchastened turbulence of youth prompted their crimes, and their good deeds were inspired by the purity and whole–heartedness and divine simplicity of youth. For every heroic vice, the Vikings laid upon the opposite scale an heroic virtue. If they plundered and robbed, as most men did in the times when Might made Right, yet the heaven–sent instinct of hospitality was as the marrow of their bones. No beggar went from their doors without alms; no traveller asked in vain for shelter; no guest but was welcomed with holiday cheer and sped on his way with a gift. As cunningly false as they were to their foes, just so superbly true were they to their friends. The man who took his enemy's last blood–drop with relentless hate, gave his own blood with an equally unsparing hand if in so doing he might aid the cause of some sworn brother. Above all, they were a race of conquerors, whose knee bent only to its proved superior. Not to the man who was king–born merely, did their allegiance go, but to the man who showed himself their leader in courage and their master in skill. And so it was with their choice of a religion, when at last the death–day of Odin dawned. Not to the God who forgives, nor to the God who suffered, did they give their faith; but they made their vows to the God who makes men strong, the God who is the never–dying and all–powerful Lord of those who follow Him.

The Thrall of Leif the Lucky

CHAPTER I. WHERE WOLVES THRIVE BETTER THAN LAMBS

```
Vices and virtues
The sons of mortals bear
In their breasts mingled;
No one is so good That no failing attends him,
Nor so bad as to be good for nothing.
     Ha'vama'l (High Song of Odin).
```

It was back in the tenth century, when the mighty fair–haired warriors of Norway and Sweden and Denmark, whom the people of Southern Europe called the Northmen, were becoming known and dreaded throughout the world. Iceland and Greenland had been colonized by their dauntless enterprise. Greece and Africa had not proved distant enough to escape their ravages. The descendants of the Viking Rollo ruled in France as Dukes of Normandy; and Saxon England, misguided by Ethelred the Unready and harassed by Danish pirates, was slipping swiftly and surely under Northern rule. It was the time when the priests of France added to their litany this petition: "From the fury of the Northmen, deliver us, good Lord."

The old, old Norwegian city of Trondhjem, which lies on Trondhjem Fiord, girt by the river Nid, was then King Olaf Trygvasson's new city of Nidaros, and though hardly more than a trading station, a hamlet without streets, it was humming with prosperity and jubilant life. The shore was fringed with ships whose gilded dragon–heads and purple–and–yellow hulls and azure–and–scarlet sails were reflected in the waves until it seemed as if rainbows had been melted in them. Hillside and river–bank bloomed with the gay tents of chieftains who had come from all over the North to visit the powerful Norwegian king. Traders had scattered booths of tempting wares over the plain, so that it looked like fair–time. The broad roads between the estates that clustered around the royal residence were thronged with clanking horsemen, with richly dressed traders followed by covered carts of precious merchandise, with beautiful fair–haired women riding on gilded chair–like saddles, with monks and slaves, with white–bearded lawmen and pompous landowners.

Along one of those roads that crossed the city from the west, a Danish warrior came riding, one keen May morning, with a young English captive tied to his saddle–bow.

The Thrall of Leif the Lucky

The Northman was a great, hulking, wild-maned, brute-faced fellow, capped by an iron helmet and wrapped in a mantle of coarse gray, from whose folds the handle of a battle-axe looked out suggestively; but the boy was of the handsomest Saxon type. Though barely seventeen, he was man-grown, and lithe and well-shaped; and he carried himself nobly, despite his clumsy garments of white wool. His gold-brown hair had been clipped close as a mark of slavery, and there were fetters on his limbs; but chains could not restrain the glance of his proud gray eyes, which flashed defiance with every look.

Crossing the city northward, they came where a trading-booth stood on its outskirts—an odd looking place of neatly built log walls tented over with gay striped linen. Beyond, the plain rose in gentle hills, which were overlooked in their turn by pine-clad snow-capped mountains. On one side, the river hurried along in surging rapids; on the other, one could see the broad elbow of the fiord glittering in the sun. At the sight of the booth, the Saxon scowled darkly, while the Dane gave a grunt of relief. Drawing rein before the door, the warrior dismounted and pulled down his captive.

It was a scene of barbaric splendor that the gay roof covered. The walls displayed exquisitely wrought weapons, and rare fabrics interwoven with gleaming gold and silver threads. Piles of rich furs were heaped in the corners, amid a medley of gilded drinking-horns and bronze vessels and graceful silver urns. Across the back of the booth stretched a benchful of sullen-looking creatures war-captives to be sold as slaves, native thralls, and two Northmen enslaved for debt. In the centre of the floor, seated upon one of his massive steel-bound chests, gorgeous in velvet and golden chains, the trader presided over his sales like a prince on his throne.

The Dane saluted him with a surly nod, and he answered with such smooth words as the thrifty old Norse proverbs advise every man to practise.

"Greeting, Gorm Arnorsson! Here is great industry, if already this Spring you have gone on a Viking voyage and gotten yourself so good a piece of property! How came you by him?"

Gorm gave his "property" a rough push forward, and his harsh voice came out of his bull-thick neck like a bellow. "I got him in England last Summer. We ravaged his lather's castle, I and twenty ship-mates, and slew all his kinsmen. He comes of good blood; I am told for certain that he is a jarl's son. And I swear he is sound in wind and limb. How

4

much will you pay me for him, Karl Grimsson?"

The owner of the booth stroked his long white beard and eyed the captive critically. It seemed to him that he had never seen a king's son with a haughtier air. The boy wore his letters as though they had been bracelets from the hands of Ethelred.

"Is it because you value him so highly that you keep him in chains?" he asked.

"In that I will not deceive you," said the Dane, after a moment's hesitation. "Though he is sound in wind and limb, he is not sound in temper. Shortly after I got him, I sold him to Gilli the Wealthy for a herd–boy; but because it was not to his mind on the dairy–farm, he lost half his herd and let wolves prey on the rest, and when the headman would have flogged him for it, he slew him. He has the temper of a black elf."

"He does not look to be a cooing dove," the trader assented. "But how came it that he was not slain for this? I have heard that Gilli is a fretful man."

The Dane snorted. "More than anything else he is greedy for property, and his wife Bertha advised him not to lose the price he had paid. It is my belief that she has a liking for the cub; she was an English captive before the Wealthy One married her. He followed her advice, as was to be expected, and saddled me with the whelp when I passed through the district yesterday. I should have sent him to Thor myself," he added with a suggestive swing of his axe, "but that silver is useful to me also. I go to join my shipmates in Wisby. And I am in haste, Karl Grimsson. Take him, and let me have what you think fair."

It seemed as if the trader would never finish the meditative caressing of his beard, but at last he arose and called for his scales. The Dane took the little heap of silver rings weighed out to him, and strode out of the tent. At the same time, he passed out of the English boy's life. What a pity that the result of their short acquaintance could not have disappeared with him!

The trader surveyed his new possession, standing straight and slim before him. "What are you called?" he demanded. "And whence come you? And of what kin?"

"I am called Alwin," answered the thrall; "and I come from Northumbria." He hesitated, and the blood mounted to his face. "But I will not tell you my father's name," he finished proudly, "that you may shame him in shaming me."

The trader's patience was a little chafed. Peaceful merchants were also men of war between times in those days.

Suddenly he unsheathed the sword that hung at his side, and laid its point against the thrall's breast.

"I ask you again of what kin you come. If you do not answer now, it is unlikely that you will be alive to answer a third question."

Perhaps young Alwin's bronzed cheeks lost a little of their color, but his lip curled scornfully. So they stood, minute after minute, the sharp point pricking through the cloth until the boy felt it against his skin.

Gradually the trader's face relaxed into a grim smile. "You are a young wolf," he said at last, sheathing his weapon; "yet go and sit with the others. It may be that wolves thrive better than lambs in the North."

CHAPTER II. THE MAID IN THE SILVER HELMET

```
In a maiden's words
No one should place faith,
Nor in what a woman says;
For on a turning wheel
Have their hearts been formed,
And guile in their breasts been laid.
    Ha'vama'l
```

Day after day, week after week, Alwin sat waiting to see where the next turn of misfortune's wheel would land him. Interesting people visited the booth continually. Now it was a party of royal guardsmen to buy weapons,—splendid mail-clad giants who ate at King Olaf's board, slept a his hall, and fought to the death at his side. Again it was a minstrel, with a harp at his back, who stopped to rest and exchange a song for a horn of mead. Once the Queen herself, riding in a shining gilded wagon, came in and bought some of the graceful spiral bracelets. She said that Alwin's eyes were as bright as a young serpent's; but she did not buy him.

The Thrall of Leif the Lucky

The doorway framed an ever changing picture,—budding birch trees along the river–bank; men ploughing in the valley; shepherds tending flocks that looked like dots of cotton wool on the green hillsides. Sometimes bands of gay folk from the King's house rode by to the hunt, spurs jingling, horns braying, falcons at their wrists. Sometimes brawny followers of the visiting chiefs swaggered past in groups, and the boy could hear their shouting and laughter as they held drinking–bouts in the hostelry near by. Occasionally their rough voices would grow rougher, and an arrow would fly past the door; or there would be a clash of weapons, followed by a groan.

One day, as Alwin sat looking out, his chin resting in his hand, his elbow on his knee, his attention was caught by two riders winding swiftly down a hill–path on the right. At first, one was only a blur of gray and the other a flame of scarlet; they disappeared behind a grove of aspens, then reappeared nearer, and he could make out a white beard on the gray figure and a veil of golden hair above the scarlet kirtle. What hair for a boy, even the noblest born! It was the custom of all free men to wear their locks uncut; but this golden mantle! Yet could it be a girl? Did a girl ever wear a helmet like a silver bowl, and a kirtle that stopped at the knee? If it was a girl, she must be one of those shield–maidens of whom the minstrels sang. Alwin watched the pair curiously as they galloped down the last slope and turned into the lane beside the river. They must pass the booth, and then...

His brain whirled, and he stood up in his intense interest. Something had startled the white steed that bore the scarlet kirtle; he swerved aside and rose on his haunches with a suddenness that nearly unseated his rider; then he took the bronze bit between his teeth and leaped forward. Whitebeard and his bay mare were left behind. The yellow hair streamed out like a banner; nearer, and Alwin could see that it was indeed a girl. She wound her hands in the reins and kept her seat like a centaur. But suddenly something gave way. Over she went, sidewise; and by the wrist, tangled in the reins, the horse dragged her over the stony road.

Forgetting his manacled limbs, Alwin started forward; but it was all over in an instant. One of the trader's servants flew at the animal's head and stopped him, almost at the door of the booth. In another moment a crowd gathered around the fallen girl and shut her from his view. Alwin gazed at the shifting backs with a dreadful vision of golden hair torn and splashed with blood. She must be dead, for she had not once screamed. His head was still ringing with the shrieks of his mother's waiting–women, as the Danes bore them out of the burning castle.

The Thrall of Leif the Lucky

Whitebeard came galloping up, puffing and panting. He was a puny little German, with a face as small and withered as a winter apple, but a body swaddled in fur–trimmed tunics until it seemed as fat as a polar bear's. He rolled off his horse; the crowd parted before him. Then the English youth experienced another shock.

Bruised and muddy, but neither dead nor fainting, the girl stood examining her wrist with the utmost calmness. Though her face was white and drawn with pain, she looked up at the old man with a little twisted smile.

"It is nothing, Tyrker," she said quickly; "only the girth broke, and it appears that my wrist is out of joint. We will go in here, and you shall set it."

Tyrker blinked at her for a moment with an expression of mingled affection and wonder; then he drew a deep breath. "Donnerwetter, but you are a true shield–maiden!" he said in a wavering treble.

The trader received them with true Norse hospitality; and Alwin watched in speechless amazement while the old man ripped up the scarlet sleeve and wrenched the dislocated bones into position, without a murmur from the patient. Despite her strange dress and general dishevelment, he could see now that she was a beautiful girl, a year or two younger than himself. Her face was as delicately pink–and–pearly as a sea–shell, and corn–flowers among the wheat were no bluer than the eyes that looked out from under her rippling golden tresses.

When the wrist was set and bandaged, the trader presented them with a silken scarf to make into a sling, and had them served with horns of sparkling mead. This gave a turn to the affair that proved of special interest to Alwin. There is an old Norse proverb which prescribes "Lie for lie, laughter for laughter, gift for gift;" so, while he accepted these favors, Tyrker began to look around for some way to repay them.

His gaze wandered over fabrics and furs and weapons, till it finally fell upon the slaves' bench. "Donnerwetter!" he said, setting down his horn. "To my mind it has just come that Leif a cook–boy is desirous of, now that Hord is drowned."

The girl saw his purpose, and nodded quickly. "It is unlikely that you can make a better bargain anywhere."

The Thrall of Leif the Lucky

She turned to examine the slaves, and her eyes immediately encountered Alwin's. She did not blush; she looked him up and down critically, as if he were a piece of armor, or a horse. It was he who flushed, with sudden shame and anger, as he realized that in the eyes of this beautiful Norse maiden he was merely an animal put up for sale.

"Yonder is a handsome thrall," she said; "he looks as though his strength were such that he could stand something."

"True it is that he cannot a lame wolf be who with the pack from Greenland is to run," Tyrker assented. "That it was, which to Hord was a hindrance. For sport only, Egil Olafson under the water took him down and held him there; and because to get away he was not strong enough, he was drowned. But to me it seems that this one would bite. How dear would this thrall be?"

"You would have to pay for him three marks of silver," said the trader. "He is an English thrall, very strong and well-shaped." He came over to where Alwin sat, and stood him up and turned him round and bent his limbs, Alwin submitting as a caged tiger submits to the lash, and with much the same look about his mouth.

Tyrker caught the look, and sat for a long while blinking doubtfully at him. But he was a shrewd old fellow, and at last he drew his money-bag from his girdle and handed it to the trader to be weighed. While this was being done, he bade one of the servants strike off the boy's fetters.

The trader paused, scales in hand, to remonstrate. "It is my advice that you keep them on until you sail. I will not conceal it from you that he has an unruly disposition. You will be lacking both your man and your money."

The old man smiled quietly. "Ach, my friend," he said, "can you not better read a face? Well is it to be able to read runes, but better yet it is to know what the Lord has written in men's eyes." He signed to the servant to go on, and in a moment the chains fell clattering on the ground.

Alwin looked at him in amazement; then suddenly he realized what a kind old face it was, for all its shrewdness and puny ugliness. The scowl fell from him like another chain.

9

"I give you thanks," he said.

The wrinkled, tremulous old hand touched his shoulder with a kindly pressure. "Good is it that we understand each other. _Nun_! Come. First shall you go and Helga's horse lead, since it may be that with her one hand she cannot manage him. Why do you in your face so red grow?"

Alwin grew still redder; but he could not tell the good old man that he would rather follow a herd of unbroken steers all day, than walk one mile before a beautiful young Amazon who looked at him as if he were a dog. He mumbled something indistinctly, and hastened out after the horses.

Helga rose stiffly from the pile of furs; it was evident that every new motion revealed a new bruise to her, but she set her white teeth and held her chin high in the air. When she had taken leave of the trader, she walked out without a limp and vaulted into her saddle unaided. The sunlight, glancing from her silver helm, fell upon her floating hair and turned it into a golden glory that hid rents and stains, and redeemed even the kirtle, which stopped at the knee.

As he helped the old man to mount, Alwin gazed at her with unwilling admiration. Perhaps some day he would show her that he was not so utterly contemptible as...

She made him an imperious gesture; he stalked haughtily forward, he took his place at her bridle rein, and the three set forth.

CHAPTER III. A GALLANT OUTLAW

```
Two are adversaries;
The tongue is the bane of the head;
Under every cloak
I expect a hand.
     Ha'vama'l
```

For a while the road of the little party ran beside the brawling Nid, whose shores were astir with activity and life. Here was a school of splashing swimmers; there, a fleet of fishing-smacks; a provision-ship loading for a cruise as consort to one of the great war vessels. They passed King Olaf's ship–sheds, where fine new boats were building, and one brilliantly–painted cruiser stood on the rollers all ready for the launching. Along the opposite bank lay the camps of visiting Vikings, with their long ships'–boats floating before them.

The road bent to the right, and wound along between the high fences that shut in the old farm–like manors. Ail the houses had their gable–ends faced to the front, like soldiers at drill, and little more than their tarred roofs showed among the trees. Most of the commons between the estates were enlivened by groups of gaily–ornamented booths. Many of them were traders' stalls; but in one, over the heads of the laughing crowd, Alwin caught a glimpse of an acrobat and a clumsy dancing bear; while in another, a minstrel sang plaintive love ballads to a throng that listened as breathlessly as leaves for a wind. The wild sweet harp–music floated out and went with them far across the plain.

The road swerved still farther to the right, entering a wood of spicy evergreens and silver–stemmed birches. In its green depths song–birds held high carnival, and an occasional rabbit went scudding from hillock to covert. From the south a road ran up and crossed theirs, on its way to the fiord.

As they reached this cross–road, a horseman passed down it at a gallop. He only glanced toward them; and all Alwin had time to see was that he was young and richly dressed. But Helga started up with a cry.

"Sigurd! Tyrker, it was Sigurd!"

Slowly drawing rein, the old man blinked at her in bewilderment. "Sigurd? Where? What Sigurd?"

"Our Sigurd—Leif's foster–son! Oh, ride after him! Shout!" She stretched her white throat in calling, but the wind was against her.

"That is now impossible that Jarl Harald's son it should be," Tyrker said soothingly. "On a Viking voyage he is absent. Besides, out of breath it puts me fast to ride. Some one else have you mistaken. Three years it has been since you have seen—"

"Then I will go myself!" She snatched the reins from Alwin, but Tyrker caught her arm.

11

"Certain it is that you would be injured. If you insist, the thrall shall go. He looks as though he would run well."

"But what message?" Alwin began.

Helga tried to stamp in her stirrups. "Will you stand there and talk? Go!"

They were fast runners in those days, by all accounts. It is said that there were men in Ireland and the North so swift−footed that no horse could overtake them. In ten minutes Alwin stood at the horseman's side, red, dripping, and furious.

The stranger was a gallant young cavalier, with floating yellow locks and a fine high−bred face. His velvet cloak was lined with ermine, his silk tunic seamed with gold; he had gold embroidery on his gloves, silver spurs to his heels, and a golden chain around his neck. Alwin glared up at him, and hated him for his splendor, and hated him for his long silken hair.

The rider looked down in surprise at the panting thrall with the shaven head.

"What is your errand with me?" he asked.

It was not easy to explain, but Alwin framed it curtly: "If you are Sigurd Haraldsson, a maiden named Helga is desirous that you should turn back."

"I am Sigurd Haraldsson," the youth assented, "but I know no maiden in Norway named Helga."

It occurred to Alwin that this Helga might belong to "the pack from Greenland," but he kept a surly silence.

"What is the rest of her name?"

"If there is more, I have not heard it."

"Where does she live?"

The Thrall of Leif the Lucky

"The devil knows!"

"Are you her father's thrall?"

"It is my bad luck to be the captive of some Norse robber."

The straight brows of the young noble slanted into a frown. Alwin met it with a black scowl. Suddenly, while they faced each other, glowering, an arrow sped out of the thicket a little way down the road, and whizzed between them. A second shaft just grazed Alwin's head; a third carried away a tress of Sigurd's fair hair. Instantly after, a man crashed out of the underbrush and came running toward them, throwing down a bow and drawing a sword as he ran.

Forgetting that no weapon hung there now, Alwin's hand flew to his side. Young Haraldsson, catching only the gesture, stayed him peremptorily.

"Stand back,—they were aimed at me! It is my quarrel." He threw himself from his saddle, and his blade flashed forth like a sunbeam.

Evidently there was no need of explanations between the two. The instant they met, that instant their swords crossed; and from the first clash, the blades darted back and forth and up and down like governed lightnings. Alwin threw a quieting arm around the neck of the startled horse, and settled himself to watch.

Before many minutes, he forgot that he had been on the point of quarrelling with Sigurd Haraldsson. Anything more deft or graceful than the swiftness and ease with which the young noble handled his weapon he had never imagined. Admiration crowded out every other feeling.

"I hope that he will win!" he muttered presently. "By St. George, I hope that he will win!" and his soothing pats on the horse's neck became frantic slaps in his excitement.

The archer was not a bad fighter, and just now he was a desperate fighter. Round and round went the two. A dozen times they shifted their ground; a dozen times they changed their modes of attack and defence. At last, Sigurd's weapon itself began to change from one hand to the other. Without abating a particle of his swiftness, in the hottest of the fray he made a feint with his left. Before the other could recover from parrying it, the weapon leaped back to his right, darted like a hissing snake at the opening, and pierced the archer's shoulder.

He fell, snarling, and lay with Sigurd's point pricking his throat and Sigurd's foot pressing his breast.

"I think you understand now that you will not stand over my scalp," young Haraldsson said sternly. "Now you have got what you deserved. You managed to get me banished, and you shot three arrows at me to kill me; and all because of what? Because in last fall's games I shot better than you! It was in my mind that if ever I caught you I would drive a knife through you."

He kicked him contemptuously as he took his foot away.

"Sneaking son of a wolf," he finished, "I despise myself that I cannot find it in my heart to do it, now that you are at my mercy; but I have not been wont to do such things, and you are not worth beginning on. Crawl on your miserable way."

While the archer staggered off, clutching his shoulder, Sigurd came back to his horse, wiping his sword composedly. "It was obliging of you to stay and hold High—flyer," he said, as he mounted. "If he had been frightened away, I should have been greatly hindered, for I have many miles before me."

That brought them suddenly back to their first topic; but now Alwin handled it with perfect courtesy.

"Let me urge you again to turn back with me. It is not easy for me to answer your questions, for this morning is the first time I have seen the maiden; but she is awaiting you at the cross—roads with the old man she calls Tyrker, and—"

"Tyrker!" cried Sigurd Haraldsson. "Leif's foster—father had that name. It is not possible that it is my little foster—sister from Greenland!"

"I have heard them mention Greenland, and also the name of Leif," Alwin assured him.

14

The Thrall of Leif the Lucky

Sigurd smote his knee a resounding thwack. "Strangest of wonders is the time at which this news comes! Here have I just been asking for Leif in the guardroom of the King's house; and because they told me he was away on the King's business, I was minded to ride straight out of the city. Catch hold of the strap on my saddle−girth, and we will hurry."

He wheeled Highflyer and spurred him forward. Alwin would not make use of the strap, but kept his place at the horse's shoulder without much difficulty. Only the pace did not leave him breath for questions, and he wished to ask a number.

It was not long, however, before most of his questions were asked and answered for him. Rounding a curve, they came face to face with the riders, who had evidently tired of waiting at the cross−roads. Tyrker, peering anxiously ahead, uttered an exclamation of relief at the sight of Alwin, whom he had evidently given up as a runaway. Helga welcomed Sigurd in a delighted cry.

The young Northman greeted her with frank affection, and saluted Tyrker almost as fondly.

"This meeting gladdens me more than tongue can tell. I do not see how it was that I did not recognize you as I passed. And yet those garments, Helga! By St. Michael, you look well−fitted to be the Brynhild we used to hear about!"

Helga's fair face flushed, and Alwin smiled inwardly. He was curious to know what the young Viking would do if the young Amazon boxed his ears, as he thought likely. But it seemed that Helga was only ungentle toward those whom she considered beneath her friendliness. While she motioned Alwin with an imperious gesture to hand her the rein she had dropped, she responded good−naturedly to Sigurd: "Nay, now, my comrade, you will not be mean enough to scold about my short kirtle, when it was you who taught me to do the things that make a short kirtle necessary! Have you forgotten how you used to steal me away from my embroidery to hunt with you?"

"By no means," Sigurd laughed. "Nor how Thorhild scolded when we came back! I would give a ring to know what she would say if she were here now. It is my belief that you would get a slap, for all your warlike array."

The Thrall of Leif the Lucky

Helga's spur made her horse prance and rear defiantly. "Thorhild is not here, nor do I expect that she will ever rule over me again. She struck me once too often, and I ran away to Leif. For two years now I have lived almost like the shield–maidens we were wont to talk of. Oh, Sigurd, I have been so happy!" She threw back her head and lifted her beautiful face up to the sunlit sky and the fresh wind. "So free and so happy!"

Alwin thrilled with sudden sympathy. He understood then that it was not boldness, nor mere waywardness, that made her what she was. It was the Norse blood crying out for adventure and open air and freedom. It did not seem strange to him, as he thought of it. It occurred to him, all at once, as a stranger thing that all maidens did not feel so,—that there were any who would be kept at spinning, like prisoners fettered in trailing gowns.

Tyrker nodded in answer to Sigurd's look of amazement. "The truth it is which the child speaks. Over winters, stays she at the King's house with one of the Queen's women, who is a friend of Leif; and during the summer, voyages she makes with me. But to me it appears that of her we have spoken enough. Tell to us how it comes that you are in Norway, and—whoa! Steady!—Wh—o—a!"

"And tell us also that you will ride on to the camp with us now," Helga put in, as Tyrker was obliged to transfer his attention to his restless horse. "Rolf Erlingsson and Egil Olafsson, whom you knew in Greenland, are there, and all the crew of the 'Sea–Deer'."

"The 'Sea–Deer'!" ejaculated Sigurd. "Surely Leif has got rid of his ship, now that he is in King Olaf's guard."

The backing and sidling and prancing of Tyrker's horse forced him to leave this also to Helga.

"Certainly he has not got rid of his ship. When he does not follow King Olaf to battle with her, Tyrker takes her on trading voyages, and she lies over–winter in the King's ship–shed. There are forty of the crew, counting me,—there is no need for you to smile, I can take the helm and stand a watch as well as any. Can I not, Tyrker?"

The old man relaxed his vigilance long enough to nod assent; whereupon his horse took instant advantage of the slackened rein to bolt off homeward, despite all the swaying and sawing of the rider.

16

That set the whole party in motion once more.

"You will come with me to camp, Sigurd my comrade?" Helga urged. "It is but a little way, on the bank across the river. Come, if only for a short time."

Sigurd gathered up his rein with a smile and a sigh together. "I will give you a favorable answer to that. It seems that you have not heard of the mishap that has befallen me. The lawman has banished me from the district."

It pleased Alwin to hear that he was likely to see more of the young Norseman. Helga was filled with amazement. On the verge of starting, she stopped her horse to stare at him.

"It must be that you are jesting," she said at last. "You, who are the most amiable person in the world,—it is not possible that you can have broken the law!"

Sigurd laughed ruefully. "In my district I am not spoken of as amiable, just now. Yet there is little need to take it heavily, my foster-sister. I have done nothing that is dishonorable,—should I dare to come before Leif's face if I had? It will blow over in time to come."

Helga leaned from her saddle to press his hand in a friendly grasp. "You have come to the right place, for nowhere in the world could you be more welcome. Only wait and see how Rolf and Egil will receive you!"

She gave the thrall a curt shake of her head, as he stepped to her bridle-rein; and they rode off.

As Helga had said, the camp was not far away. Once across the river, they turned to the left and wound along the rolling woody banks toward the fiord. Entering a thicket of hazel-bushes on the crest of the gentle slope, they were met by faint sounds of shouting and laughter. Emerging into a green little valley, the camp lay before them.

Half a dozen wooden booths tented over with gay striped linen and adorned with streaming flags, a leaping fire, a pile of slain deer, a string of grazing horses, and a throng of brawny men skinning the deer, chasing the horses, scouring armor, drinking, wrestling, and lounging,—these were Alwin's first confused impressions.

"There it is!" cried Helga. "Saw you ever a prettier spot? There is Tyrker under that ash tree. And there,—do you remember that black mane? Yonder, bending over that shield? That is Egil Olafsson. Now it comes to my mind again! To-night we go to a feast at the King's house; that is why he is so busy. And yonder! Yonder is Rolf wrestling. He is the strongest man in Greenland; did you know that? Even Valbrand cannot stand against him. Whistle now as you were wont to for the hawks, and see if they will not remember."

They swept down the slope, the high sweet notes rising clear above the clatter. One man glanced up in surprise, then another and another; then suddenly every man dropped what he was doing, and leaped up with shouts of greeting and welcome. Sigurd disappeared behind a hedge of yellow heads and waving hands.

Alwin felt himself clutched eagerly. "Donnerwetter, but I have waited a long time for you!" said the old German, short-breathed and panting. "That beast was like the insides of me to have out-shaken. Bring to me a horn of ale; but first give me your shoulder to yonder booth."

CHAPTER IV. IN A VIKING LAIR

```
Leaving in the field his arms,
Let no man go
A fool's length forward:
For it is hard to know
When, on his way,
A man may need his weapon.
    Ha'vama'l
```

The camp lay red in the sunset light, and the twilight hush had fallen upon it so that one could hear the sleepy bird-calls in the woods around, and the drowsy murmur of the river. Sigurd lay on his back under a tree, staring up into the rustling greenery. From the booth set apart for her, Helga came out dressed for the feast. She had replaced her scarlet kirtle and hose by garments of azure-blue silk, and changed her silver helmet for a golden diadem such as high-born maidens wore on state occasions; but that was her only ornament, and her skirt was no longer than before. Sigurd looked at her critically.

The Thrall of Leif the Lucky

"It does not appear to me that you are very well dressed for a feast," said he. "Where are the bracelets and gold laces suitable to your rank? It looks ill for Leif's generosity, if that is the finest kirtle you own."

"That is unfairly spoken," Helga answered quickly. "He would dress me in gold if I wished it; it is I who will not have it so. Have you forgotten my hatred against clothes so fine that one must be careful of them? But this was to be expected," she added, flushing with displeasure; "since the Jarl's son has lived in Normandy, a maiden from a Greenland farm must needs look mean to him."

She was turning away, but he leaped up and caught her by her shoulders and shook her good−naturedly. "Now are you as womanish as your bondmaid. You know that all the gold on all the women in Normandy is not so beautiful as one lock of this hair of yours."

At least Helga was womanish enough to smile at this. "Now I understand why it is that men call you Sigurd Silver−Tongue," she laughed. Suddenly she was all earnestness again. "Nay, but, Sigurd, tell me this,—I do not care how you scold about my dress,—tell me that you do not despise me for it, or for being unlike other maidens."

Sigurd's grasp slipped from her shoulders down to her hands, and shook them warmly. "Despise you, Helga my sister? Despise you for being the bravest comrade and the truest friend a man ever had?"

She grew rosy red with pleasure. "If that is your feeling, I am well content."

She took a step toward the place where her horse was tethered, and looked back regretfully. "It seems inhospitable to leave you like this. Will you not come with us, after all?"

Sigurd threw himself down again with an emphatic gesture of refusal. "I like better to be left so than to be left in a mound with my head cut off, which is what would happen were an outlaw to visit the King uninvited."

"I shall not deny that that would be disagreeable," Helga assented. "But do not let your mishap stand in the way of your joy. Leif has great favor with King Olaf; there is no doubt in my mind that he will be able to plead successfully for you."

19

"I hope so, with all my heart," Sigurd murmured. "When all brave men are fighting abroad or serving the King at home, it is great shame for me to be idling here." And he sighed heavily as Helga passed out of hearing.

As she went by the largest of the booths, which was the sleeping–house of the steersman Valbrand and more than half the crew, Alwin came out of the door and stood looking listlessly about. He had spent the afternoon scouring helmets amid a babble of directions and fault–finding, accented by blows. Helga did not see him; but he gazed after her, wondering idly what sort of a mistress she was to the young bond–girl who was running after her with the cloak she had forgotten,—wondering also what there was in the girl's brown braids that reminded him of his mother's little Saxon waiting–maid Editha.

The sound of a deep–drawn breath made him turn, to find himself face to face with a young mail–clad Viking, in whose shaggy black locks he recognized the Egil Olafsson whom Helga had that morning 'pointed out. But it was not the surprise of the meeting that made Alwin leap suddenly backward into the shelter of the doorway; it was the look that he caught in the other's dark face,—a look so full of hate and menace that, instead of being strangers meeting for the first time, one would have supposed them lifelong enemies.

Still eying him, Egil said slowly in a voice that trembled with passion: "So you are the English thrall,—and looking after her already! It seems that Skroppa spoke some truth—" He broke off abruptly, and stood glaring, his hand moving upward to his belt.

For once Alwin was fairly dazed. "Either this fellow has gotten out of his wits," he muttered, crossing himself, "or else he has mistaken me for some—"

He had not time to finish his sentence. Young Olafsson's fingers had closed upon the haft of his knife; he drew it with a fierce cry: "But I will make the rest of it a lie!" Throwing himself upon Alwin, he bore him over backwards across the threshold.

It is likely that that moment would have seen the end of Alwin, if it had not happened that Valbrand the steersman was in the booth, arraying himself for the feast. He was a gigantic warrior, with a face seamed with scars and as hard as the battle–axe at his side. He caught Egil's uplifted arm and wrested the blade from his grasp.

20

The Thrall of Leif the Lucky

"It is not likely that I will allow Leif's property to be damaged, Egil the Black. Would you choke him? Loose him, or I will send you to the Troll, body and bones!"

Egil rose reluctantly. Alwin leaped up like a spring released from a weight.

"What has he done," demanded Valbrand, "that you should so far forget the law as to attack another man's thrall?"

Instead of bursting into the tirade Alwin expected, Egil flushed and looked away. "It is enough that I am not pleased with his looks," he said sullenly.

Valbrand tossed him his knife with a scornful grunt. "Go and get sense! Is he yours, that you may slay him because you dislike the tilt of his nose? Go dress yourself. And you," he added, with a nod over his shoulder at Alwin, "do you take yourself out of his sight somewhere. It is unwisdom to tempt a hungry dog with meat that one would keep."

"If I had so much as a hunting–knife," Alwin cried furiously, "I swear by all the saints of England, I would not stir—"

Valbrand wasted no time in argument. He seized Alwin and threw him out of the door, with energy enough to roll him far down the slope.

The force with which he struck inclined Alwin to stay where he was for a while; and gradually the coolness and the quietness about him soothed him into a more reasonable temper. Egil Olafsson was mad; there could be no question of that. Undoubtedly it was best to follow Valbrand's advice and keep out of his way,—at least until he could secure a weapon with which to defend himself. He stretched himself comfortably in the soft, dewy grass and waited until the revellers, splendid in shining mail and gay–hued mantles, clanked out to their horses and rode away. When the last of them shouted his farewell to Sigurd and disappeared amid the shadows of the wood–path, Alwin arose and walked slowly back to the deserted camp.

Even the sunset light had left it now; a soft grayness shut it in, away from the world. The air was full of night–noises; and high in the pines a breeze was whispering softly. Very softly and sweetly, from somewhere among the booths, the voice of the bond–girl arose in a plaintive English ballad.

The Thrall of Leif the Lucky

Alwin recognized the melody with a throb that was half of pleasure, half of pain. In the old days, Editha had sung that song. Poor little gentle–hearted Editha! The last time he had seen her, she had been borne past him, white and unconscious, in the arms of one of the marauding Danes. He shook himself fiercely to drive off the memory. Turning the corner of Helga's booth, he came suddenly upon the singer, a slender white–robed figure leaning in the shadow of the doorway. Sigurd still lounged under the trees, half dozing, half listening.

As the thrall stepped out of the shadow into the moonlight, the singer sprang to her feet, and the song merged into a great cry.

"My lord Alwin!"

It was Editha herself. Running to meet him, she dropped on her knees before him and began to kiss his hands and cry over them. "Oh, my dear lord," she sobbed, "you are so changed! And your hair—your beautiful hair! Oh, it is well that Earl Edmund and your lady mother are dead,—it would break their hearts, as it does mine!" Forgetting her own plight, she wept bitterly over his, though he tried with every gentle word to soothe her.

It was a sad meeting; it could not be otherwise. The memory of their last terrible parting, the bondage in which they found each other, the shameful, hopeless future that stretched before them,—it was all full of bitterness. When Editha went in at last, her poor little throat was bursting with sobs. Alwin sank down on the trunk of a fallen tree and buried his head in his hands, and the first groan that his troubles had wrung from him was forced now from his brave lips.

He had forgotten Sigurd's presence. In their preoccupation, neither of them had noticed the young Viking watching them curiously. Now Alwin started like a colt when a hand fell lightly on his shoulder. "It appears to me," came in Sigurd's voice, "that a man should be merry when he has just found a friend."

Alwin looked up at him with eyes full of savage despair.

"Merry! Would you be merry, had you found Helga the drudge of an English camp?" He shook off the other's hand with a fierce motion.

22

But Sigurd answering instantly, "No, I would look even blacker than you, if that were possible," the thrall was half appeased.

The young Viking dropped down beside him, and for a while they sat in silence, staring away where the moonlit river showed between the trees. At last Sigurd said dreamily: "It came to my mind, while you two were talking, how unevenly the Fates deal things. It appears, from what the maiden said, that you are the son of an English jarl who has often fought the Northmen. Now I am the son of a Norwegian jarl who has not a few times met the English in battle. It would have been no more unlikely than what has happened had I been the captive and you the victor."

"That is true," said Alwin slowly. He did not say more, but in some odd way the idea comforted and softened him. Neither of the young men turned his eyes from the river toward the other, yet in some way something friendly crept into their silence.

After a while Sigurd said, still without looking around, "It seems to me that the right–minded thing for me in this matter is to do what I should desire you to do if you were in my place; therefore I offer you my friendship."

Something blurred the bright river for an instant from Alwin's sight. "I give you thanks," he said huskily. "Save Editha, I have not a friend in the world."

He hesitated a while; then slowly, bit by bit, he set forth the story that he had never expected to unfold to Northern ears. "The Danes set fire to my father's castle, and he was burned with many of my kinsmen. The robbers came in the night, and a Danish churl opened the gates to them,—though he had been my father's man for four seasons. It was from him that I learned to speak the Northern tongue. They took me while I slept, bound me, and carried me out to their boats. They carried out also the young maidens who attended my mother,—Editha among them,—and not a few of the youth of the household, all that they chose for captives. They took out all the valuables that they wanted. After that, they threw great bales of hay into the hall, and set fire to them, and—"

"The bloody wolves!" Sigurd burst out. "Did they not offer your mother to go out in safety?"

23

"Nay, they had the most hatred against her." The bearing of his head grew more haughty. "My mother was a princess of the blood of Alfred."

It happened that Sigurd had heard of that great monarch. His face kindled with enthusiasm.

"Alfred! He who got the victory over the Danes? Small wonder they did not love his kin after they had known his cunning! I know a fine song about him,—how he went alone into the Danish camp, though they were hunting him to kill him; and while they thought him a simple—minded minstrel, he learned all their secrets. By my troth, that is good blood to have in one's veins! Were I English, I would rather be his kinsman than Ethelred's."

He stared at Alwin with glowing eyes; they were facing each other now. Suddenly he stretched out his hand.

"It is naught but a piece of bad luck that you are Leif's thrall. It might just as easily have happened that I were in your place. Now I will make a bargain with you that hereafter I will remember this, and never hold your thraldom against you."

Such a concession as that, few of the proud Viking race were generous enough to make. Alwin could not but be moved by it. He took the outstretched hand in a hard grip.

"Will you do that?" he said; and it seemed for a time as though he could not find words to answer. At last he spoke: "If you will do that, I promise on my side that I will forgive your Northern blood and your lordship over me, and love you as my own brother."

CHAPTER V. THE IRE OF A SHIELD–MAIDEN

```
With insult or derision
Treat thou never
A guest or wayfarer;
They often little know,
Who sit within,
Of what race they are who come.
    Ha'vama'l
```

The Thrall of Leif the Lucky

Alwin was sitting on the ground in front of the provision-shed, grinding meal on a small stone hand-mill, when Editha came to seek him.

"If it please you, my lord—"

He broke into a bitter laugh. "By Saint George, that fits me well! 'If it please you,' and 'my lord,' to a short-haired, callous-handed hound of a slave!"

Tears filled her eyes, but her gentle mouth was as obstinate as gentle mouths can often be. "Have they drawn Earl Edmund's blood out of you? Until they have done that, you will be my lord. Your lady mother in heaven would curse me for a traitor if I denied your nobility."

Alwin ground out a resigned sigh with his last handful of meal. "Go on then, if you must. We spoke enough of the matter last night. Only see to it that no one hears you. I warn you that I shall kill the first who laughs,—and who could help laughing?"

She was too wise to answer that. Instead, she motioned over her shoulder toward the group of late-risen revellers who were lounging under the trees, breaking their fast with an early meal. "Tyrker bids you come and serve the food."

"If it please me?"

"My dear lord, I pray you give over all bitterness. I pray you be prudent toward them. I have not been a shield-maiden's thrall for nearly a year without learning something."

"Poor little dove in a hawk's nest! Certainly I think you have learned to weep!"

"You need not pity me thus, Lord Alwin. It is likely that my mistress even loves me in her own way. She has given me more ornaments than she keeps for herself. She would slay anyone who spoke harshly to me. What is it if now and then she herself strikes me? I have had many a blow from your mother's nurse. I do not find that I am much worse than before. No, no; my trouble is all for you. My dearest lord, I implore you not to waken their anger. They have tempers so quick,—and hands even quicker."

The Thrall of Leif the Lucky

Remembering his encounter with Egil the evening before, Alwin's eyes flared up hotly. But he would make no promises, as he arose to answer the summons.

The little maid carried an anxious heart to her task of mending Helga's torn kirtle.

No one seemed to notice the young thrall when he came among them and began to refill the empty cups. The older men, sprawling on the sun-flecked grass and over the rude benches, were still drowsy from too deep soundings in too many mead horns. The four young people were talking together. They sat a little apart in the shade of some birch trees which served as rests for their backs,—Helga enthroned on a bit of rock, Rolf and Sigurd lounging on either side of her, the black-maned Egil stretched at her feet. Between them a pair of lean wolf-hounds wandered in and out, begging with glistening eyes and poking noses for each mouthful that was eaten,—except when a motion of Helga's hand toward a convenient riding-switch made them forget hunger for the moment.

"I wonder to hear that Leif was not at the feast last night," Sigurd was saying, as he sipped his ale in the leisurely fashion which some of the old sea-rovers in the distance condemned as French and foolish.

Swallowing enough of the smoked meat in her mouth to make speaking practicable, Helga answered: "He will be away two days yet; did I not tell you? He has gone south with a band of guardsmen to convert a chief to Christianity."

"Then Leif himself has turned Christian?" Sigurd exclaimed in astonishment. "The son of the pagan Eric a Christian! Now I understand how it is that he has such favor with King Olaf, for all that he comes of outlawed blood. In Wisby, men thought it a great wonder, and spoke of him as 'Leif the Lucky,' because he had managed to get rid of the curse of his race."

Rolf the Wrestler shook his head behind his uplifted goblet. He was an odd-looking youth, with chest and shoulders like the forepart of an ox, and a face as mild and gently serious as a lamb's. As he put down the curious gilded vessel, he said in the soft voice that matched his face so well and his body so ill: "If you have a boon to ask of your foster-father, comrade, it is my advice that you forget all such pagan errors as that story of the curse. Egil, here, came near being spitted on Leif's sword for merely mentioning

Skroppa's name."

Alwin recognized the name with a start. Egil scowled in answer to Sigurd's curious glance.

"Odin's ravens are not more fond of telling news, than you," the Black One growled. "At meal-time I have other uses for my jaws than babbling. Thrall, bring me more fish."

Alwin waited long enough to possess himself of a sharp bronze knife that lay among the dishes; then he advanced, alertly on his guard, and shovelled more herrings upon the flat piece of hard bread that served as a plate. Egil, however, noticed him no more than he did the flies buzzing around his food. Whatever the cause of their enmity, it was evidently a secret.

The English youth was retiring in surprise, when Rolf took it into his head to accost him. The wrestler pointed to a couple of large flat stones that he had placed, one on top of the other, beside him. "This is very tough bread that you have given me, thrall," he said reproachfully.

Their likeness to bread was not great, and the jest struck Alwin as silly. He retorted angrily: "Do you suppose that my wits were cut off with my hair, so that I cannot tell stones from bread?"

Not a flicker stirred the seriousness of Rolf's blue eyes. "Stones?" he said. "I do not know what you mean. Can they be stones that I am able to treat like this?" His fist arose in the air, doubled itself into the likeness of a sledge-hammer, and fell in a mighty blow. The upper stone lay in fragments.

Whereupon Alwin realized that it had all been a flourish to impress him. So, though unquestionably impressed, he refused to show it. A second time he was turning his back on them, when Helga stopped him.

"You must bring something that I want, first. In the northeast corner of the provision shed, was it not, Sigurd?"

The Thrall of Leif the Lucky

Young Haraldsson was scrambling to his feet in futile grabs after one of the hounds that was making off with his herring, but he nodded back over his shoulder. Helga looked from one to the other of her companions with an ecstatic smack of her lips. "Honey," she informed them. "Sigurd ran across a jar of it last night. That pig of an Olver yonder hid it on the highest shelf. Very likely the goldsmith's daughter gave it to him and it was his intention to keep it all for himself. We will put a trick upon him. Bring it quickly, thrall. Yet have a care that he does not see it as you pass him. That is he with the bandaged head. If he looks sharply at you, hide the jar with your arm and it is likely he will think that you have been stealing some food for yourself, and be too sleepy to care."

Lord Alwin of Northumbria lost sight of the lounging figures about him, lost sight of Sigurd chasing the circling hound, lost sight of everything save the imperious young person before him. He stared at her as though he could not believe his ears. She waved him away; but he did not move.

"Let him think that _I_ am _stealing_!" he managed to gasp at last.

The grass around Helga's foot stirred ominously.

"I have told you that he is too sleepy to care. If he threatens to flog you, I promise that I will interfere. Coward, what are you afraid of?"

She caught her breath at the blazing of his face. He said between his clenched teeth: "I will not let him think that I would steal so much as one dried herring,—were I starving!"

The fire shot out of Helga's beautiful eyes. Egil and the Wrestler sprang up with angry exclamations; but words would not suffice Helga. Leaping to her feet, she caught up the riding—whip from the grass beside her and lashed it across the thrall's face with all her might. A bar of livid red was kindled like a flame along his cheek.

"You are cracking the face of Leif's property," Rolf murmured in mild remonstrance.

Egil laughed, a hateful gloating laugh, and settled himself against a tree to see the finish. As Helga's arm was flung up the second time, the thrall leaped upon her and tore the whip from her grasp and broke it in pieces. He would that he might have broken her as well; he thirsted to,—when he caught sight of the laughing Egil, and everything else was blotted out of his vision. Without a sound, but with the animal passion for killing upon his white face, he wheeled and leaped upon the Black One, crushing him, pinioning him against the tree, strangling him with the grip of his hands.

CHAPTER VI. THE SONG OF SMITING STEEL

```
To his friend
A man should be a friend,—
To him and to his friend;
But no man
Should be the friend
Of his foe's friend.
     Ha'vama'l
```

In the madness of his rush, Alwin blundered. Springing upon Egil from the left, he left his enemy's right arm free. Instantly this arm began forcing and jamming its way downward across Egil's body. Should it find what it sought—!

Alwin saw what was coming. He set his teeth and struggled desperately; but he could not prevent it. Another moment, and the Black One's fingers had closed upon his sword–hilt; the blade hissed into the air. Only an instant wrenching away, and a lightning leap aside, saved the thrall from being run through. His short bronze knife was no match for a sword. He gave himself up for lost, and stiffened himself to die bravely,—as became Earl Edmund's son. He had yet to learn that there are crueler things than sword–thrusts.

As Egil advanced with a jeering laugh, Helga caught his sleeve; and Rolf laid an iron hand upon his shoulder.

"Think what you do!" the Wrestler admonished. "This will make the third of Leif's thralls that you have slain; and you have no blood–money to pay him."

"Shame on you, Egil Olafsson!" cried Helga. "Would you stain your honorable sword with a thing so foul as thrall–blood?"

Rolf's grip brought Egil to a standstill. The contempt in Helga's words was reflected in his face. He sheathed his sword with a scornful gesture.

The Thrall of Leif the Lucky

"You speak truth. I do not know how it was that I thought to do a thing so unworthy of me. I will leave Valbrand to draw the fellow's blood with a stirrup leather."

He turned away, and the others followed. Those of the crew who had raised their muddled heads to see what the trouble was, laid them down again with grunts of disappointment. Alwin was left alone, untouched.

Yet truly his anguish would not have been greater had they cut him in pieces. Without knowing what he did, he sprang after them, crying hoarsely: "Cowards! Churls! What know you of my blood? Give me a weapon and prove me. Or cast yours aside,—man to man." His voice broke with his passion and the violence of his heart—beats.

But the mocking laughter that burst out died in a sudden hush. A moment before, Sigurd had concluded his pursuit of the thieving hound and rejoined the group,—in time to gather something of what had passed. The instant Alwin ceased, he stepped out and placed himself at the young thrall's side. He was no longer either the courteous Sigurd Silver—Tongue or Sigurd the merry comrade; his handsome head was thrown up with an air of authority which reminded all present that Sigurd, the son of the famous Jarl Harald, was the highest—born in the camp.

He said sternly: "It seems to me that you act like fools in this matter. Can you not see that he is no more thrall—born than you are? Or do you think that ill luck can change a jarl's son into a dog? He shall have a chance to prove his skill. I myself will strive against him, to any length he chooses. And what I have thought it worth while to do, let no one else dare scorn!"

He unbuckled his own gold—mounted weapon and forced it into Alwin's hands, then turned authoritatively to the Wrestler: "Rolf, if you count yourself my friend, lend me your sword."

It was yielded him silently; and they stepped out face to face, the young noble and the young thrall. But before their steel had more than clashed, Egil came between and knocked up their blades with his own.

"It is enough," he said gruffly. "What Sigurd Haraldsson will do, I will not disdain. I will meet you honorably, thrall. But you need not sue for mercy." A gleam of that strange

30

groundless hatred played over his savage face.

It did not daunt Alwin; it only helped to warm his blood. "This steel shall melt sooner than I ask for quarter!" he cried defiantly, springing at his enemy.

Whish–clash! The song of smiting steel rang through the little valley. The spectators drew back out of the way. Again the half–drunken loungers rose upon their elbows.

They were well matched, the two. If Alwin lacked any of the Black One's strength, he made it up in skill and quickness. The bright steel began to fly fast and faster, until its swish was like the venomous hiss of serpents. The color came and went in Helga's cheek; her mouth worked nervously. Sigurd's eyes were fixed upon the two like glowing lamps, as to and fro they went with vengeful fury. In all the valley there was no sound but the fierce clash and clatter of the swords. The very trees seemed to hold their breath to listen.

Egil uttered a panting gasp of triumph; his, blade had bitten flesh. A widening circle of red stained the shoulder of Alwin's white tunic. The thrall's lips set in a harder line; his blows became more furious, as if pain and despair gave him an added strength. Heaving his sword high in the air, he brought it down with mighty force on Egil's blade. The next instant the Black One held a useless weapon, broken within a finger of the hilt.

A murmur rose from the three watchers. Helga's hand moved toward her knife.

Rolf shook his head gently. "Fair play," he reminded her; and she fell back.

Tossing away his broken blade, Egil folded his arms across his breast and waited in scornful silence; but in a moment Alwin also was empty–handed.

"I do no murder," he panted. "Man to man we will finish it."

With lowered heads and watchful eyes, like beasts crouching for a spring, they moved slowly around the circle. Then, like angry bears, they grappled; each grasping the other below the shoulder, and striving by sheer strength of arm to throw his enemy.

Only the blood that mounted to their faces, the veins that swelled out on their bare arms, told of the strain and struggle. So evenly were they matched, that from a little distance it

31

looked as if they were braced motionless. Their heels ground deep into the soft sod. Their breath began to come in labored gasps. It could not last much longer; already the great drops stood on Alwin's forehead. Only a spurt of fury could save him.

Suddenly, in changing his hold, Egil grasped the other's wounded shoulder. The grip was torture,—a spur to a fainting horse. The blood surged into Alwin's eyes; his muscles stiffened into iron. Egil swayed, staggered, and fell headlong, crashing.

Mad with pain, Alwin knelt on his heaving breast. "If I had a sword," he gasped; "if I had a sword!"

Shaken and stunned, Egil still laughed scornfully. "What prevents you from getting your sword? I shall not run away. Do you think it matters to me how soon my death-day comes?"

Alwin was still crazy with pain. He snatched the bronze knife from his belt and laid it against Egil's throat. Sigurd's brow darkened, but no one spoke or moved,—least of all, Egil; his black eyes looked back unshrinkingly.

It was their calmness that brought Alwin to himself. As he felt their clear gaze, it came back to him what it meant to take a human life,—to change a living breathing body like his own into a heap of still, dead clay. His hand wavered and fell away. The passion died out of his heart, and he arose.

"Sigurd Haraldsson," he said, "for what you have done for me, I give you your friend's life."

Sigurd's fine face cleared.

"Only," Alwin added, "I think it right that he should explain the cause of his enmity toward me, and—"

Egil leaped to his feet; his proud indifference flamed into sudden fury. "That I will never do, though you tear out my tongue-roots!" he shouted.

Even his comrades regarded him in amazement.

Alwin tried a sneer. "It is my belief that you fear to speak of Skroppa."

"Skroppa?" a chorus of. astonishment repeated. But only two scarlet spots on Egil's cheeks showed that he heard them. He gave Alwin a long, lowering look. "You should know by this time that I fear nothing."

Helga made an unfortunate attempt. "I think it is no more than honorable, Egil, to tell him why you are his enemy."

Unconsciously she spoke of the thrall now as of an equal. He noticed it; Egil also saw it. It seemed to enrage him beyond bearing.

"If you speak in his favor," he thundered, seizing her wrist, "I will sheathe my knife in you!" But even before she had freed herself, and Rolf and Sigurd had turned upon him, he realized that he had gone too far. Leaving them abruptly, he went and stood a little way off with his back toward them, his head bowed, his hands clenched, struggling with himself.

For a long time no one spoke. Sigurd questioned with his eyes, and Rolf answered by a shrug. Once, as Helga offered to approach the Black One, Sigurd made a warning gesture. They waited in dead silence. While the voices of the other men came to them faintly, and the insects chirped about their feet, and the birds called in the trees above them.

At last Egil came slowly back, sullen−eyed and grim−mouthed. He held a branch in his hands and was bending and breaking it fiercely. "It is shame enough," he began after a while, "that any man should have had it in his power to spare me. I wonder that I do not die of the disgrace! But it would be a still fouler shame if, after he had spared my life, I let myself keep a wolf's mind toward him." His eyes suddenly blazed out at Alwin, but he controlled himself and went on. "The reason for my enmity I will not tell; wild steers should not tear it out of me. But,—" He stopped and drew a hard breath, and set his teeth afresh; "but I will forego that enmity. It is more than my life is worth. It is worth a dozen lives to him,—" his voice broke with rage,—"yet because it is honorable, I will do it. If you, Sigurd Haraldsson, and you, Rolf, will pledge your friendship to this man, I will swear him mine." It was well that he had reached the end, for he could not have spoken another syllable.

The Thrall of Leif the Lucky

Bewilderment tied Alwin's tongue. Sigurd was the first to speak.

"That seems to me a fair offer; and half the condition is already fulfilled. I clasped his hand last night."

Rolf answered with less promptness. "I say nothing against the Englishman's courage or his skill; yet—I will not conceal it—even in payment for a comrade's life, I do not like to give my friendship to one of thrall–birth."

That loosened Alwin's tongue. "In my own country," he said haughtily, "you would be done honor by a look from me. Editha will tell you that my father was Earl of Northumbria, and my mother a princess of the royal blood of Alfred."

Helga uttered an exclamation of surprise and interest; but he would not deign to look at her. For a while longer Rolf hesitated, looking long and strangely at Egil, and long and keenly at Sigurd. But at last he put forth his huge paw.

"Alwin of England," he said slowly, "though you little know how much it means, I offer you my hand and my friendship."

Alwin took it a little coldly. "I will not give you thanks for a forced gift; yet I pledge you my faith in return."

Though his face still worked with passion, Egil's hand was next extended. "However much I hate you, I swear that I will always act as your friend."

In his secret heart Alwin murmured, "The Fiend take me if ever I turn my back on your knife!" But aloud he merely repeated his former compact.

When it was finished, Sigurd laid an affectionate hand upon his shoulder. "We cannot bind our friend–ship closer, but it is my advice that you do not leave Helga out of the bargain. Truer friend man never had."

The bar across Alwin's cheek grew fiery with his redder flush. He stood before her, rigid and speechless. Helga too blushed deeply; but there was nothing of a girl's shyness about her. Her beautiful eyes looked frankly back into his.

34

"I will not offer you my friendship," she said simply, "because I read in your face that you have not forgiven the foul wrong I put upon you,—not knowing that you were brave, high-born and accomplished. I can understand your anger. Were I a man, and a woman should do such a thing to me, it is likely that I should kill her on the spot. But it may be that, in time to come, the memory will fade out of your mind, even as the scar will fade from your face. Then, if you have seen that my friendship is worth having, do you come and ask me for it, and I will give it to you."

Before Alwin had time to think of an answer that would say neither more nor less than he meant, she had walked away with Sigurd. He looked after her with a scowl,—because he saw Egil watching him. But it surprised him that, search as he would, he could nowhere find that great soul-stirring rage which he had first felt against her.

CHAPTER VII. THE KING'S GUARDSMAN

```
Something great
Is not always to be given.
Praise is often for a trifle bought.
   Ha'vama'l
```

It was the day after this brawl, when the guardsman Leif returned to Nidaros. Alwin was brought to the notice of his new master in a most unexpected fashion.

For one reason or another, the camp had been deserted early. At day-break, Egil slung his bow across his back, provided himself with a store of arrows and a bag of food, and set out for the mountains,—to hunt, he told Tyrker, sullenly, as he passed. Two hours later, Valbrand called for horses and hawks, and he and young Haraldsson, with Helga and her Saxon waiting-maid, rode south for a day's sport in the pine woods.

Helga was the best comrade in the camp, whether one wished to go hawking, or wanted a hand at fencing, or only asked for a quiet game of chess by the leaping firelight. Her ringing laugh, her frank glance, and her beautiful glowing face made all other maidens seem dull and lifeless. Alwin dimly felt that hating her was going to be no easy task, and he dared not raise his eyes as she rode past him. Instead he forced himself to stare at the reflection of his scarred face in the silver horn he was wiping; and he blew and blew upon the sparks of his anger.

The Thrall of Leif the Lucky

Noticing it, Helga frowned regretfully. "I cannot blame him if he will not speak to me," she said to Sigurd Haraldsson. "The nature of a high-born man is such that a blow is like poison in his blood. It must rankle and fester and break out before he can be healed. I do not think he could have been more lordlike in his father's castle than he was yesterday. Hereafter I shall treat him as honorably as I treat you, or any other jarl-born man."

"In this you show yourself as high-minded as I have always thought you," answered Sigurd, turning toward her a face aglow with pleasure.

By the middle of the forenoon, everyone had gone, this way or that, to hunt, or fish, or swim, or loiter about the city. There were left only a man with a broken leg and a man with a sprained shoulder, throwing dice on a bench in the sun; Alwin, whistling absently as he swept out the sleeping-house; and Rolf the Wrestler sitting cross-legged under a tree, sharpening his sword and humming snatches of his favorite song:

```
"Hew'd we with the Hanger!
Hard upon the time 't was
When in Gothlandia going
To give death to the serpent."
```

Rolf had declined to go hunting, on the plea of his horse's lameness. Now, as he sat working and humming, he was presumably thinking up some other diversion,—and the frequent glances he sent toward the thrall seemed to indicate that the latter was to be concerned in it.

Finally Rolf called to Alwin: "Ho there, Englishman! Come hither and tell me what you think of this for a weapon."

It needed no urging to make Alwin exchange a broom for a sword. He came and lifted the great blade, and made passes in the air, and examined the hilt of brass-studded wood.

"Saw I never a finer weapon," he admitted. "The hilt fits to one's hand better than those gold things on Sigurd Haraldsson's sword. What is it called?" For in those days a good blade bore a name as certainly as a horse or a ship.

Rolf answered, in his soft voice: "It is called 'The Biter.' And it has bitten not a few,—but it is fitting that others should speak of that. Since the handle fits your grasp so well, will you not hold it a little longer, while I borrow Long Lodin's weapon here, and we try each other's skill?" He made a motion to rise, then checked himself and hesitated: "Or it may be," he added gently, "that you do not care to strive against one as strong as I?"

"Now, by St. Dunstan, you need not spare me thus!" Alwin cried hotly. "Never have I turned my back on a challenge; and never will I, while the red blood runs in my veins. Get your weapon quickly." He shook the big blade in the air, and threw himself into a posture of defence.

But the Wrestler made no move to imitate him. He remained sitting and slowly shaking his head.

"Those are fine words, and I say nothing against your sincerity; but my appetite has changed. I will tell you what we will do instead. When your work is done, we will betake ourselves across the river to Thorgrim Svensson's camp and see the horse–fight he is going to have. He has a black stallion of Keingala's breed, named Flesh–tearer, that it is not necessary to prod with a stick. When he stands on his hind legs and bites, you would swear he had as many feet as Odin's gray Sleipnir. Do you not think that would be good entertainment?"

For a moment Alwin did not know what to think. He did not believe that Rolf was afraid of him; and if the challenge was withdrawn, surely that ended the matter. A horse fight? He had enjoyed no such spectacle as that since the Michaelmas Day when his father had the great bear–baiting in the pit at his English castle. And a ramble through the sun and the wind, a taste of liberty—!

"It seems to me that it would be very enjoyable," he agreed. He started eagerly to finish his work, when a thought caught him like a lariat and whirled him back. "I am forgetting the yoke upon my neck, for the first time in a twelvemonth! Is it allowed a dog of a slave to seek entertainment?"

Mild displeasure stiffened Rolf's big frame. He said gravely: "It is plain your thoughts do not do me much honor, since you think I have so little authority. I tell you now that you will always be free to do whatever I ask of you. If there is anything wrong in the doing, it is I who must answer for it, not you. That is the law, while you are bound and I am free."

The Thrall of Leif the Lucky

A fresh sense of the shame of his thraldom broke over Alwin like a burning wave. It benumbed him for a second; then he laughed with jeering bitterness.

"It is true that I have become a dog. I can follow any man's whistle, and it is the man who is responsible. I ask you to forget that for a moment I thought myself a man." In sudden frenzy, he whirled the great sword around his head and lunged at the pine tree behind Rolf, so that the blade was left quivering in the trunk.

It was weather to gladden a man's heart,—a sunlit sky overhead, and a fresh breeze blowing that set every drop of blood a–leaping with the desire to walk, walk, walk, to the very rim of the world. The thrall started out beside the Wrestler in sullen silence; but before they had gone a mile, his black mood had blown into the fiord. River bank and lanes were sweet with flowers, and every green hedge they passed was a–flutter with nesting birds. The traders' booths were full of beautiful things; musicians, acrobats, and jugglers with little trick dogs, were everywhere,—one had only to stop and look. A dingy trading vessel lay in the river, loaded with great red apples, some Norman's winter store. One of the crew who knew Rolf threw some after him, by way of greeting; and the two munched luxuriously as they walked along. They passed many Viking camps, gay with streamers and striped linens, where groups of brawny fair–haired men wrestled and tried each other's skill, or sat at rough tables under the trees, drinking and singing. In one place they were practising with bow and arrow; and, being quite impartial in their choice of a target, one of the archers sent a shaft within an inch of Rolf's head, purely for the expected pleasure of seeing him start and dodge. Finding that neither he nor Alwin would go a step faster, they rained shafts about their ears as long as they were within bow–shot, and saw them out of range with a cheer.

The road branched into one of the main thoroughfares, and they met pretty maidens who smiled at them, melancholy minstrels who frowned at them, and grim–mouthed warriors whose eyes were too intent on future battles even to see them. Occasionally Rolf quietly saluted some young guardsman; and, to the thrall's surprise, the warrior answered not only with friendliness but even with respect. It seemed strange that one of Rolf's mild aspect should be held in any particular esteem by such young fire–eaters. Once they encountered a half–tipsy seaman, who made a snatch at Rolf's apple, and succeeded in knocking it from his hand into the dust. The Wrestler only fixed his blue eyes upon him in a long look, but the man went down on his knees as though he had been hit.

"I did not know it was you, Rolf Erlingsson," he hiccoughed over and over in maudlin terror. "I beg you not to be angry."

"It is seldom that I have seen such a coward as that," Alwin said in disgust as they walked on.

Rolf turned upon him his gentle smile. "It is your opinion, then, that a man must he a coward to fear me?"

Alwin did not answer immediately: of a sudden it occurred to him to doubt the Wrestler's mild manner.

While he was still hesitating, Rolf caught him lightly around the waist and swung him over a hedge into a field where a dozen red–and–yellow tented booths were clustered. "These are Thorgrim Svensson's tents," he explained, following as coolly as though that were the accepted mode of entrance. "Yonder he is,—that lean little man with the freckled face. He is a great seafaring man. I promise you that you will see many precious things from all over the world."

Approaching the booths, Alwin had immediate proof of this statement, for bench and bush and ground were littered with garments and furs and weapons, and odds–and–ends of spoil, as if a ship had been overturned on the spot. The lean little man whom Rolf had pointed out stood in the midst of it all, examining and directing. He was dressed in coarse homespun of the dingy colors of trading vessels, gray and brown and rusty black, which contrasted oddly with the mantle of gorgeous purple velvet he was at that moment trying on. His little freckled face was wrinkled into a hundred shrewd puckers, and his eyes were two twinkling pin–points of sharpness. He seemed to thrust their glance into Alwin, as he advanced to meet his visitors; and the men who were helping him paused and looked at the thrall with expectant grins.

Rolf said blandly, "Greeting, Thorgrim Svensson! We have come to see your horse–fight. This is Alwin, Edmund Jarl's son, of England. Bad luck has made him Leif's thrall, but his accomplishments have made me his friend."

He spoke with the utmost mildness, merely glancing at the grinning crew; yet they sobered as though their mirth had been turned off by a faucet, and Thorgrim gave the thrall a civil welcome.

"It is a great pity," he continued, addressing the Wrestler, "that you cannot see the Flesh–Tearer, since you came for that purpose; but it has happened that he has lamed himself, and will not be able to fight for a week. Do not go away on that account, however. My ship has brought me some cloaks even finer than the one you covet,"—here it seemed to Alwin as if the little man winked at Rolf,—"and if the Englishman is as good a swordsman as you have said—ahem!" He broke off with a cough, and endeavored to hide his abruptness by turning away and picking a fur mantle off a pile of costly things.

Alwin's momentary surprise was forgotten at sight of the treasure thus disclosed. Beneath the cloak, thrown down like a thing of little value, lay an open book. It was written in Anglo–Saxon letters of gold and silver; its crumpled pages were of rarest rose–tinted vellum; its covers, sheets of polished wood gold–embossed and adorned with golden clasps. Even Alfred's royal kinswoman had never owned so splendid a volume. The English boy caught it up with an exclamation of delight, and turned the pages hungrily, trying whether his mother's lessons would come back to him.

He was brought to himself by the touch of Rolf's hand on his shoulder. They were all looking at him, he found,—once more with expectant grins. Opposite him an ungainly young fellow in slave's garb—and with the air of belonging in it—stood as though waiting, a naked sword in his hand.

"Now I have still more regard for you when I see that you have also the trick of reading English runes," the Wrestler said. "But I ask you to leave them a minute and listen to me. Thorgrim here has a thrall whom he holds to be most handy with a sword; but I have wagered my gold necklace against his velvet cloak that you are a better man than he."

The meaning of the group dawned on Alwin then: he drew himself up with freezing haughtiness. "It is not likely that I will strive against a low–born serf, Rolf Erlingsson. You dare to put an insult upon me because luck has left your hair uncut."

A sound like the expectant drawing–in of many breaths passed around the circle. Alwin braced himself to withstand Rolf's fist; but the Wrestler only drew back and looked at him reprovingly.

The Thrall of Leif the Lucky

"Is it an insult, Alwin of England, to take you at your word? It is not three hours since you vowed never to turn your back on a challenge while the red blood ran in your veins. Have witches sucked the blood out of you, that your mind is so different when you are put to the test?"

At least enough blood was left to crimson Alwin's cheeks at this reminder. Those had been his very words, stung by Rolf's taunt.

The smouldering doubt he had felt burst into flame and burned through every fibre. What if it were all a trap, a plot?—if Rolf had brought him there on purpose to fight, the horses being only a pretext? Thorgrim's wink, his allusion to Alwin's swordsmanship, it had all been arranged between them; the velvet cloak was the clew! Rolf had wished to possess it. He had persuaded Thorgrim to stake it on his thrall's skill,—then he had brought Alwin to win the wager for him. _Brought_ him, like a trained stallion or a trick dog!

He turned to fling the deceit in the Wrestler's teeth. Rolf's fair face was as innocent as those of the pictured saints in the Saxon book. Alwin wavered. After all, what proof had he?

Jeering whispers and half–suppressed laughter became audible around him. The group believed that his hesitation arose from timidity. Ignoring the smart of yesterday's wound, he snatched the sword Rolf held out to him, and started forward.

His foot struck against the Saxon book which he had let fall. As he picked it up and laid it reverently aside, it suggested something to him.

"Thorgrim Svensson," he said, pausing, "because I will not have it said that I am afraid to look a sword in the face, I will fight your serf,—on one condition: that this book, which can be of no use to you, you will give me if I get the better of him."

The freckled face puckered itself into a shrewd squint. "And if you fail?"

"If I fail," Alwin returned promptly, "Rolf Erlingsson will pay for me. He has told me that while he is free and I am bound, he is answerable for what I do."

At this there was some laughter—when it was seen that the Wrestler was not offended. "A quick wit answered that, Alwin of England," Rolf said with a smile. "I will pay willingly, if you do not save us both, as I expect."

Anxious to be done with it, Alwin fell upon the thrall with a fierceness that terrified the fellow. His blade played about him like lightning; one could scarce follow its motions. A flesh−wound in the hip; and the poor churl, who had little real skill and less natural spirit, began to blunder. A thrust in the arm that would have only redoubled Alwin's zeal, finished him completely. With a roar of pain, he threw his weapon from him, broke through the circle of angry men, and fled, cowering, among the booths.

There were few words spoken as the cloak and the book were handed over. The set of Thorgrim's mouth suggested that if he said anything, it would be something which he realized might be better left unsaid. His men were like hounds in leash. Rolf spoke a few smooth phrases, and hurried his companion away.

The sense that he had been tricked to the level of a performing bear came upon Alwin afresh. When they stood once more in the road, he looked at the Wrestler accusingly and searchingly.

Rolf began to talk of the book. "Nothing have I seen which I think so fine. I must admit that you men of England are more skilful than we of the North in such matters. It is all well enough to scratch pictures on a rock or carve them on a door; but what will you do when you wish to move? Either you must leave them behind, or get a yoke of oxen. To have them painted on kid−skin, I like much better. You are in great luck to come into possession of such property."

Alwin forgot his resentful suspicions in his pleasure. "Let us sit down somewhere and examine it," said he. "Yonder, where those trees stretch over the fence and make the grass shady,—that will be a good place."

"Have it your own way," Rolf assented. To the shady spot they proceeded accordingly.

Rolf stretched himself comfortably in the long grass and made a pillow of his arms. Alwin squatted down, his back planted against the fence, the book open on his knees.

The Thrall of Leif the Lucky

The reading-matter was attractive enough, with its glittering characters and rose-tinted pages, and every initial letter inches high and shrined in azure-blue traceries. But the splendor of the pictures!—no barbaric heart could resist them. What if the straight lines were crooked,—if the draperies were wooden,—the hands and the feet ungainly? They had been drawn with sparkles of gold and gleams of silver, in blue and scarlet and violet, until nothing less than a stained-glass window glowing in the sun could even suggest their radiance. Rolf warmed into unusual heartiness.

"By the hilt of my sword, he was an accomplished man who was able to make such pictures! Look at that horse,—it does not keep you guessing a moment to tell what it is. And yonder man with the red flames leaping about him,—I wish I knew why he was bound to that post!"

Alwin also was bitten with curiosity. "I tell you what I will do," he offered. "You must not suppose that reading is as easy as swimming, or handling a sword. My father did not have the accomplishment, and his hair was gray. Neither would my mother have learned it, had it not been that Alfred was her kinsman and she was proud of his scholarship. Nor should I have known how, if she had not taught me. And I have forgotten much. But this I will offer you: I will read the Saxon words to myself, and then tell you in the Northern tongue what they mean."

He spread the book open on a spot of clean turf, stretched himself on his stomach, gripped one leg around the other, planted his chin on his clenched fists, and began.

It was slow work. He had forgotten a good deal; and every other word was linked with distracting memories: his mother leaning from her embroidery frame to follow the line with her bodkin; his mother, erect and stern, bidding Brother Ambrose bear him away and flog him for his idleness; his mother hearing his lesson with one arm around him and the other hand holding the sweetmeat she would give him if he succeeded. He did not notice that Rolf's eyes were gradually closing, and his bated breath lengthening into long even sighs. He plodded on and on.

All at once a thunder of approaching hoof-beats reached him from up the road. Nearer and nearer they came; and around the curve swept a party of the King's guardsmen,—yellow hair and scarlet cloaks flying in the wind, spurs jingling, weapons clattering, armor clashing. Alwin glanced up and saw their leader,—and his interest in pale pictured saints dropped dead.

"It must be King Olaf himself!" he murmured, staring.

A head taller than the other tall men, with shoulders a palm's–width broader, the leader sat on his mighty black horse like a second Thor. Light flashed from his steel tunic and gilded helmet. His bronzed face had an eagle's beak for a nose, and eyes of the blue of ice or steel, piercing as a two–edged sword. A white cross was painted on his shield of gold.

As he swept past, he glanced toward the pair by the fence. Catching sight of the sleeping Rolf, he checked his horse sharply, made a motion bidding the others go on without him, and, wheeling, rode back, followed only by a mounted thrall who was evidently his personal attendant. Alwin leaped up and attempted to arouse his companion, but the guardsman saved him the trouble. Leaning out of his saddle, he struck the Wrestler a smart blow with the flat of his sword.

"What now, Rolf Erlingsson!" he demanded, in tones of thunder. "Because I go on a five days' journey, must it happen that my men lie like drunken swine along the roadside? For this you shall feel—"

Before his eyes were fairly open, Rolf was on his feet, tugging at his sword. Luckily, before he thrust, he got a glimpse of his assailant.

"Leif, the son of Eric!" he cried, dropping his weapon. "Welcome! Hail to you!"

The warrior's frown relaxed into a grim smile, as he yielded his hand to his young follower's hearty grip.

"Is it possible that you are sober after all? What in the Fiend's name do you here, asleep by the road in company with a thrall and a purple cloak?"

Rolf relaxed into his customary drawl. "That is unjustly spoken, chief. I have not been asleep. I have found a new and worthy enjoyment. I have been listening while this Englishman read aloud from a Saxon book of saints."

"A Saxon book of saints!" exclaimed the guardsman. "I would see it."

When its owner had handed it up, he looked it through hastily, yet turning the leaves with reverence, and crossing himself whenever he encountered a pictured cross. As he handed it back, he turned his eyes on Alwin, blue and piercing as steel.

"It is likely that you are a high-born captive. That you can read is an unusual accomplishment. It is not impossible that you might be useful to me. Who is your master? Is it of any use to try to buy you from him?"

Rolf laughed. "Certainly you are well named 'the Lucky,' since you only wish for what is already yours. This is the cook-boy whom Tyrker bought to fill the place of Hord."

"So?" said Leif, in unconscious imitation of his old German foster-father. He sat staring down thoughtfully at the boy,—until his attendant took jealous alarm, and put his horse through a manoeuvre to arouse him.

The guardsman came to himself with a start and a hasty gathering up of his rein. "That is a good thing. We will speak further of it. Now, Olaf Trygvasson is awaiting my report. Tell them I will be in camp to-morrow. If I find drunken heads or dulled weapons—!" He looked his threat.

"I will heed your orders in this as in everything," Rolf answered, in the courtier-phrase of the day. His chief gave him a short nod, struck spurs to his horse, and galloped after his comrades.

CHAPTER VIII. LEIF THE CROSS-BEARER

```
Inquire and impart
Should every man of sense,
Who will be accounted sage.
Let one only know,—
A second may not;
If three, all the world knows.
    Ha'vama'l
```

It was early the next morning, so early that the world was only here and there awake. The town was silent; the fields were empty; the woods around the camp slept in darkness and silence. Only the little valley lay fresh and smiling in the new light, winking back at the sun from a million dewy eyes.

Under the trees the long white—scoured tables stood ready with bowl and trencher, and Alwin carried food to and fro with leisurely steps. From Helga's booth her voice arose in a weird battle—chant; while from the river bank came the voices and laughter and loud splashing of many bathers.

Gradually the shouts merged into a persistent roar. The roar swelled into a thunder of excitement. Alwin paused, in the act of ladling curds into the line of wooden bowls, and listened smiling.

"Now they are swimming a race back to the bank. I wonder whom they will drive out of the water today." For that was the established penalty for being last in the race.

The thunder of cheering reached its height; then suddenly it split into scattered jeers and hootings. There was a crackling of dead leaves, a rustling of bushes, and Sigurd appeared, dripping and breathless. Panting and spent, he threw himself on the ground, his shining white body making a cameo against the mossy green.

"You! You beaten!" Alwin cried in surprise.

Sigurd gave a breathless laugh. "Even I myself. Certainly it is a time of wonders!" He looked eagerly at the spread table, and held up his hand. "And I am starving besides! Toss me something, I beg of you." When Alwin had thrown him a chunk of crusty bread, he consented to go on and explain his defeat between mouthfuls. "It was because my shoulder is still heavy in its movements. I broke it wrestling last winter. I forgot about it when I entered the race."

"That is a pity," said Alwin. But he spoke absently, for he was thinking that here might be an opening for something he wished to say. He filled several bowls in silence, Sigurd watching over his bread with twinkling eyes. After a while Alwin went on cautiously: "This mishap is a light one, however. I hope it is not likely that you will have to endure a heavier disappointment when Leif arrives today."

Back went Sigurd's yellow head in a peal of laughter. "I would have wagered it!" he shouted. "I would have wagered my horse that you were aiming at that! So every speech ends, no matter where it begins. I talk with Helga of what we did as children and she answers: 'You remember much, foster-brother; do not forget the sternness of Leif's temper.' I enter into conversation with Rolf, and he returns, 'Yes, it is likely that Leif has got greater favor than ever with King Olaf. I cannot be altogether certain that he will shelter one who has broken Olaf's laws.' Tyrker advises me,—by Saint Michael, you are all as wise as Mimir!" He flung the crust from him with a gesture of good-humored impatience. "Do you all think I am a fool, that I do not know what I am doing? It appears that you forget that Leif Ericsson is my foster-father."

Alwin deposited the last curd in the last bowl, and stood licking the horn-spoon, and looking doubtfully at the other. "Do you mean by that that you have a right to give him orders? I have heard that in the North a foster-son does not treat his foster-father as his superior, but as his servant. Yet Leif did not look to be—"

Sigurd shouted with laughter. "He did not! I will wager my head he did not! Certainly the foster-son who would show disrespect to Leif the Lucky would be putting his life in a bear's paw. It makes no difference that it is customary for many silly old men of lower birth to allow themselves to be trampled upon by fiery young men of higher rank, like old wolves nipped by young ones. King Olaf's heir dare not do so to Leif Ericsson. No; what I would have you understand is that I know what I am doing because I know Leif's temper as you know your English runes. From the time I was five winters old to the time I was fifteen, I lived under his roof in Greenland, and he was as my father to me. I know his sternness, but I know also his justice and what he will dare for a friend, though Olaf and all his host oppose him."

He let fly a Norman oath as, splod! a handful of wet clay struck between his bare shoulders. Turning, he saw among the bushes a mischievous hand raised for a second throw, and scrambled laughing to his feet.

"The trolls! First to drive me from my bath and then to throw mud on me! Poison his bowl, if you love me, Alwin. Ah, what a throw! It is not likely that you could hit a door. What bondmaids' aiming! Shame!" Mocking, and dodging this way and that, he gained the welcome shelter of the sleeping-house.

A rush of big white bodies, a gleam of dampened yellow hair, an outburst of boisterous merriment, and the camp was swarming with hungry uproarious giants, who threw shoes at each other and shoved and quarrelled around the polished shield, before which they parted their yellow locks, stamping, singing and whistling as they pulled on their tunics and buckled their belts.

"Leif is coming!—the Lucky, the Loved One!" Helga sang from her booth; and the din was redoubled with cheering.

"By Thor, it seems to me that he is coming now!" said Valbrand, suddenly. He had finished his toilet, and sat at the table, facing the thicket. Every one turned to look, and beheld Leif's thrall—attendant gallop out of the shadows toward them. No one followed, however, and a murmur of disappointment went round.

"It is nobody but Kark!"

Kark rose in his stirrups and waved his hand. He was of the commonest type of colorless blond, and coarse and ignorant of face; but his manners had the assurance of a privileged character.

"It is more than Kark," he shouted. "It is news that is worth a hearing. Ho, for Greenland! Greenland in three days!"

"Greenland?" echoed the chorus.

"Greenland?" cried Helga, appearing in her doorway, with blanching cheeks.

They rushed upon the messenger, and hauled him from his horse and surged about him. And what had seemed Babel before was but gentle murmuring compared with what now followed.

"Greenland! What for?"—"You are jesting." "That pagan hole!"—"In three days? It is impossible!"—"Is the chief witch—ridden?"—" Has word come that Eric is dead?"—" Has Leif quarrelled with King Olaf, that the King has banished him?"—" Greenland, grave—mound for living men!"—"What for?"—"In the Troll's name, why?"—" You are lying; it is certain that you are."—" Speak, you raven!"

The Thrall of Leif the Lucky

"In a moment, in a moment,—give me breath and room, my masters," the thrall answered boldly. "It is the truth; I myself heard the talk. But first,—I have ridden far and fast, and my throat is parched with—"

A dozen milk-bowls were snatched from the table and passed to him. He emptied two with cool deliberation, and wiped his mouth on his sleeve.

"I give you thanks. I shall not keep you waiting. It happened last night when Leif came in to make his report to the King. Olaf was seated on the throne in his hall, feasting. Many famous chiefs sat along the walls. You should have heard the cheer they gave when it was known that Leif had the victory!"

Here Kark's roving eyes discovered Alwin among the listeners; he paused, and treated him to a long insolent stare. Then he went on:

"I was saying that they cheered. It is likely that the warriors up in Valhalla heard, and thought it a battle-cry. Olaf raised his drinking-horn and said, 'Hail to you, Leif Ericsson! Health and greeting! Victory always follows your sword.' Then he drank to him across the floor, and bade him come and sit beside him, that he might have serious speech with him."

A second cheer, loud as a battle-cry, went up to Valhalla. But mingling with its echo there arose a chorus of resentment.

"Yet after such honors why does he banish him?"—"Did they quarrel?"—"Is it possible that there is treachery?"—"Tell us why he is banished!"—"Yes, why?" —"Answer that!"

The messenger laughed loudly. "Who said that he was banished? Rein in your tongues. As much honor as is possible is intended him. It happened after the feast—"

"Then pass over the feast; come to your story!" was shouted so impatiently that even Kark saw the wisdom of complying.

"It shall be as you like. I shall begin with the time when every warrior had gone to bed, except those lying drunk upon the benches. I sat on Leif's foot-stool, with his horn. It is likely that I also had been asleep, for what I first remember was that Leif and the King

49

had ceased speaking together, and sat leaning back staring at the torches, which were burning low. It was so still that you could hear the men snore and the branches scraping on the roof. Then the King said, while he still looked at the torch, 'Do you purpose sailing to Greenland in the summer?' It is likely that Leif felt some surprise, for he did not answer straightway; but he is wont to have fine words ready in his throat, and at last he said, 'I should wish to do so, if it is your will.' Then the King said nothing for a long time, and they both sat looking at the pine torch that was burning low, until it went out. Then Olaf turned and looked into Leif's eyes and said, 'I think it may well be so. You shall go my errand, and preach Christianity in Greenland.'"

From Kark's audience burst another volley of exclamations.

"It is because he is always lucky!"—"It cannot be done. Remember Eric!"—"The Red One will slay him!"—"You forget Thorhild his mother!" "Hail to the King!" —"It is a great honor!"

"Silence!" Valbrand commanded. Kark went on: "Leif said that he was willing to do whatever the King wished; yet it would not be easy. He spoke the name of Eric, and after that they lowered their voices so that I could not hear. Then at last Olaf leaned back in his high–seat and Leif stood up to go. Olaf stretched forth his hand and said, 'I know no man fitter for the work than you. You shall carry good luck with you.' Leif answered: 'That can only be if I carry yours with me.' Then he grasped the King's hand and they drank to each other, looking deep into each other's eyes."

There was a pause, to make sure the messenger had finished. Then there broke out cheers and acclamations and exulting.

"Hail to Leif! Hail to the Lucky One!"—"Leif and the Cross!"—"Down with the hammer sign!"—"Down with Thor!"—"Victory for Leif, Leif and the Cross!"

Shields clashed and swords were waved. Kark was thrown bodily into the air and tossed from hand to hand. A wave of mad enthusiasm swept over the group. Only Helga stood like one stunned, her hands wound in her long tresses, her face set and despairing.

The Black One was the first to notice her amid the confusion. He dropped the cloak he was waving and stared at her wonderingly for a moment; then he burst into a boisterous laugh.

"Look at the shield-maiden, comrades,—look at the shield-maiden! It has come into her mind that she is going back to Thorhild!"

For a moment Alwin wondered who Thorhild might be. Then vaguely he remembered hearing that it was to escape a strong-minded matron of that name that Helga had fled from Greenland. That now she must go back to be civilized, and made like other maidens, struck him also as an excellent joke; and he joined in the laugh. One after another caught it up with jests and mocking.

"Back to Thorhild the Iron-Handed!"—"No more short kirtles!"—"She has speared her last boar!"—"After this she will embroider boar-hunts on tapestry!"—"Embroider? Is it likely that she knows which end of the needle to put the thread through?"—"It will be like yoking a wild steer!"—"Taming a shield-maiden!"—"There will be dagger-holes in Thorhild's back!"—They crowded around her, bandying the jest back and forth, and roaring with laughter.

Always before, Helga had taken their chaff in good part; always before, she had joined them in making merry at her expense. But now she did not laugh. She rose slowly and stood looking at them, her breast heaving, her eyes like glowing coals.

At last she said shrilly, "Oh, laugh! If you see a jest in it—laugh! Because I am going to lose my freedom—my rides over the green country,—never to stand in the bow and feel the deck bounding under me,—is it such sport to you, you stupid clods? Would you think it a jest if the Franks should carry me off, and shut me up in one of their towers, and load me with fetters, and force me to toil day and night for them? You would take that ill enough. How much better is it that I am to be shut in a smothering women's-house and wound around with cloth till I trip when I walk, and made to waste the daylight, baking to fill your swinish stomachs, and sewing tapestries that your dull eyes may have something to look at while you swallow your ale? Clods! I had rather the Franks took me. At least they would not call themselves my friends while they ill-used me. Heavy-witted churls, laugh if you want to! Laugh till you burst!"

She whirled away from them into her booth, and the door-curtain fell behind her.

All day long she sat there, neither eating nor speaking, Editha crouching in a corner, afraid to approach her.

CHAPTER IX. BEFORE THE CHIEFTAIN

```
At home let a man be cheerful,
And toward a guest liberal;
Of wise conduct he should be,
Of good memory and ready speech.
    Ha'vama'l
```

In the river, on the city–side, the "Sea–Deer" lay at anchor, stripped to her hulk, as the custom was. Her oars and her rowing–benches, her scarlet–and–white sail, her gilded vanes and carven dragon–head, were all carefully stored in the booths at the camp. With the eagerness of lovers, her crew rushed down to summon her from her loneliness and once more hang her finery about her. All day long their brushes lapped her sides caressingly, and their hammers rang upon her decking. All day long the ship's boat plied to and fro, bringing her equipments across the river. All day long Alwin was hurried back and forth with messages, and tools, and coils of rope.

The last trip he made, Sigurd Haraldsson walked with him across the bridge and along the city–bank of the river. The young Viking had spent the day riding around the country with Tyrker, getting prices on a ship–load of corn. Corn, it seemed, was worth its weight in gold in Greenland.

"Leif shows a keen wit in taking Eric a present of corn," Sigurd explained, as they dodged the loaded thralls running up and down the gangways. "He will like it better than greater valuables. His pleasure will come near to converting him."

Alwin shook his head doubtfully,—not at this last observation, but at the prospect in general. "The more I think of going to Greenland," he said, "the more excellent a place I find Norway."

He looked appreciatively at the river beside them, and ahead at the great shining fiord. Scattered over its sunlit waters trim clipper–built craft rode at anchor; between them, long–oared skiffs darted back and forth like long–legged water–bugs. Along the shore a chain of ships stretched as far as eye could reach,—graceful war cruisers, heavily–laden provision ships, substantial trading vessels. On the flat beach and along the wooded banks rose great storehouses and lines of fine new ship–sheds. Rich merchandise was piled before them; rows of covered carts stood in waiting. Everywhere were busy throngs of traders and seamen and slaves. His eye kindled as it passed from point to point.

"It seems that Northmen are something more than pirates," he said, thoughtfully.

"It seems that your speech is something more than free," said Sigurd, in displeasure.

Alwin realized that it had been, and explained: "I but spoke of you as southerners do who have not seen your country. I tell you truly that, after England, I believe Norway to be the finest country in the world."

Sigurd swung along with recovered good–humor. "I will not quarrel with you over that exception. And yonder is Valbrand just come ashore,—at the fore–gangway. Go and do your errand with him, and then we will walk over to that pier and see what it is that the crowd is gathered about, to make them shout so."

The attraction proved to be a chattering brown ape that some sailor had brought home from the East. Part of the spectators regarded it as a strange pagan god; part believed it to be an unfortunate being deformed by witchcraft; and the rest took it for a devil in his own proper person,—so there was great shrieking and scattering, whichever way it turned its ugly face. It happened that Sigurd was better informed, having seen a similar specimen kept as a pet at the court of the Norman Duke; so the terror of the others amused him and his companion mightily. They stayed until the creature put an end to the show by breaking away from its captor and taking refuge in the rigging.

It was a fascinating place altogether,—that beach,—and difficult to get away from. Almost every ship brought back from its voyage some beast or bird or fish so outlandish that it was impossible to pass it by. Twilight had fallen before the pair turned in among the hills.

Between the trees shone the red glow of the camp–fires. Through the dusk came the pleasant odors of frying fish and roasting pork, with now and then a whiff of savory garlic. Alwin turned on his companion in sudden excitement.

The Thrall of Leif the Lucky

"It is likely that Leif is already here!"

Sigurd laughed. "Do you think it advisable for me to climb a tree?"

They stepped out of the shadow into the light of the leaping flames. On the farther side of the long fire, men were busy with dripping bear–steaks and half–plucked fowls; while others bent over the steaming caldron or stirred the big mead–vat. On the near side, ringed around by stalwart forms, showing black against the fire–glow, the chief sat at his ease. The flickering light revealed his bronzed eagle face and the richness of his gold–embroidered cloak. At his elbow Helga the Fair waited with his drinking–horn. Tyrker hovered behind him, touching now his hair and now his broad shoulders with an old man's tremulous fondness. All were listening reverently to his quick, curt narrative.

Sigurd's laughing carelessness fell from him. He walked forward with the gallant air that sat so well upon his handsome figure. "Health and greeting, foster–father!" he said in his clear voice. "I have come back to you, an outlaw seeking shelter."

Helga spilled the ale in her consternation. The old German began a nervous plucking at his beard. The heads that had swung around toward Sigurd, turned back expectantly.

More than one heart sank when it was seen that the chief neither held out his hand nor moved from his seat. Silver–Tongued and sunny–hearted, the Jarl's son was well–beloved. There was a long pause, in which there was no sound but the crackling of flames and the loud sputtering of fat.

At last Leif said sternly, "You are my foster–son, and I love your father more than anyone else, kinsman or not; yet I cannot offer you hand or welcome until I know wherein you have broken the law."

Through the breathless hush, Sigurd answered with perfect composure: "That was to be expected of Leif Ericsson. I would not have it otherwise. All shall be without deceit on my side."

He folded his arms across his breast, and, standing easily before his judge, told his story. "In the games last fall it happened that I shot against Hjalmar Oddsson until he was obliged to acknowledge himself beaten; and for that he wished me ill luck. When the

The Thrall of Leif the Lucky

Assembly was held in my district this spring, he came there and three times tried to make me angry, so that I should forget that the Assembly Plain is sacred ground. The first time, he spoke lightly of my skill; but I thought that a jest, since it had proved too much for him. The second time, he spoke slightingly of my courage, saying that the reason I did not go in my father's Viking ship this spring was because I was wont to be afraid in battle. Now it had been seen by everybody that I wished to go. I had spent the winter in Normandy, yet I returned by the first ship, that I might make one of my father's crew. It was not my doing that my ship got lost in the fog and did not fetch me here until after the Jarl had sailed. It angered me that such slander should be spoken of me. Yet, remembering that men are peace–holy on the Assembly Plain, I did manage to turn it aside. A third time he threw himself in my way, and began speaking evil of a friend of mine, a man with whom I have sworn blood–brotherhood. I forgot where we stood, and what was the law, and I drew my sword and leaped upon him; and it is likely the daylight would have shone through him, but that he had friends hidden who ran out and seized me and dragged me before the law–man. Seeing me with drawn sword, he knew without question that I had broken the law; so, without caring what I urged, he passed sentence upon me, banishing me from my district for three seasons. My father and my kinsmen are away on Viking voyages; I cannot take service with King Olaf, and I will not serve under a lesser man. It was not easy to know where to go, until I thought of you, Leif Ericsson. It was you who taught me that 'He who is cold in defence of a friend, will be cold so long as Hel rules.' There is no fear in my mind that you will send me away."

He finished as composedly as he had begun, and stood waiting. But not for long. Leif rose from his seat, sweeping the circle with a keen glance. "It is likely," he said grimly, "that someone has told you that an unfavorable answer might be expected, because I feared to lose King Olaf's favor. You have done well to trust my friendship, foster–son." He stretched out his hand, a rare gleam of pleasure lighting his deep–set eyes. "You have behaved well to your friend, Sigurd Haraldsson; there is the greatest excuse for you in this affair. I bid you welcome, and I offer you a share in everything I own. If it is your choice, you shall go back to Brattahlid with me; and my home shall be your home for whatever time you wish."

Sigurd thanked him with warmth and dignity. Then a twinkle of mischief shone at the comers of his handsome mouth; after the fashion of the French court, he bent over the brawny outstretched hand and kissed it.

The Thrall of Leif the Lucky

A murmur of mingled amazement and amusement went up from the group. Leif himself gave a short laugh as he jerked his hand away.

"This is the first time that ever my fist was mistaken for a maiden's lips. It is to be hoped that this is not the most useful accomplishment you have brought from France. Now go and try your fine manners on Helga,—if you do not fear for your ears. I wish to speak with this thrall."

But Helga had not now spirit enough to avenge the salute. She drooped over the fire, staring absently into the embers; the heat toasting her delicate face rose–red, the light touching her hair into a wonderful golden web. She looked up at Sigurd with a faint frown; then dropped her chin back into her hands and forgot him.

Alwin came and placed himself before the chief's seat, where the young Viking had stood. He was not so picturesque a figure, with his shorn head and his white slaves'–dress; but he stood straight and supple in his young strength, his head haughtily erect, his eyes bright and fearless as a young falcon's.

Leif put his questions. "What are you called?"

"I am called Alwin, Edmund Jarl's son."

"Jarl–born? Then it is likely that you can handle a sword?"

"Not a few of your own men can bear witness to that."

Rolf spoke up with his quiet smile. "The boy speaks the truth. One would think that he had drunk nothing but dragon's blood since his birth."

"So?" said Leif dryly. "It may be that I should be thankful my men are not torn to pieces. But these accomplishments count for naught; none here but have them. You must accomplish something that I think of more importance, or I shall sell you and buy a man–thrall who has been trained to work. It seems that you can read runes: can you also write them?"

The Thrall of Leif the Lucky

In a flash of memory, Alwin saw again Brother Ambrose's cell, and his rebellious self toiling at the desk; and he marvelled that in this far-off place and time that toil was to be of use to him.

"To some small degree I can," he answered. "I learned in my boyhood; but last summer, on tee dairy farm of Gilli of Trondhjem, I practised on sheep-skins—"

"Gilli of Trondhjem?" Leif repeated. He sat suddenly erect, and shot a glance at the unconscious Helga; and the old German, peering from the shadows behind him, did the same.

Alwin regarded them wonderingly. "Yes, Gilli the trader, whom men call the Wealthy. It was he who first had me in my captivity."

For a long time the chief sat tugging thoughtfully at his yellow mustache. Tyrker bent over and whispered in his ear; and he nodded slowly, with another glance at Helga.

"But for this I should never have thought of him,—yet, it is certainly one way out of the matter."

Suddenly he made a motion with his hand, so that the circle fell back out of hearing. He turned and fixed his piercing eyes on the thrall as though he would probe his brain.

"I ask you to tell me what manner of man this Gilli is?"

It happened that Alwin asked nothing better than a chance to free his mind. He answered instantly: "Gilli of Trondhjem is a low-minded man who has gained great wealth, and is so greedy for property that he would give the nails off his hands and the tongue out of his head to get it. He is an overbearing churl."

Leif's eyes challenged him, but he did not recant.

"So!" said the chief abruptly; then he added: "I am told for certain that his wife is a well-disposed woman."

"I say nothing against that," Alwin assented. "She is from England, where women are taught to bear themselves gently."

His eulogy was cut short by an exclamation from the old German. "Donnerwetter! That is true! An English captive she was. Perhaps she their runes also understands?"

Finding this a question addressed to him, Alwin answered that he knew her to understand them, having heard her read from a book of Saxon prayers.

Tyrker rolled up his eyes devoutly. "Heaven itself it is that so has ordered it for the shield—maiden! You see, my son? This youth here can make runes,—she can read them; so can you speak with her without that the father shall know."

"Bring torches into the sleeping—house," Leif called, rising hastily. "Valbrand, take your horse and lay saddle on it. You of England, get bark and an arrow—point, or whatever will serve for rune writing, and follow me."

What took place behind the log walls, no one knew. When it was over, and Valbrand had ridden away in the darkness, Rolf sought out the scribe and gently gave him to understand that he was curious in the matter. But Alwin only cast a doubtful glance across the fire at Helga, and begged him to talk of something else.

Late the next afternoon, Valbrand returned, his horse muddy and spent, and was closeted for a long time with Leif and the old German. But none heard what passed between them.

CHAPTER X. THE ROYAL BLOOD OF ALFRED

```
Brand burns from brand,
Until it is burnt out;
Fire is from fire quickened.
Man to man
Becomes known by speech,
But a fool by his bashful silence.
     Ha'vama'l
```

Brave with fluttering pennant and embroidered linen and sparkling gilding, amid cheers and prayers and shouts of farewell, on the third day the "Sea—Deer" set sail for

The Thrall of Leif the Lucky

Greenland.

Newly clad from head to foot in a scarlet suit of King Olaf's giving, Leif stood aft by the great steering oar. The wind blew out his long hair in a golden banner. The sun splintered its lances upon his gilded helm. Upon his breast shone the silver crucifix that had been Olaf's parting gift. His hand was still warm from the clasp of his King's; no chill at his heart warned him that those hands had met for the last time, no thought was in him that he had looked his last upon the noble face he loved. Gazing out over the tumbling blue waves, he thought exultantly of the time when he should come sailing back, with task fulfilled, to receive the thanks of his King.

Bravely and merrily the little ship parted from the land and set forth upon her journey. Every man sat in his place upon the rowing–benches; every back bent stoutly to the oar. Dripping crystals and flashing in the sun, the polished blades rose and fell, as the "Sea–Deer" bounded forward. To those upon her decks, the mass of scarlet cloaks upon the pier merged into a patch of flame, and then became a fiery dot. The sunny plain of the city and the green slope of the camp dwindled and faded; towering cliffs closed about and hid them from the rowers' view.

Leaving the broad elbow of the fiord, they soon entered the narrow arm that ran in from the sea, like a silver lane between giant walls. Passing out with the tide, they reached the ocean. The salt wind smote their faces; the snowy sail drew in a long glad breath and swelled out with a throb of exultation, and the world of waters closed around their little craft.

It was a beautiful world, full of the shifting charms of color and of motion, of the joy of sun and wind; but Alwin found it a wearily busy world for him. Since he was not needed at the oars, they gave him the odds and ends of drudgery about the ship. He cleared the decks, and plied the bailing–scoop, and stood long tedious watches. He helped to tent over the vessel's decks at night, and to stow away the huge canvas in the morning. He ground grain for the hungry crew, and kept the great mead–vat filled that stood before the mast for the shipmates to drink from. He prepared the food and carried it around and cleared the remnants away again. He was at the beck and call of forty rough voices; he was the one shuttlecock among eighty brawny battledores.

The Thrall of Leif the Lucky

It was a peaceful world, stirred by no greater excitement than a glimpse of a distant sail or the mystery of a half–seen shore; yet things could happen in it, Alwin found. The second day out, the earl–born captive for the first time came in direct contact with the thrall–born Kark.

Kark was not deferential, even toward his superiors; there was barely enough discretion in his roughness to save him from offending. Among those of his own station, he dispensed even with discretion. And he had looked upon Alwin with unfriendly eyes ever since Leif's first manifestation of interest in his English property.

It often happens that the whole of earth's dry land proves too small to hold two uncongenial spirits peaceably. One can imagine, then, how it fared when two such opposites were limited to some hundred–odd feet of timber in mid–ocean.

"Ho there, you cook–boy!" Kark's rough voice came down to the foreroom where Alwin was working. "Get you quickly forward and wipe up the beer Valbrand has spilled over his bench."

For a moment, Alwin's eyes opened wide in amazement; then they drew together into two menacing slits, and his very clothing bristled with haughtiness. He deigned no answer whatsoever.

A pause, and Kark followed his voice. "What now, you cub of a lazy mastiff! I told you, quickly; the beer will get on his clothes."

With immovable calmness, Alwin went on with his grinding. Only after the fourth round he said coldly: "It would save time if you would do your work yourself."

Kark gasped with amazement. This to him, the slave–born son of Eric's free steward, who held the whip–hand over all the thralls at Brattahlid! His china–blue eyes snapped spitefully.

"It does not become the bowerman of Leif Ericsson to do the dirty work of a foreign whelp. If you have the ambition to be more than—"

The Thrall of Leif the Lucky

He was interrupted by the sound of approaching thunder. Valbrand descended upon them, his new tunic drenched, the scars on his battered old face showing livid red.

"Is it likely that I will wait all day while two thralls quarrel over precedence?" he roared. "The Troll take me if I do not throw one of you to Ran before the journey is over! Go instantly—"

"I am sharpening Leif's blade," Kark struck in; he had indeed drawn a knife and sharpening-stone from his girdle. "It is not becoming for me to leave the chief's work for another task."

The argument was unassailable. To the unlucky man-of-all-work the steersman's anger naturally reverted.

"Then you, idle dog that you are! What is it that keeps you? Would you have him attend on Leif and do your work as well? You may choose one of two conditions: go instantly or have your back cut into ribbons."

If he had not added that, it is possible that Alwin would have obeyed; but to yield in the face of a threat, that was too low for his stiff-necked pride to stoop. The earl-born answered haughtily, "Have your will,—and I will have mine."

If he had had any idea that they would not go so far, it was quickly dashed out of him. One moment of struggle and confusion, and he found himself stripped to the waist, his hands bound to the mast, a man standing over him with a knotted thong of walrus hide. All Sigurd's furious eloquence could not restrain the storm of sickening blows.

On the other hand, if they had had the notion that their victim's obstinacy would run from him with his blood, they also were mistaken. The red drops came, but no sign of weakening. At last, with the subsiding of his anger, Valbrand ordered him to be set free.

"The same shall overtake you if you are disobedient to me again," was all he said.

Stripped and bloody, dizzy with pain and blind with rage, Alwin staggered forward, caught at Sigurd to save himself from falling, and looked unsteadily about him. When he found what he sought, his wits were cleared as a foggy night by lightning. With a hoarse cry, he caught up a fragment of broken oar and struck Kark over the head so that he fell stunned upon the deck, blood reddening his colorless face.

"In the Troll's name!" Valbrand swore, after a moment of utter stupefaction.

Alwin laughed between his teeth at Sigurd's despairing glance, and waited to feel the steersman's knife between his ribs. Instead, he was dragged aft to where the chief sat on the deck beside the steering–oar.

Leif was deep in consultation with his shrewd old foster–father. Without pausing in his argument, he sent an impatient glance over his shoulder; when it fell upon the gory young madman, he turned sharply and faced the group.

Alwin was in the mood to suffer torture with a smile. The more outrageous Valbrand depicted him, the better he was pleased. Leif made no comment whatever, but sat pulling at his long mustaches and eying them from under his bushy brows.

When the steersman had finished, he asked, "Is Kark slain?"

Glancing back, Valbrand saw the bowerman sitting up and feeling of his wounds. "Except a lump on his head, I do not think he is worse than before," he answered.

"So," said Leif with an accent of relief. "Then it is not worth while to say much. If he had been killed, his father would have taken it ill; and that would have displeased Eric and hurt my mission. It would have become necessary for me to slay this boy to satisfy them. Now it is of little importance."

He straightened abruptly and waved them away.

"What more is there to do about it?" he added. "This fellow has been punished, and Kark has got one of the many knocks his insolence deserves. Let us end this talk,—only see to it that they do not kill each other. I do not wish to lose any more property." He motioned them off, and turned back to Tyrker.

But there was more to it. Something,—Leif's curtness, or the touch of Valbrand's hand upon his naked shoulder,—roused Alwin's madness afresh. Shaking off the hand, fighting it off, he bearded the chief himself.

"I will kill him if ever he utters his cur's yelp at me again. You are blind and simple to think to keep an earl-born man under the feet of a churl. You are a fool to keep an accomplished man at work that any simpleton might do. I will not bear with your folly. I will slay the hound the first chance I get." He ended breathless and trembling with passion.

Valbrand stood aghast. Leif's brows drew down so low that nothing but two fiery sparks showed of his eyes. Through Alwin went the same thrill he had felt when the trader's sword-point pricked his breast.

Yet the lightning did not strike. Alwin glanced up, amazed. While he stared, a subtle change crept over the chief. Slowly he ceased to be the grim curt Viking: slowly he became the nobleman whose stateliness minstrels celebrated in their songs, and the King spoke of with praise. A stillness seemed to gather round them. Alwin felt his anger cooling and sinking within him.

After a time, Leif said with the calmness of perfect superiority: "It may be that I have not treated you as honorably as you deserve. Yet what am I to think of these words of yours? Is it after such fashion that a jarl-born man with accomplishments addresses his lord in your country?"

To the blunt old steersman, to the ox-like Olver, to the half-dozen others who heard it, the change was incomprehensible. They stared at their master, then at each other, and finally gave it up as a whim past their understanding. It may be that Leif was curious to see whether it would be incomprehensible to Alwin as well. He sat watching him intently.

Alwin's eyes fell before his master's. The stately quietness, the noble forbearance, were like voices out of his past. They called up memories of his princess-mother, of her training, of the dignity that had always surrounded her. Suddenly he saw, as for the first time, the roughness and coarseness of the life about him, and realized how it had roughened and coarsened him. A dull red mounted to his face. Slowly, like one groping for a half forgotten habit, he bent his knee before the offended chief. Unconsciously, for the first time in his thraldom, he gave to a Northman the title a Saxon uses to his superior.

The Thrall of Leif the Lucky

"Lord, you are right to think me unmannerly. I was mad with anger so that I did not weigh my words. I will say nothing against it if you treat me like a churl."

To the others, this also was inexplicable. They scratched their heads, and rubbed their ears, and gaped at one another. Leif smiled grimly as he caught their looks. Picking a silver ring from his pouch, he tossed it to Valbrand.

"Take this to Kark to pay him for his broken head, and advise him to make less noise with his mouth in the future." When they were gone he turned to Alwin and signed him to rise. "You understand a language that churls do not understand. I will try you further. Go dress yourself, then bring hither the runes you were reading to Rolf Erlingsson."

Alwin obeyed in silence, a tumult of long-quiet emotions whirling through his brain,—relief and shame and gratification, and, underneath it all, a new-born loyalty.

All the rest of the day, until the sun dropped like a red ball behind the waves, he sat at the chief's feet and read to him from the Saxon book. He read stumblingly, haltingly; but he was not blamed for his blunders. His listener caught at the meanings hungrily, and pieced out their deficiencies with his keen wit and dressed their nakedness in his vivid imagination. Now his great chest heaved with passion, and his strong hand gripped his sword-hilt; now he crossed himself and sighed, and again his eyes flashed like smitten steel. When at last the failing light compelled Alwin to lay down the book, the chief sat for a long time staring at him with keen but absent eyes.

After a while he said, half as though he was speaking to himself: "It is my belief that Heaven itself has sent you to me, that I may be strengthened and inspired in my work." His face kindled with devout rapture. "It must have been by the guidance of Heaven that you were trained in so unusual an accomplishment. It was the hand of God that led you hither, to be an instrument in a great work."

Awe fell upon Alwin, and a shiver of superstition that was almost terror. He bowed his head and crossed himself.

But when he looked up, the thread had snapped; Leif was himself again. He was eying the boy critically, though with a new touch of something like respect.

The Thrall of Leif the Lucky

He said abruptly: "It is not altogether befitting that one who has the accomplishments of a holy priest should go garbed like a base-bred thrall. What is the color of the clothes that priests wear in England?"

Alwin answered, wondering: "They wear black habits, lord. It is for that reason that they are called Black Monks."

Rising, Leif beckoned to Valbrand. When the steersman stood before him, he said: "Take this boy down to my chests and clothe him from head to foot in black garments of good quality. And hereafter let it be understood that he is my honorable bowerman, and a person of breeding and accomplishments."

The old henchman looked at the new favorite as dispassionately as he would have looked at a weapon or a dog that had taken his master's fancy. "I would not oppose your will in this, any more than in other things; yet I take it upon me to remind you of Kark. If you make this cook-boy your bowerman, to keep the scales balancing you must make him who was your bowerman into a cook-boy. It is in my mind that Kark's father will take that as ill as—"

A sweep of Leif's arm swept Kark out of the path of his will. "Who is it that is to command me how I shall choose my servants? The Fates made Kark a cook-boy when he was born; let him go back where he belongs. I have endured his boorishness long enough. Am I to despise a tool that Heaven has sent me because a clod at my feet is jealous? What kind of luck could that bring?"

Convinced or not, Valbrand was silenced. "It shall be as you wish," he muttered.

Alwin fell on his knee, and, not daring to kiss the chief's hand, raised the hem of the scarlet cloak to his lips.

"Lord," he said earnestly; then stopped because he could not find words in which to speak his gratitude. "Lord—" he began again, and again he was at a loss. At last he finished bluntly, "Lord, I will serve you as only a man can serve whose whole heart is in his work."

CHAPTER XI. THE PASSING OF THE SCAR

```
A ship is made for sailing,
A shield for sheltering,
A sword for striking,
A maiden for kisses.
     Ha'vama'l
```

"When the sun rises tomorrow it is likely that we shall see Greenland ahead of us," growled Egil.

With Sigurd and the Wrestler, he was lounging against the side, watching the witch—fires run along the waves through the darkness. The new bower—man stood next to Sigurd, but Egil could not properly be said to be with him, for the two only spoke under the direst necessity. Around them, under the awnings, in the light of flaring pine torches, the crew were sprawled over the rowing—benches killing time with drinking and riddles.

"It seems to me that it will gladden my heart to see it," Sigurd responded. "As I think of the matter, I recall great fun in Greenland. There were excellent wrestling matches between the men of the East and the West settlements. And do you remember the fine feasts Eric was wont to make?"

Rolf gently smacked his lips and laid his hands upon his stomach. "By all means. And remember also the seal hunting and the deer—shooting!"

Sigurd's eyes glistened. "Many good things may be told of Greenland. There is no place in the world so fine to run over on skees. By Saint Michael, I shall be glad to get there!" He struck Egil a rousing blow upon the sullen hump of his shoulders.

Unmoved, the Black One continued to stare out into the darkness, his chin upon his fists.

"Ugh! Yes. Very likely," he grunted. "Very likely it will be clear sailing for you, but it is my belief that some of us will run into a squall when we have left Leif and gone to our own homes, and it becomes known to our kinsmen that we are no longer Odin—men. It is probable that my father will stick his knife into me."

The Thrall of Leif the Lucky

There was a pause while they digested the truth of this; until Rolf relieved the tension by saying quietly: "Speak for yourself, companion. My kinsman is no such fool. He has been on too many trading voyages among the Christians. Already he is baptized in both faiths; so that when Thor does not help him, he is wont to pray to the god of the Christians. Thus is he safe either way; and not a few Greenland chiefs are of his opinion."

Sigurd's merry laugh rang out. "Now that is having a cloak to wear on both sides, according to the weather! If only Eric were so minded—"

"Is Eric the ruler in Greenland?" Alwin interrupted. All this while he had been looking from one to the other, listening attentively.

The two sons of Greenland chiefs answered "No!" in one breath. Sigurd raised quizzical eyebrows.

"I admit that he is not the ruler in name, Greenland being a republic, but in fact—?"

They let him go on without contradiction.

"Thus it stands, Alwin. Eric the Red was the first to settle in Greenland, therefore he owns the most land. Besides Brattahlid, he owns many fishing stations; and he also has stations on several islands where men gather eggs for him and get what drift–wood there is. And not only is he the richest man, but he is also the highest–born, for his father's father was a jarl of Jaederan; and so—"

It is to be feared that Alwin lost some of this. He broke in suddenly: "Now I know where it is that I have heard the name of Eric the Red! It has haunted me for days. In the trader's booth in Norway a minstrel sang a ballad of 'Eric the Red and his Dwarf–Cursed Sword.' Know you of it?"

He was answered by the involuntary glances that the others cast toward the chief.

Rolf said with a shrug: "It is bondmaids' gabble. There is little need to say that a dwarf cursed Eric's sword, to explain how it comes that he has been three times exiled for manslaughter, and driven from Norway to Iceland and from Iceland to Greenland. He quarrelled and slew wherever he settled, because he has a temper like that of the dragon

Fafnir."

A faint red tinged Egil's dark cheeks. "Nevertheless, Skroppa's prophecy has come true," he muttered, "that after the blade was once sheathed in the new soil of Greenland, it would bring no more ill–luck."

"Skroppa!" cried Alwin. But he got no further, for Sigurd's hand was clapped over his mouth.

"Lower your voice when you speak that name, comrade," the Silver–Tongued warned him.

"Do not speak it at all," Egil interrupted brusquely. "The English girl is coming aft. It is likely she brings some message from Helga."

They faced about eagerly. Editha's smooth brown head was indeed to be seen threading its way between the noisy groups. They agreed that it was time they heard from the shield–maiden. For her to take advantage of her womanhood, and turn the forecastle into a woman's–house, and forbid their approach, was something unheard–of and outrageous.

"It would be treating her as she deserves if we should refuse to go now when she sends for us," Egil growled, though without any apparent intention of carrying out the threat.

To the extreme amusement of his fellows, Sigurd began to settle his ornaments and rearrange his long locks.

"It may be that she accepts my invitation to play chess. Leif spoke with her for a long time this afternoon; it is likely that he roused her from her black mood."

"It is likely that he roused her," Alwin said slowly.

There was something so peculiar in his voice that they all turned and looked at him. He had suddenly grown very red and uncomfortable.

"It seems that anyone can be foreknowing at certain times," he said, trying to smile. "Now my mind tells me that the summons will be for me."

The Thrall of Leif the Lucky

"For you!" Egil's brows became two black thunder-clouds from under which his eyes flashed lightnings at the thrall.

Alwin yielded to helpless laughter. "There is little need for you to get angry. Rather would I be drowned than go."

It was Sigurd's turn to be offended. "I had thought better of you, Alwin of England, than to suppose that you would cherish hatred against a woman who has offered to be your friend."

"Hatred?" For a moment Alwin did not understand him; then he added: "By Saint George, that is so! I had altogether forgotten that it was my intention to hate her! I swear to you, Sigurd, I have not thought of the matter these two weeks."

"Which causes me to suspect that you have been thinking very hard of something else," Rolf suggested.

But Alwin closed his lips and kept his eyes on Editha's approaching figure.

The little bondmaid came up to them, dropped as graceful a curtsey as she could manage with the pitching of the vessel, and said timidly: "If it please you, my lord Alwin, my mistress desires to speak with you at once."

"Hail to the prophet!" laughed Sigurd, pretending to rumple the locks that he had so carefully smoothed.

"Now Heaven grant that I am a false prophet in the rest of my foretelling," Alwin murmured to himself, as he followed the girl forward. "If I am forced to tell her the truth, I think it likely she will scratch my eyes out."

She did not look dangerous when he came up to her. She was sitting on a little stool, with her hands folded quietly in her lap, and on her beautiful face the dazed look of one who has heard startling news. But her first question was straight to the mark.

"Leif has told me that Gilli and Bertha of Trondhjem are my father and mother. He says that you have seen them and know them. Tell me what they are like."

69

It was an instant plunge into very deep water. Alwin gasped. "Lady, there are many things to be said on the subject. It may be that I am not a good judge."

He was glad to stop and accept the stool Editha offered, and spend a little time settling himself upon it; but that could not last long.

"Bertha of Trondhjem is a very beautiful woman," he began. "It is easy to believe that she is your mother. Also she is gentle and kind-hearted—"

Helga's shoulders moved disdainfully. "She must be a coward. To get rid of her child because a man ordered it! Have you heard that? Because when I was born some lying hag pretended to read in the stars that I would one day become a misfortune to my father, he ordered me to be thrown out—for wolves to eat or beggars to take. And my mother had me carried to Eric, who is Gilli's kinsman, and bound him to keep it a secret. She is a coward."

"It must be remembered that she had been a captive of Gilli," Alwin reminded the shield-maiden. "Even Norse wives are sometimes—"

"She is a coward. Tell me of Gilli. At least he is not witless. What is he like?"

Again the deep water. Alwin stirred in his seat and fingered at the silver lace on his cap. He was dressed splendidly now. Left's wardrobe had contained nothing black that was also plain, so the bowerman's long hose were of silk, his tunic was seamed with silver, his belt studded with steel bosses, his cloak lined with fine gray fur.

"Lady," he stammered, "as I have said, it may be that I am not a fair judge. Gilli did not behave well to me. Yet I have heard that he is very kind to his wife. It is likely that he would give you costly things—"

Helga's foot stamped upon the deck. "What do I care for that?"

He knew how little she cared. He gave up any further attempts at diplomacy.

But her next words granted him a respite. "What was the message that you wrote to my mother for Leif?"

The Thrall of Leif the Lucky

"I think I can remember the exact words," he answered readily, "it gave me so much trouble to spell them. It read this way, after the greeting: 'Do you remember the child you sent to Eric? She is here in Norway with me. She is well grown and handsome. I go back the second day after this. It will be a great grief to her if she is obliged to go also. If her father could see her, it is likely he would be willing to give her a home in Norway. It would even be worth while coming all the way to Greenland after her. It is certain that Gilli would think so, if you could manage that he should see her.' I think that was all, lady."

"If Gilli is what I suspect him to be, that is more than enough," Helga said slowly. She raised her head and looked straight into his eyes. "Answer me this,—you know and must tell,—is he a high-minded warrior like Leif, or is he a money-loving trader?"

"Lady," said Alwin desperately, "if you will have the truth, he is a mean-spirited churl who thinks that the only thing in the world is to have property."

Helga drew a long breath, and her slender hands clenched in her lap. "Now I have found what I have suspected. Answer this truthfully also: If I go back to him, is it not likely that he will marry me to the first creature who offers to make a good bargain with him?"

"Yes," said Alwin.

For days he had been watching her with uneasy pity, whenever in his mind's eye he saw her in the power of the unscrupulous trader, It had made him uncomfortable to feel that he was the tool that had brought it about, even though he knew he was as innocent as the bark on which he had written.

Drop by drop the blood sank out of Helga's face. Spark by spark, the light died out of her eyes. Like some poor trapped animal, she sat staring dully ahead of her.

It was more than Alwin could bear in silence. He leaned forward and shook her arm. "Lady, do anything rather than despair. Get into a rage with me,—though Heaven knows I never intended your misfortune! Yet it is natural you should feel hard toward me. I—"

She stared at him dully. "Why should I be angry with you? You could not help what you did; and Leif thought I would wish rather to go to my own mother than to Thorhild."

71

The Thrall of Leif the Lucky

It had never occurred to Alwin that she would be reasonable. His remorse became the more eager. He bethought himself of some slight comfort. "At least it cannot happen for a year, lady. And in—"

She raised her head quickly. "Why can it not happen for a year?"

"Because Gilli is away on a trading voyage, and will not be back until fall, when it will be too late to start for Greenland. Nor will he come early in spring and so lose the best of his trading season. It is sure to be more than a year."

Youth can construct a lifeboat out of a straw. Hope crept back to Helga's eyes.

"A year is a long time. Many things can happen in a year. Gilli may be slain, —for every man a mistletoe−shaft grows somewhere. Or I may marry someone in Greenland. Already two chiefs have asked my hand of Leif, so it is not likely that I shall lack chances."

"That is true; and it may also happen that the Lady Bertha will never get my runes. She was absent on a visit when Valbrand left them at her farm. Or even if she gets them, she may lack courage to tell the news to Gilli. Or he may dislike the expense of a daughter. Surely, where there are so many holes, there are many good chances that the danger will fall through one of them."

Helga flung up her head with a gallant air. "I will heed your advice in this matter. I will not trouble myself another moment; and I will love Brattahlid as a bird loves the cliff that hides it! And Thorhild? What if her nature is such that she is cross? She is no coward. She would defend those she loved, though she died for it. I should like to see Eric bid her to abandon a child. There would not be a red hair left in his beard. Better is it to be brave and true than to be gentle like your Lady Bertha. Is it because she is my mother that you give that title to me also?"

Alwin hesitated and reddened. "Yes. And because I like to remember that there is English blood in you."

Helga paused in the midst of her excitement, and her face softened. She looked at him, and her starry eyes were full of frank good−will.

72

She said slowly, "Since there is English blood in me, it may be that you will some time ask for the friendship I have offered you."

At that moment, it seemed to Alwin that such simplicity and frankness were worth more than all the gentle graces of his country–women. He put out his hand.

"You need not wait long for me to ask that," he said. "I would have asked it a week ago, but I could not think it honorable to call myself your friend when I had injured you so."

Helga's slim fingers gave his a firm clasp, but she laughed merrily.

"That is where you are mistaken. If you had not injured me, you would never have forgotten that I had injured you. Now we are even, and we start afresh. That is a good thing."

CHAPTER XII. THROUGH BARS OF ICE

```
A day should be praised at night;
A sword when it is tried;
Ice when it is crossed.
   Ha'vama'l
```

A dim line of snowy islands, so far apart that it was hard to believe they were only the ice–tipped summits of Greenland's towering coast, stretched across the horizon. Standing at Helga's side in the bow, Alwin gazed at them earnestly.

"To think," he marvelled, "that we have come to the very last land on this side of the world! Suppose we were to sail still further west? What is it likely that we would come to? Does the ocean end in a wall of ice, or would we fall off the earth and go tumbling heels over head through the darkness—? By St. George, it makes one dizzy!"

Helga's ideas were not much clearer. It was nearly five hundred years before the time of Columbus. But she knew one thing that Alwin did not know.

"Greenland is not the most western land," she corrected. "There is another still further west, though no one knows how big it is or who lives in it."

She turned, laughing, to where young Haraldsson sat counting the wealth of his pouch and calculating how valuable could be the presents he could afford to bestow on his arrival.

"Sigurd, do you remember that western land Biorn Herjulfsson saw? and how we were wont to plan to run away to it, when I grew tired of embroidering and Leif kept you overlong at your exercises?"

"I have not thought of it since those days," laughed Sigurd. He swept the mass of gold and silver trinkets back into the velvet pouch at his belt, and came over and joined them. "What fine times we had planning those trips, over the fire in the evenings! By Saint Michael, I think we actually started once; have you forgotten?—in the long–boat off Thorwald's whaling vessel! And you wore a suit of my clothes, and fought me because I said anyone could tell that you were a girl."

Helga's laughter rang out like a chime of bells. "Oh, Sigurd I had forgotten it! And we had nothing with us to eat but two cheeses! And Valbrand had to launch a boat and come after us!"

They abandoned themselves to their mirth, and Alwin laughed with them; but his curiosity had been aroused on another subject.

"I wish you would tell me something concerning this farther land," he said, as soon as he could get them to listen. "Does it in truth exist, or is it a tale to amuse children with?"

They both assured him that it was quite true.

"I myself have talked with one of the sailors who saw it," Sigurd explained. "He was Biorn's steersman. He saw it distinctly. He said that it looked like a fine country, with many trees."

"If it was a real country and no witchcraft, it is strange that he contented himself with looking at it. Why did he not land and explore?"

"Biorn Herjulfsson is a coward," Helga said contemptuously. "Every man who can move his tongue says so."

Sigurd frowned at her. "You give judgment too glibly. I have heard many say that he is a brave man. But he was not out on an exploring voyage; he was sailing from Iceland to Greenland, to visit his father, and lost his way. And he is a man not apt to be eager in new enterprises. Besides, it may be that he thought the land was inhabited by dwarfs."

"There, you have admitted that I am right!" Helga cried triumphantly. "He was afraid of the dwarfs; and a man who is afraid of anything is a coward."

But Sigurd could fence with his tongue as well as with his sword. "What then is a shield—maiden who is afraid of her kinswoman?" he parried. And they fell to wrangling laughingly between themselves.

Unheeding them, Alwin gazed away at the mysterious blue west. His eyes were big with great thoughts. If he had a ship and a crew,—if he could sail away exploring! Suppose kingdoms could be founded there! Suppose—his imaginings became as lofty as the drifting clouds, and as vague; so vague that he finally lost interest in them, and turned his attention to the approaching shore. They had come near enough now to see that the scattered islands had connected themselves into a peaked coast, a broken line of dazzling whiteness, except where dark chasms made blots upon its sides.

But sighting Greenland and landing upon it were two very different matters, he found. A little further, and they encountered the border of drift—ice that, travelling down from the northeast in company with numerous icebergs, closes the fiord—mouths in summer like a magic bar.

"I shall think it great luck if this breaks up so that we can get through it in a month," Valbrand observed phlegmatically.

"A month?" Alwin gasped, overhearing him.

The old sailor looked at him in contempt. "Does a month seem long to you? When Eric came here from Iceland, he was obliged to lie four months in the ice."

Four months on shipboard, with nothing more cheerful to look at than barren cliffs and a gray sea paved with grinding ice—cakes! The consternation of Alwin's face was so great that Sigurd took pity on him even while he laughed.

"It will not be so bad as that. And we will steer to a point north of the fiord and lie there in the shelter of an island."

"Shelter!" muttered the English youth. "Twelve eiderdown beds would be insufficient to shelter one from this wind."

Nor was the island of any more inviting appearance when finally they reached it. What of it was not barren boulders was covered with black lichens, the only hint of green being an occasional patch of moss nestling in some rocky fissure. To heighten the effect, icy gales blew continually, accompanied by heavy mists and chilling fogs.

Amid these inhospitable surroundings they were penned for two weeks,—Norse weeks of but five days each, but seemingly endless to the captives from the south. Editha retired permanently into the big bear–skin sleeping–bag that enveloped the whole of her little person and was the only cure for the chattering of her teeth. Alwin wrapped himself in every garment he owned and as many of Sigurd's as could be spared, and strove to endure the situation with the stoicism of his companions; but now and then his disgust got the better of his philosophy.

"How intelligent beings can find it in their hearts to return to this country after the good God has once allowed them to leave it, passes my understanding!" he stormed, on the tenth day of this sorry picnicking. "At first it was in my mind to fear lest such a small ship should sink in such a great sea; now I only dread that it will not, and that we will be brought alive to land and forced to live there."

Rolf regarded him with his amiable smile. "If your eyes were as blue as your lips, and your cheeks were as red as your nose, you would be considered a handsome man," he said encouragingly.

And again it was Sigurd who took pity on Alwin. "Bear it well; it will not last much longer," he said. "Already a passage is opening. And inside the fiord, much is different from what is expected."

Alwin smiled with polite incredulity.

The Thrall of Leif the Lucky

The next day's sun showed a dark channel open to them, so that before noon they had entered upon the broad water–lane known as Eric's Fiord. The silence between the towering walls was so absolute, so death–like, as to be almost uncanny. Mile after mile they sailed, between bleak cliffs ice–crowned and garbed in black lichens; mile after mile further yet, without passing anything more cheerful than a cluster of rocky islands or a slope covered with brownish moss. The most luxuriant of the islands boasted only a patch of crowberry bushes or a few creeping junipers too much abashed to lift their heads a finger's length above the earth.

Alwin looked about him with a sigh, and then at Sigurd with a grimace. "Do you still say that this is pleasanter than drowning?" he inquired.

Sigurd met the fling with obstinate composure. "Are you blind to the greenness of yonder plain? And do you not feel the sun upon you?"

All at once it occurred to Alwin that the icy wind of the headlands had ceased to blow; the fog had vanished, and there was a genial warmth in the air about him. And yonder,—certainly yonder meadow was as green as the camp in Norway. He threw off one of his cloaks and settled himself to watch.

Gradually the green patches became more numerous, until the level was covered with nothing else. In one place, he almost thought he caught a gleam of golden buttercups. The verdure crept up the snow–clad slopes, hundreds and thousands of feet; and here and there, beside some foaming little cataract tumbling down from a glacier–fed stream, a rhododendron glowed like a rosy flame. They passed the last island, covered with a copse of willows as high as a tall man's head, and came into an open stretch of water bordered by rolling pasture lands, filled with daisies and mild–eyed cattle. Sigurd clutched the English boy's arm excitedly.

"Yonder are Eric's ship–sheds! And there—over that hill, where the smoke is rising—there is Brattahlid!"

"There?" exclaimed Alwin. "Now it was in my mind that you had told me that Eric's house was built on Eric's Fiord."

"So it is,—or two miles from there, which is of little importance. Oh, yes, it stands on the very banks of Einar's Fiord; but since that is a route one takes only when he visits the other parts of the settlement, and seldom when he runs out to sea—Is that a man I see upon the landing?"

"If they have not already seen us and come down to meet us, their eyes are less sharp than they were wont to be three years ago," Rolf began; when Sigurd answered his own question.

"They are there; do you not see? Crowds of them—between the sheds. Someone is waving a cloak. By Saint Michael, the sight of Normandy did not gladden me like this!"

"Let down sail! drop anchor, and make the boats ready to lower," came in Valbrand's heavy drone.

CHAPTER XIII. ERIC THE RED IN HIS DOMAIN

```
Givers, hail!
A guest is come in;
Where shall he sit?

Water to him is needful
Who for refection comes,
A towel and hospitable invitation,
A good reception;
If he can get it,
Discourse and answer.
    Ha'vama'l
```

Ten by ten, the ship's boat brought them to land, and into the crowd of armed retainers, house servants, field hands, and thralls. A roar of delight greeted the appearance of Helga; and Sigurd was nearly overturned by welcoming hands. It seemed that the crowd stood too much in awe of Leif to salute him with any familiarity, but they made way for him most respectfully; and a pack of shaggy dogs fell upon him and almost tore him to pieces in the frenzy of their joyful recognition. A fusillade of shoulder–slapping filled the air. Not a buxom maid but found some brawny neck to fling her arms about, receiving a hearty smack for her pains. Nor were the men more backward; it was only by clinging like a burr to her mistress's side that Editha escaped a dozen vigorous caresses. Alwin, with his short hair and his contradictorily rich dress, was stared at in outspoken curiosity. The men whispered that Leif had become so grand that he must have a page to carry his cloak, like the King himself. The women said that, in any event, the youth looked handsome, and black became his fair complexion. Kark scowled as he stepped ashore and heard their comments.

"Where is my father, Thorhall?" he demanded, giving his hand with far more haughtiness than the chief.

"He has gone hunting with Thorwald Ericsson," one of the house thralls informed him. "He will not be back until to-night."

Whereupon Kark's colorless face became mottled with red temper-spots, and he pushed rudely through the throng and disappeared among the ship-sheds.

"Is my brother Thorstein also in Greenland?" Leif asked the servant.

But the man answered that Eric's youngest son was absent on a visit to his mother's kin in Iceland. When the boat had brought the last man to land, the "Sea-Deer" was left to float at rest until the time of her unloading; and they began to move up from the shore in a boisterous procession.

Between rich pastures and miniature forests of willow and birch and alder, a broad lane ran east over green hill and dale. Amid a babel of talk and laughter, they passed along the lane, the rank and file performing many jovial capers, slipping bold arms around trim waists and scuffling over bundles of treasure. Over hill and dale they went for nearly two miles; then, some four hundred feet from the rocky banks of Einar's Fiord, the lane ended before the wide-thrown gates of a high fence.

If the gates had been closed, one might have guessed what was inside; so unvarying was the plan of Norse manors. A huge quadrangular courtyard was surrounded by substantial buildings. To the right was the great hall, with the kitchens and storehouses. Across the inner side stood the women's house, with the herb-garden on one hand, and the guest-chambers on the other. To the left were the stables, the piggery, the sheep-houses, the cow-sheds, and the smithies.

The Thrall of Leif the Lucky

No sooner had they passed the gates than a second avalanche of greetings fell upon them. Gathered together in the grassy space were more armed retainers, more white–clad thralls, more barking dogs, more house servants in holiday attire, and, at the head of them, the far–famed Eric the Red and his strong–minded Thorhild.

One glance at the Red One convinced Alwin that his reputation did not belie him. It was not alone his floating hair and his long beard that were fiery; his whole person looked capable of instantaneous combustion. His choleric blue eyes, now twinkling with good humor, a spark could kindle into a blaze. A breath could fan the ruddy spots on his cheeks into flames.

As Alwin watched him, he said to himself, "It is not that he was three times exiled for manslaughter which surprises me,—it is that he was not exiled thirty times."

Alwin looked curiously at the plump matron, with the stately head–dress of white linen and the bunch of jingling keys at her girdle, and had a surprise of a different kind. Certainly there were no soft curves in her resolute mouth, and her eyes were as keen as Leif's; yet it was neither a cruel face nor a shrewish one. It was full of truth and strength, and there was comeliness in her broad smooth brow and in the unfaded roses of her cheeks. Ah, and now that the keen eyes had fallen upon Leif, they were no longer sharp; they were soft and deep with mother–love, and radiant with pride. Her hands stirred as though they could not wait to touch him.

There was a pause of some decorum, while the chief embraced his parents; then the tumult burst forth. No man could hear himself, much less his neighbor.

Under cover of the confusion, Alwin approached Helga. Having no greetings of his own to occupy him, he made over his interest to others. The shield–maiden was standing on the very spot where Leif had left her, Editha clinging to her side. She was gazing at Thorhild and nervously clasping and unclasping her hands.

Alwin said in her ear: "She will make you a better mother than Bertha of Trondhjem. It is my advice that you reconcile yourself to her at once."

"It was in my mind," Helga said slowly, "it was in my mind that I could love her!"

Shaking off Editha, she took a hesitating step forward. Thorhild had parted from Leif, and turned to welcome Sigurd. Helga took another step. Thorhild raised her head and looked at her. When she saw the picturesque figure, with its short kirtle and its shirt of steel, she drew herself up stiffly, and it was evident that she tried to frown; but Helga walked quickly up to her and put her arms about her neck and laid her head upon her breast and clung there.

By and by the matron slipped an arm around the girl's waist, then one around her shoulders. Finally she bent her head and kissed her. Directly after, she pushed her off and held her at arm's length.

"You have grown like a leek. I wonder that such a life has not ruined your complexion. Was cloth so costly in Norway that Leif could afford no more for a skirt? You shall put on one of mine the instant we get indoors. It is time you had a woman to look after you."

But Helga was no longer repelled by her severity; she could appreciate now what lay beneath it. She said, "Yes, kinswoman," with proper submissiveness, and then looked over at Alwin with laughing eyes.

Eric's voice now made itself heard above the din. "Bring them into the house, you simpletons! Bring them indoors! Will you keep them starving while you gabble? Bring them in, and spread the tables, and fill up the horns. Drink to the Lucky One in the best mead in Greenland. Come in, come in! In the Troll's name, come in, and be welcome!"

Rolf smiled his guileless smile aside to Egil. "It is likely that he will say other things 'in the Troll's name' when he finds out why the Lucky One has come," he murmured.

CHAPTER XIV. FOR THE SAKE OF THE CROSS

```
A wary guest
Who to refection comes
Keeps a cautious silence;
With his ears listens,
And with his eyes observes:
So explores every prudent man.
    Ha'vama'l
```

The Thrall of Leif the Lucky

In accordance with the fashion of the day, Brattahlid was a hall not only in the sense of being a large room, but in being a building by itself,—and a building it was of entirely unique appearance. Instead of consisting of huge logs, as Norse houses almost invariably did, three sides of it had been built of immense blocks of red sandstone; and for the fourth side, a low, perpendicular, smooth rock had been used, so that one of the inner walls was formed by a natural cliff between ten and twelve feet high. Undoubtedly it was from this peculiarity that the name Brattahlid had been bestowed upon it, Brattahlid signifying 'steep side of a rock.' Its style was the extreme of simplicity, for a square opening in the roof took the place of a chimney, and it had few windows, and those were small and filled with a bladder–like membrane instead of glass; yet it was not without a certain impressiveness. The hall was so large that nearly two hundred men could find seats on the two benches that ran through it from end to end. Its walls were of a symmetry and massiveness to outlast the wear of centuries; and the interior had even a certain splendor.

To–night, decked for a feast, it was magnificent to behold. Gay–hued tapestries covered the sides, along which rows of round shields overlapped each other like bright painted scales. Over the benches were laid embroidered cloths; while the floor was strewn with straw until it sparkled as with a carpet of spun gold. Before the benches, on either side of the long stone hearth that ran through the centre of the hall, stood tables spread with covers of flax bleached white as foam. The light of the crackling pine torches quivered and flashed from gilded vessels, and silver–covered trenchers, and goblets of rarely beautiful glass, ruby and amber and emerald green.

"I have nowhere seen a finer hall," Alwin admitted to Sigurd, as they pushed their way in through the crowd. "If the high–seats were different, and the fire–place was against the wall, and there were reeds upon the floor instead of straw, it would not be unlike what my father's castle was."

"If I were altogether different, would I look like a Saxon maiden also?" Helga's voice laughed in his ear. She had come in through the women's door, with Thorhild and a throng of high–born women. Already she was transformed. A trailing gown of blue made her seem to have grown a head taller. Bits of finery—a gold belt at her waist, a gold brooch on her breast, a string of amber beads around the white neck that showed coquettishly above the snowy kerchief—banished the last traces of the shield–maiden, For the first time, it occurred to Alwin that she was more than a good comrade,—she was a girl, a beautiful girl, the kind that some day a man would love and woo and win. He

82

gazed at her with wonder and admiration, and something more; gazed so intently that he did not see Egil's eyes fastened upon him.

Helga laughed at his surprise; then she frowned. "If you say that you like me better in these clothes, I shall be angry with you," she whispered sharply.

Fortunately, Alwin was not obliged to commit himself. At that moment the headwoman or housekeeper, who was also mistress of ceremonies in the absence of the steward, came bustling through the crowd, and divided the men from the women, indicating to every one his place according to the strictest interpretation of the laws of precedence.

If there had been more time for preparation there would have been a larger company to greet the returned guardsman. Yet the messengers Thorhild had hastily despatched had brought back nearly a score of chiefs and their families; and what with their additional attendants, and Leif's band of followers, and Eric's own household, there were few empty places along the walls.

According to custom, Eric sat in his high–seat between two lofty carved pillars midway the northern length of the hall. Thorhild sat in the seat with him; the high–born men were placed upon his right; the high–born women were upon her left. Opposite them, as became the guest of honor and his father's eldest son, Leif was established in the other high–seat. Tyrker, weazened and blinking, and swaddled in furs, sat on one side of him; Jarl Harald's son was on the other, merry–eyed, fresh–faced, and dressed like a prince. On either hand, like beads on a necklace, the crew of the "Sea–Deer" were strung along. Kark came the very last of the line, in the lowest seat by the door. Alwin had fresh cause to be grateful to the fate that had changed their stations. His place was on the foot–stool before Leif's high–seat, guarding the chief's cup. It was an honorable place, and one from which he could see and hear, and even speak with Sigurd when anything happened that was too interesting to keep to himself.

Among Leif's men there were many temptations to consult together. Not one but was waiting in tense expectancy for the move that should disclose the guardsman's mission. They had sternest commands from Leif to take no step without his order. They had equally positive word from Valbrand to defend their chief at all hazards. Between the two, they sat breathless and strained, even while they swallowed the delicacies before them.

The Thrall of Leif the Lucky

When the towels and hand–basins had gone quite around, and all the food had been put upon the table, and the feast was well under way, three musicians were brought in bearing fiddles and a harp. Their performance formed a cover under which the guests could relieve their minds.

"Do you observe that he has let his crucifix slide around under his cloak where it is not likely to be noticed?" one whispered to another. "It is my belief that he wishes to put off the evil hour."

"When the horse–flesh is passed to him he will be obliged to refuse, and that will betray him," the other answered.

But Eric did not see when Leif shook his head at the bearer of the forbidden meat; and that danger passed.

Rolf murmured approvingly in Sigurd's ear: "He is wise to lie low as long as possible. It is a great thing to get a good foothold before the whirlwind overtakes one."

Sigurd shook his head in his goblet. "When you wish to disarm a serpent, it is best to provoke him into striking at once, and so draw the poison out of his fangs."

Under the shelter of some twanging chords, Alwin whispered up to them: "If you could sit here and see Kark's face, you would think of a dog that is going to bite. And he keeps watching the door. What is it that he expects to come through it?"

Neither could say. They also took to watching the entrance.

Meanwhile the feasting went merrily on. The table was piled with what were considered the daintiest of dishes,—reindeer tongues, fish, broiled veal, horse–steaks, roast birds, shining white pork; wine by the jugful, besides vats of beer and casks of mead; curds, and loaves of rye bread, mounds of butter, and mountains of cheese. Toasts and compliments flew back and forth. Alwin was kept leaping to supply his master's goblet, so many wished the honor of drinking with him. His news of Norway was listened to with breathless attention; his opinion was received with deference. Often it seemed to Alwin that he had only to speak to have his mission instantly accomplished. The English youth noticed, however, that amid all Leif's flowing eloquence there was no reference to the new faith.

The feast waxed merrier and noisier. One of the fiddlers began to shout a ballad, to the accompaniment of the harp. It happened to be the "Song of the Dwarf–Cursed Sword." Sigurd swallowed a curd the wrong way when the words struck his ear; even Valbrand looked sideways at his chief. But Leif's face was immovable; and only his followers noticed that he did not join in the applause that followed the song. Some of the crew let out sighs of impatience. They could fight,—it was their pleasure next after drinking,—but these waits of diplomacy were almost too much for them. It was fortunate that some trick–dogs were brought in at this point. Watching their antics, the spectators forgot impatience in boisterous delight.

While they were cheering the dog that had jumped highest over his pole, and pounding on the table to express their approval, through chinks in the uproar there came from outside a sound of voices, and horses neighing.

"It is Thorwald, home from hunting!" Sigurd said eagerly, looking toward the door. In a moment he was proved correct, for the door had opened and admitted the sportsman and his companion.

Thorwald Ericsson was as unlike his brother Leif as the guardsman was different from some of the plain farmers around him. He was long and lean and wiry, and his thin lips were set in cruel lines. His dress was shabby, and out of all decent order. Patches of fur had been torn out of his cloak; he was muddy up to his knees, and there was blood on his tunic and on his hands. He stood staring at the gay company in surprise, blinking in the sudden light, until his gaze en–countered Leif, when he cried out joyously and hastened forward to seize his hand.

Alwin drew away in disgust from the touch of his ill–smelling garments. As he did so, his eye fell upon Kark, who had laid hold of Thorwald's companion and was talking rapidly in his ear.

The new–comer was not an amiable–looking man. Above his gigantic body was a lowering face that showed a capacity for slyness or viciousness, whichever better served his turn. As Kark talked to him, his brow grew blacker and he plucked savagely at his knife–hilt. It dawned upon Alwin then that he must be Kark's father, the steward Thorhall of whom Valbrand had spoken.

"In which case it is likely that something is about to happen," he told himself, and tried to communicate the news to Sigurd. But Thorwald stood between them, still pressing Leif's hand.

When the hunter had passed on down the line of the crew, Thorhall came forward and greeted Leif with great civility. Only as he was retiring his eye appeared to fall upon Alwin for the first time; he stopped in pained surprise.

"What is this I see, chief? You have got another bowerman in place of my son, whom your father gave to you? It must be that Kark has done something which you dislike. Tell me what it is, and I will slay him with my own hand."

Again Valbrand looked sideways at his master, as if to remind him that he had warned him of this. Tyrker began to fumble at his beard with shaking hands, and to blink across at Eric. This time they had attracted the Red One's attention. His palm was curved around his ear that he might not lose a word; his eyes were fastened upon Leif.

The guardsman's face was as inscrutable as the side of his goblet. "If Kark had deserved to be slain, he would not be living now. He is less accomplished than this man, therefore I changed them."

The steward bent his head in apparent submission. "Now, as always, you are right. Rather than a boorish Odin−man, better is it to have a man of accomplishments,—even though he be a hound of a Christian." He turned away, as one quite innocent of the barb in his words.

An audible murmur passed down the line of Leif's men. No one doubted that this was Thorhall's trap to avenge the slights upon his son. Would the chief let this also pass by? Though their faces remained set to the front, their eyes slid around to watch him.

Leif drew himself up haughtily and also very quietly. "It is unadvisable for you to speak such words to me," he said. "I also am a Christian."

Flint had struck steel. Eric leaped to his feet in a blaze.

86

The Thrall of Leif the Lucky

"Say that again!"

Thorwald and a dozen of the guests shook their heads frantically at him, but Leif repeated the declaration.

Crash! Down went Eric's goblet, to shiver into a thousand pieces on the table edge. With a furious curse he flung himself back in his chair, and leaned there, panting and glaring.

A hum of voices arose around the room. Men called out soothing words to the Red One and expostulations to Leif. Others felt furtively for their weapons. Some of the women turned pale and clung to each other. Helga arose, her beautiful face shining like a star, and left their ranks and came over and seated herself on Leif's foot–stool, though the voice of Thorhild rose high and shrill in scolding. Leif's men straightened themselves alertly, and fixed upon their master the eyes of expectant dogs. Thorwald hurried to his brother, and laid hands on his shoulders, and endeavored to argue with him.

Leif put him aside, as he arose and faced his father. Through the tumult his voice sounded quiet and strong, the quiet of perfect self–command, the strength of a fearless heart and an iron will.

"It is a great grief to me that you dislike what I have done; yet now I think it best to tell you the whole truth, that you cannot feel that I have acted underhanded in anything."

Eric gave vent to a sound between a growl and a snarl, and flounced in his chair. Thorhild made her son a gesture of entreaty. But Lei/, looking back into the frowning faces, calmly continued:

"Olaf Trygvasson converted me to Christianity two winters ago, and I tell you truly that I was never so well helped as I have been since then. And not only am I a Christian, but every man who calls himself mine is also one, and will let blood–eagles be cut in his back rather than change his faith."

No sound came from Eric; but his mouth was half open, as though his rage were choking him, and his face was purple and twitched with passion. He had picked up the ugly little bronze battle–axe that leaned against his chair, and was hefting it and fingering it and shifting it from hand to hand. Gradually the eyes of all the company centred upon the

87

gleaming wedge, following it up and down and back and forth, expecting, dreading.

"If he does not wish to go so far as to slay his own son, he has yet an easy mark in me," Alwin murmured, his eyes following the motions like snake–charmed birds. "If he raises it again like that, I think I shall dodge." Out of the corners of his eyes, he could see many movements of uneasiness among Leif's men.

Only Leif went on quietly: "You have always known that your gods must die, so it should not surprise you to be told now that they are dead; and it should gladden your hearts to know that One has been found who is both ever–living and willing to help. Therefore King Olaf has sent me to lay before you, that if you will accept this faith as the men of Trondhjem have done—"

Helga sprang aside with a shriek of warning. Eric's arm had shot up and back. With a bellow of rage, he leaped to his feet and hurled the axe at his son's head. Simultaneously came an oath from Valbrand and a roar from the crew; then a thundering blow, as the axe, missing the Lucky One by ever so small a space, buried itself deep in the wall behind him.

Instantly every man of the crew was on his feet, and there was clashing of weapons and a tumult of angry voices. Eric's men were not behindhand, and many of the guests drew swords to protect themselves. They were on the verge of a bloody scene, when again Leif's voice sounded above the uproar. He had drawn no weapon, nor swerved nor moved from his first position.

"Put up your swords!" he said to his men.

Those who caught the under–note in his voice hastened to obey, even while they protested.

He turned again to his father, and into his manner came that strange new gentleness that is known as courtesy, which set him above the raging Red One as a man is above a beast.

"It seems strange to me that the one who taught me the laws of hospitality should be the one to break them with me. Nevertheless, now that I have been frank with you, I will not anger you by speaking further of my mission. And since you do not wish to lodge us, I and my men will go back to my ship and sleep there until my errand is accomplished. Valbrand, do you go first, that the others may follow you in order."

The old warrior hesitated as he wheeled. "It is you who should go first, my chief. The heathens will murder you. We—"

"You will do as I command," Leif interrupted him distinctly; and after one glance at his face, they obeyed.

Nothing like this had ever been seen before. A hush of awe fell upon Eric's men and Eric's guests. One by one the crew filed out, with rumbling threats and scowling faces, but wordless and empty–handed. Alwin took advantage of his close attendance to be the last to go, but finally even he was forced to leave. Helga marched out beside him, her head held very high, her eyes dealing sharper stabs than her dagger, Leif's scar–let colors flying in her cheeks. Thorhild called to her, but she swept on, unheeding.

At the door, Alwin paused to look back. Ne would not be denied that. Leif still stood before his high–seat, holding Eric with his keen calm eyes as a man holds a mad dog at bay. Never had he looked grander. Alwin silently swore his oath of fealty anew.

That no one should accuse him of cowardice, the guardsman waited until the door had closed upon the last one of his men. Then, slowly, with the utmost composure, he walked out alone between the ranks of his enemies.

An involuntary murmur applauded him as he passed. Thorhild, torn as she was between anger and pride, was quick to catch its meaning and to use it. Whatever Leif's faith, she was still his mother. Taking her life in her hand, she bent over and whispered in Eric's ear.

The darkness of his face became midnight blackness,—then was suddenly rent apart as with lightning. He brought his fist down upon the table with a mighty crash.

"Stop! When did I say anything against lodging you? Do you think to throw shame upon my hospitality before my guests? I will have none of your religion,—I spit upon it. You are no longer my son,—I disown you. But you shall sleep under my roof and eat at my board so long as you remain in Greenland, you and your following. No man shall breathe a word against the hospitality of Eric of Brattahlid. Thorhall, light them to sleeping rooms!" His breath, which had been growing shorter and shorter, failed him utterly. He finished with a savage gesture, and threw himself back in his chair.

If Leif had consulted his pride, it is likely that that night Greenland would have seen the last of him. But foremost in his heart, before any consideration for himself, was the success of his mission. After a moment's hesitation, he accepted the offer courteously, and permitted Thorhall's obsequious attendance.

One can imagine the amazement of his followers when he came out to them, not only unharmed, but waited upon by the steward and a dozen torch-bearers.

"It is because he is the Lucky One," they whispered to each other. "His God helps him in everything. It is a faith to live and die for."

They followed him across the grassy courtyard to the foot of the steps leading up to his sleeping-room, and would not leave him until he had consented that Valbrand and Olver should go in with him for a bodyguard.

"And this boy also," he added, signing to Alwin.

As Alwin approached, Kark had the impudence to shoulder himself forward also.

"Chief, are you going to turn me out to lie with the swine in the kitchen?" he said boldly. "Remember that every time you have slept in this room before, I have lain across your threshold."

Leif's glance pierced him through and through. "Is it sense for a man to trust his slumbers to a dog that has bitten him once? Go lie in the kennel. If it were not for provoking Eric, you would not wait long to feel my blade." He turned and walked up the steps, with his hand on Alwin's shoulder.

CHAPTER XV. A WOLF-PACK IN LEASH

```
He utters too many
Futile words
```

The Thrall of Leif the Lucky

```
Who is never silent;
A garrulous tongue,
If it be not checked,
Sings often to its own harm.
     Ha'vama'l
```

Out in the courtyard the four juniors of Leif's train were resting in the shade of the great hall, after a vigorous ball–game. It was four weeks since the crew of the "Sea–Deer" had come into shore–quarters; and though the warmth of August was in the sunshine, the chill of dying summer was already in the shadow. Sigurd drew his cloak around him with a shiver.

"Br–r–r! The sweat drops are freezing on me. What a place this is!"

Rolf, leaning against the door–post, whittling, finished his snatch of song,

```
"'Hew'd we with the Hanger!
 It happed that when I young was
 East in Eyrya's channel
 Outpoured we blood for grim wolves,'"–
```

and looked down with his gentle smile. "If you mean that it is this doorstep that is not to your mind, you take too much trouble. We must leave it in a moment; do you not hear that?" He jerked his head toward the gateway, from which direction they suddenly caught the faint notes of hunters' horns. "It is Eric's men returning from their sport. In a little while they will be here, and we must try our luck elsewhere."

He straightened himself lazily, flicking the chips from his dress; but the other three sat doggedly unmoved.

Alwin said, testily: "I do not see why we must be kept jumping like frightened rabbits because Leif has ordered us to avoid quarrels. What trouble can we get into if we remain here without speaking, and give them plenty of room to pass by us into the hall?"

Rolf smiled amiably at the three scowling faces. "Certainly you are good mates to Ann the Simpleton, if you cannot tell any better than that what would happen? They would go a rod out of their way to bump into one of us. If they have been successful, their blood will be up so that they will wish to fight for pleasure. If they have failed, they will be murderous with anger. It took less than that to start the brawl in which Olver was slain,—which I dare say you have not forgotten."

Alwin winced, and Sigurd shivered with something besides the cold. It was not the bloody tumult of the fight that they remembered the most clearly; it was what came after it. True to his interpretation of hospitality, Eric had punished the murder of his guest's servant by lopping off, with his own sword, the right hand of the murderer; whereupon Leif had sworn to mete the same justice to any man of his who should slay a follower of Eric.

Slowly, as the blaring horns and trampling hoofs drew nearer, the three rose to their feet. Only Alwin struck the ground a savage blow with the bat he still held.

"By Saint George! it is unbearable that we should be forced to act in such a foolish way! Has Leif less spirit than a wood–goat? I do not see what he means by it."

"Nor I," echoed Sigurd.

"Nor I," growled Egil. "I believed he had some of Eric's temper in him."

"I do not see why, myself," Rolf admitted; "but I see something that seems to me of greater importance, and that is how he looked when he gave the order."

They followed him across the grassy enclosure, though they still grumbled.

"Where shall we go?"

"The stable also is full of Eric's men."

"Before long we shall be shoved off the land altogether. We will have to swim over to Biorn's dwarf–country."

"I propose that we go to the landing place," exclaimed Sigurd. "It may be that the ship which Valbrand sighted this morning is nearly here."

"I say nothing against that," Rolf assented.

They wheeled promptly toward a gate. But at that moment, Alwin caught sight of a blue-gowned figure watering linen in front of the women's-house.

"Do you go on without me," he said, drawing back. "I will follow in a moment."

Sigurd threw him a keen glance. "Is it your intention to do anything exciting, like quarrelling with Thorhall as you did last night? Let me stay and share it."

There was a little embarrassment in Alwin's laugh. "No such intention have I. I wish to see the hunters ride in."

The hunters were an imposing sight, as they swept into the court, and broke ranks with a cheer that brought heads to every door. White-robed thralls ran among the champing horses, unsaddling them; scarlet-cloaked sportsmen tumbled heaps of feathered slain out of their game-bags upon the grass; horns brayed, and hounds bayed and struggled in the leash. But Alwin forgot to notice it, he was hurrying so eagerly to where Helga, Gilli's daughter, walked between her strips of bleaching linen, sprinkling them with water from a bronze pan with a little broom of twigs.

The outline of her face was sharper and the roses glowed more faintly in her cheeks, but she welcomed him with her beautiful frank smile.

"I was hoping some of you would think it worth while to come over here. It is a great relief for me to speak to a man again. I am so tired of women and their endless gabble of brewing and spinning. Yesterday Freydis, Eric's daughter, drove over, and all the while she was here she talked of nothing but—"

"Eric's daughter?" Alwin repeated in surprise. "Not until now have I heard that Leif had a sister. Why is she never spoken of? Where does she live?"

Helga shrugged impatiently. "She lives at Gardar with a witless man named Thorvard, whom she married for his wealth. She is a despisable creature. And the reason no one speaks of her is that if he did he would feel Thorhild's hands in his hair. There is great hatred between them. Yesterday they quarrelled before Freydis had been here any time at all. And I was about to say that I was glad of it, since it brought about Freydis' departure: all the time she was here she spoke of nothing save her ornaments and costly things. Oh, I do not see why Odin had the wish to create women! It would have been pleasanter if they had remained elm–trees."

Alwin regarded her with eyes of the warmest good–will. "It would become a heavy misfortune to me if you were an elm–tree,—though it is likely that I should speak with you then quite as often as I do now. Except at meals, I seldom see you. But I never pass your window that I do not remember that you are toiling within, and say to myself that I am sorry for your bad luck."

"I give you thanks," answered Helga, with her friendly smile. "Where have the other men gone? I wished to speak with Sigurd."

"They have gone to the landing–place, to watch for a ship that Valbrand sighted this morning from the rocks."

She cried out joyfully: "A ship in Einar's Fiord? Then it belongs to some chief of the settlement, who is returning from a Viking voyage! There will be a fine feast made to welcome him."

Alwin followed her doubtfully up the lane between the white patches. "Is it likely that that will do us any good? It is possible that Leif will not be invited."

The heat of her scorn was like to have dried the drops she was scattering. "You are out of your senses. Do you think men who trade among the Christians are so little–minded as Eric? Leif is known to be a man of renown, and the friend of Olaf Trygvasson. They will be proud to sit at table with him."

"It may be that he will refuse to feast with heathens."

"That is possible," Helga admitted. She emptied her pan with a little flirt of impatience, and sighed. "How tiresome everything is! To sit at a table where one is afraid to move lest there be a fight! I speak the truth when I say that this is the merriest diversion I have,—standing out here, watering linen, and watching who comes and goes. And now that my pan is empty, I must betake myself indoors again. Yonder is Valbrand beckoning you."

It is probable that Alwin would not have hurried to obey the summons, but with a nod and a smile Helga turned away, and there was nothing for him but to go forward to meet the steersman.

The old warrior regarded the young favorite with his usual apathy. "It is the wish of Leif that you attend upon him directly."

"Is he in his sleeping–room?"

"Yes."

It occurred to Alwin to wonder at this summons. His usual hour for reading came after Leif had retired for the night. If the chief had overheard the dispute with Thorhall! He lingered, meditating a question; but a second glance at Valbrand's battered face dissuaded him. He turned sharply on his heel, and strode across to the storehouse that had become Leif's headquarters.

A loft that could be reached only by a ladder–like outer stairway, and was without fireplace or stove or means of heating, does not appear inviting. But one has a keener sense of appreciation when he considers that the other alternative was a bed in the great hall, where the air was as foul as it was warm, and the room was shared with drunken men and spilled beer and bones and scraps left from feasting. Alwin had no inclination to hold his nose high in regard to his master's new lodgings. England itself offered nothing more comfortable.

When he had come up the long flight of steps and swung open the heavy door, he had even an impulse of admiration. This, the state guest–chamber, was not without softening details. It was large and high and weather–proof, and boasted three windows. The box–like straw–filled beds, that were built against the wall, were spread with snowy linen and covers of eiderdown. The long brass–bound chests that stood on either side the door were piled with furs until they offered the softest and warmest of resting–places. A score of Leif's rich dresses, hanging from a row of nails, covered the bare walls as with a gorgeous tapestry. The table was provided with graceful bronze water–pitchers and wash–basins of silver, and was littered over with silver scissors and gold–mounted combs and bright–hilted knives, and a medley of costly trinkets. Near the table stood a great carved arm–chair.

At the sight of the man who leaned against its flaming red cushions of eiderdown, Alwin forgot his admiration. The chief's eyebrows made a bushy line across his nose. The young bowerman knew, without words, why he had been sent for. He stopped where he was, a pace within the door, angry and embarrassed.

After a while, Leif said sternly: "You are very silent now, but it appears to me that I heard your voice loud enough in the hall last night."

"It was only that I was accusing Thorhall of a trick that he tried to put upon me. He allowed me to go up to the loft above the provision house without telling me that the flooring had been taken up, so that they might pour the new mead into the vat in the room below. In one more step I should have fallen through the opening and been drowned. It is plain he did it to avenge Kark. I should have burst if I had not told him so."

"I have commanded that my men shall not hold speech with the men of Eric except on friendly matters; that they shall avoid a quarrel as they would avoid death."

His tone of quiet authority had begun to have its usual effect upon his young follower; Alwin's head had bent before him. But suddenly he looked up with a daring flash.

"Then I have not been disobedient to you, lord; for I would not avoid death if it seemed to me that such shirking were cowardly."

A moment the retort brought a grim smile to Leif's lips; then suddenly his face froze into a look of terrible anger. He half started from his chair.

"Do you dare tell me to my face that, because I order you to keep the peace, I am a coward?"

Alwin gave a great gasp. "Lord, there is no man in the world who would dare speak such words to you. I but meant that I cannot bear such treatment as Thorhall's in silence."

Had another said this, the answer might have been swift and fierce; but Leif's manner toward this follower was always different from his way with others,—whether out of respect for his accomplishment, or a fancy for him, or because he discerned in him some refinement that was rare in that brutal age. The anger faded from his face and he said quietly: "Can you not bear so small a thing as that, for so great a cause as the spreading of your faith?"

The boy started.

"Without peace in which to gain their friendship so that they will hear us willingly, our cause is lost. It is not because I am a craven that I bear to be the guest of the man who sought my life, who turns his face from me when I sit at his board, who allows his servants to insult me. Sometimes I think it would be easier to bear the martyrdom of the blessed saints!" He made a sudden fierce movement in his chair, as though the fire in his veins had leaped out and burnt his flesh.

Then, for the first time, Alwin understood. He bent before him, rebuked and humbled.

"Lord, I see that I have done wrong. I ask you to pardon it. Say what you would have me do."

"Put my commands ahead of your desires, as I put King Olaf's wish before my pride, and as he sets the will of God before his will."

"I promise I will not fail you again, lord."

"See that you do not," Leif answered, with a touch of sternness.

CHAPTER XVI. A COURTIER OF THE KING

```
A better burden
No man bears on the way
Than much good sense;
That is thought better than riches
In a strange place:
Such is the recourse of the indigent.
    Ha'vama'l
```

The Thrall of Leif the Lucky

The next afternoon when Helga came out to water the linen, she found Alwin waiting for her, on the pretext of hunting in the long grass for a lost arrow–head.

He greeted her gayly: "I will offer you three chances to guess my news."

She paused, with her twig broom raised and dripping, and scanned him eagerly. "Is it anything about the ship that came yesterday? I heard among the women that it is the war–vessel of Eric's kinsman, Thorkel Farserk, just come back from ravaging the Irish coast. Is his wife going to make a feast to welcome him?"

"I will not deny that you have proved a good guesser. And, by Dunstan! he deserves to be received well. Never saw I such a sight as that landing! There were more slaves than there were men in the crew. Not a man but had a bloody bandage on his head or his body, and the arms and legs of some were lacking. Two of the crew were not there at all, and their sweethearts had come down to the shore to meet them; and when they found that they had been slain, they tore their hair and tried to kill themselves with knives."

"That was foolish of them," said Helga, calmly. "Better was it that their lovers should die in good repute than live in the shame of cowardice. But tell me the news. Has it happened, as I supposed, that there is going to be a feast, and Leif is asked to it?"

"Messengers came this morning from Farserk's wife. But you dare not guess the rest."

"I dare throw this pan of water over you if you do not tell me instantly."

"It would not matter much if you did. I am to have new clothes,—of black velvet with bands of ermine. But hearken now: Leif has accepted the invitation! Even Valbrand thinks this a great wonder. At this moment Sigurd is selecting the chief's richest dress, and Rolf is getting out the most costly of the gifts that were brought from Norway."

Helga set down her pan for the express purpose of clapping her hands. "Now I am well content; for at last they will see him in all his glory, and know what manner of man they have treated with disrespect. I have hoped with all my heart for such a thing as this, but by no means did I think he cared enough to do it."

Alwin shook his head hastily. "You must not get it into your mind that it is to improve his own honor that he does it now. I know that for certain. It is to give his mission a good appearance."

Helga picked up her pan with a sigh. "When he begins to preach that to them, he will knock it all over again."

Alwin considered it his duty to frown at this; but it must be confessed that something very similar was in his own thoughts as he followed his lord into Thorkel Farserk's feasting–hall that night. Whatever his religion, the guardsman's rank and his gallant appearance and fine manners compelled admiration and respect. It could not but seem a pity to his admirers that soon, with one word, he would he forced to undo it all.

"It is harder than the martyrdom of the saints," Alwin murmured bitterly. Then his eye fell upon the silver crucifix, shining pure and bright on Leif's breast, and he realized the unworthiness of his thoughts, and resigned himself with a sigh.

But he found that even yet Leif's purposes were beyond him. Never, by so much as a word, did the guardsman refer to the subject of the new religion,—though again and again his skilful tongue won for him the attention of all at the table. He spoke of battles and of feasts, and of the grandeur of the Northmen. With the old men he discussed Norwegian politics; with the young ones he talked of the famous champions of King Olaf's guard. To the women who wished to know concerning the King's house, and the Queen, he answered with the utmost patience. He described everything, from weddings to burials, with the skill of a minstrel and the weight of an authority, and always with the tact of a courtier.

Gradually whispers of praise circled around the board, whispers that fell like sweetest music on the jealous ears of Leif's followers. Thorhild leaned back from her food and watched him with open pride,—and though Eric kept his face still turned away, he set his ear forward so that he should hear everything.

Alwin was almost beside himself with nervousness. "If the crash does not come soon, I shall go out of my wits," he whispered to Rolf.

The Wrestler turned upon him a face of such unusual excitement that he was amazed. "Do you not see?" he whispered. "There will not be any crash. I have just begun to understand. It was this he meant when he spoke to you of gaining their friend—ship that they might hear him willingly. Do you not see?"

Alwin's relief was so great that at first he dared not believe it. When the truth of it dawned upon him, he was overcome with wonder and admiration. In those days, nine men out of every ten could draw their swords and rave and die for their principles; it was only the tenth man that was strong enough to keep his hand off his weapon, or control his tongue and live to serve his cause.

"Luck obeys his will as the helm his hand. I shall never worry over him again," he said contentedly, as with the others he waited in the courtyard for Leif to come out of the feasting—hall.

Sigurd laughed gayly. "Do you know what I just overheard in the crowd? Some of Thorkel's men were praising Leif, and one of Eric's churls thought it worth while to boast to them how he had known the Lucky One when he was a child. Certainly the tide is beginning to turn."

"Leif Ericsson is an ingenious man," Rolf said, with unusual decision. "I take shame upon me that ever I doubted his wisdom."

Egil uttered the kind of sullen grunt with which he always prefaced a disagreeable remark. "Ugh! I do not agree with you. I think his behavior was weak—kneed. Knowing their hatred against the word Christian, all the more would I have dinged it into their ears; that they might not think they had got the better of me. Now they believe he has become ashamed of his faith and deserted it."

The three broke in upon him in an angry chorus. Alwin said sternly: "You speak in a thoughtless way, Egil Olafsson. You forget that he still wears the crucifix upon his breast. How can they believe that he has forgotten his faith or given it up, when they cannot look at him without seeing also the sign of his God?"

Egil turned away, silenced.

This feast of Thorkel Farserk was the first of a long line of such events. With the approach of autumn, ships became a common sight in the fiords—Those chieftains who had left Greenland in summer to spear whales in the northern ocean, or make trading voyages to eastern countries, or cruise over the high seas on pirates' missions, now came sailing home again with increased wealth and news-bags bursting. For every traveller, wife or kinsman made a feast of welcome—a bountiful entertainment that sometimes lasted three days, with tables always spread, and horns always filled, and games and horse-races, and gifts for everyone. At each of these celebrations, Leif appeared in all his splendor; and his tactful tongue held for him the place of honor. His popularity grew apace. The only thing that could keep step with it was the exultation of his followers.

CHAPTER XVII. THE WOOING OF HELGA

```
At love should no one
Ever wonder
In another;
A beauteous countenance
Oft captivates the wise,
Which captivates not the foolish.

A man must not
Blame another
For what is many men's weakness;
For mighty love
Changes the sons of men
From wise into fools.
      Ha'vama'l
```

It happened, one day, that an accidental discovery caused Alwin to regard these festivities in a new light.

It was a morning in November when he was in the hall, kneeling before master to lace his high boots. Leif stood before the fire, wrapping himself up for a ride across the Settlement. Some unknown cause had made the atmosphere of the breakfast-table so particularly ungenial,—Thorhild sitting with her back to her spouse, and Eric manifesting a growing desire to hurl goblets at the heads of all who looked at him,—that the courtier had judged it discreet to absent himself from the next meal. He now stood arraying himself from a pile of furs, and talking with Tyrker, who sat near him blinking in the fire–glow. Save a couple of house–thralls scrubbing at the lower end of the room, no one else was present, Eric having started on his morning round of the stables, the smithies, and the cow–houses.

As he pulled on his fur gloves, Leif smiled satirically. "It is a good thing that I was present last summer when King Olaf converted Kjartan the Icelander. It was then I learned that those who cannot be dealt with by force may often be led by the nose without their knowing it. Olaf said to the fellow, 'The God I worship does not wish that any should be brought to Him by force. As you are averse to the doctrines of Christianity, you may depart in peace.' Whereupon Kjartan immediately replied: 'In this manner I may be induced to be a Christian.' So, because I have kept my promise to speak no more concerning Christianity, men have become curious about it, and yesterday two chiefs came of their own will and asked me questions concerning it."

Tyrker poked his head out to say "So?" then snuggled back into his wraps again, to chuckle contentedly. He was so wound up in furs that he looked like a sharp little needle in a fuzzy haystack.

Leif's smile gave way to a frown. "Another man came to me also, on a different errand,—Ragner Thorkelsson,—it may be that you saw him? He wished to make a bargain concerning Helga."

Alwin gave a great start, so that the leather thong snapped in his hand; but his master went on unheeding.

"You know it is my wish that she shall marry as soon as she can make a good match, since she is not happy while she sits at home with Thorhild, and it is not likely that she will like her father much better. It has been in my mind through every feast; but until now, none of the men who have asked for her has seemed to me a good match."

Though his hands kept mechanically at their work, Alwin's brain seemed to have come to a standstill. It must be a dream, a foolish dream. It was not possible that such a thing could have been planned without his even suspecting it. He listened numbly.

"The first man was too old. The second was not of good enough kin; and the other two had not enough property. Ragner Thorkelsson lacks none of these. He is young; his father's father was a lawman; and he owns eighteen farms and many ships."

Though he did not in the least know why, Alwin felt a hot desire to seek out Ragner Thorkelsson and kill him.

"So?" said Tyrker, peering forth inquiringly. "Yet never have I heard that he any accomplishments had, or that in battle enemies he had overcome."

"No," Leif assented.

He did not finish immediately, and there was a pause. From the courtyard came a clashing and jingling of bells, as servants brought the reindeer from the feeding–ground to harness them to the boat–like sledges that stood waiting.

"It may be that I have acted unwisely," Leif said at last; "but because I did not believe it would be according to Helga's wish, I told him that I would not bargain with him."

Alwin buried a gulping laugh in the fur cloak he had picked up. He had known that it would end in some such way. Of course; it had been idiotic to expect anything else. He listened smilingly for what else Leif had to say.

The guardsman drew the last strap through the last buckle on his double fur jacket, and turned toward the door. "It may be that I was unwise, but it may also be that it will not matter much. The most desirable men come home latest; we have not seen them all. It is likely that the next feast will decide it."

Long after the door had closed upon Leif, and he had entered the sledge and been whirled through the gate in a flurry of snow and a clamor of bells, Alwin stood there, motionless. Tyrker dozed in the comfort–able warmth, and woke to find him still staring down into the fire.

"What hast thou, my son?" he questioned, kindly. Alwin came to himself with a start and a stare, and catching up his cloak, hurried out of the room without replying.

"I will find Helga and tell her that she must put a stop to it," he was saying to himself as he went. "That is what I will do. I will tell her that she must stop it."

The Thrall of Leif the Lucky

Pulling his cap lower as the keen wind cut his face, he hurried across the courtyard toward the women's–house, trying to frame some excuse that should bring Helga to the door where he could speak to her.

Half–way across, he bumped into Rolf.

"Hail, comrade! Have you left your eyes behind you in your hurry?" the Wrestler greeted him, catching him by the shoulders and spinning him round and round as he attempted to pass. "You look as sour as last night's beer. What will you give to hear good tidings?"

"Nothing. Let me go. I am in a hurry," Alwin fumed.

"You have not outrun your curiosity, have you? I have just learned why it is that Thorhild no longer speaks to Eric, and why he is in a mood to smash things."

"Why?" asked Alwin, impatiently; but he no longer struggled, for he knew it was useless in Rolf's grip.

"Because last night Thorhild told Eric that she had become a Christian. Her bowerwoman told Helga, and when I met Helga—"

"Met her? Where? Is she in the women's–house?"

Rolf shook him by the shoulders he still held. "Is that all you have to say to news of such importance? Do you not see that now that Thorhild has been converted, Eric's men will no longer dare oppose us; lest in time to come, when she has brought Eric round—"

"I say, where did you meet Helga?" roared Alwin.

Rolf released him, and stood looking at him with an inscrutable smile. "If I were not your sworn friend, I should enjoy wringing your neck," he said. "I met Helga at the gate yonder. She was going over to Glum Starkadsson's to get something for Thorhild, and also because she wished a walk over the hard snow."

"Is it far from here? And in what direction?"

The Thrall of Leif the Lucky

"For what purpose do you wish to know that?"

"I ask you in what direction it lies."

"The Troll take you!" Rolf gave it up with a laugh. "It lies to the north of the fiord,—beyond a bridge that crosses a river that runs through a valley. And it is not far. Have you not yet learned that in Greenland people do not take long strolls in the winter–time?"

Alwin pulled a hood over his cap, strapped his cloak still tighter, drew a pair of down–lined mittens from under his girdle and put them on over his gloves, and, without another syllable, turned and made for the gate.

It was glorious weather, dry and clear, and so still that very little of the cold penetrated his fur–lined garments. Snow covered everything, fine and firm and dazzling. The smooth white expanse suggested a wish that he had brought the skees he was learning to use; then the sight of the line of boulders he would have had to steer around made him rejoice that he had not. Far ahead of him rose the glittering wall of inland ice,—that mysterious frozen sea that covers all of Greenland except its very border, and never advances and never recedes. What made it stop there, he wondered? And what lay beyond it? And could those tales be true that the old women told, of terrible magical beings living on its silent frozen peaks?

The sight of a dark speck moving over the white plain far ahead of him banished every other thought. It might be that it was Helga. He crunched on eagerly. Then he dipped into the valley and lost sight of the speck, found it on the bridge, dipped again, and again it was lost to view.

It was not until the fence of Glum Starkadsson's farm was plainly in sight, that he caught another glimpse of it. But this time it was coming toward him, from the gateway.

Certainly that long crimson cloak and full crimson hood belonged to Helga. In a moment, she waved her hand at him. Soon he could see her face under the white fur border. Her scarlet lips were curving in a smile. The snow–glare brought out the dazzling fairness of her pearly skin, and her eyes were like two radiant blue stars. It seemed to Alwin that he had never known before how beautiful she was. A strange shyness came over him, that weighted his feet and left him without a word to say when they met.

But Helga greeted him cheerily. "Did you ever breathe finer air? I wish Thorhild would run out of gold thread every day in the week. Are you in a hurry?"

"No," Alwin began hesitatingly, "I—"

She did not wait for the end. "Then turn back with me a little way, and I will tell you something worth hearing."

He turned obediently and walked beside her, trying to think how to put what he had come to say.

"You remember hearing of Egil's father Olaf, who was so ill–tempered that Egil dared not go home and confess that he had become a Christian? Gunnlaug Starkadsson returned this morning from visiting his wife, and she says that last night the old man's horse threw him so that his head hit against a stone, and it caused his death."

She made an impressive pause; but Alwin stalked along in silence, grinding his heels deep into the snow.

"Do you not see what that means?" she asked, impatiently. "Egil will now come into his inheritance, and become one of the richest men in the Settlement."

The trouble was that, in the first flash, Alwin had seen it all too plainly. He had seen that now Egil would become just such a man as Leif was wishing to bargain with. The thought burnt him like a hot iron, and he opened his lips to pour out his frenzy; but he could not find the words.

After a moment he said, sullenly: "I should be thankful if he would leave Leif's service, so that I could sometimes speak to you without having him watch me like a dog at a rabbit–hole."

Helga turned toward him with frank interest. "I wonder at that also. He does not act so when I speak to Sigurd or Rolf. But then, he has behaved very strangely to me ever since he talked with Skroppa in Iceland, two seasons ago."

"He spoke to me of Skroppa the first time I saw him," Alwin said, absently. Then a flicker of curiosity awoke in him. "I wish that you would tell me what 'Skroppa' stands for. I do not know whether it is man or beast or demon."

Even out there in the open, Helga glanced about for listeners before she answered. "Skroppa is a fore–knowing woman, who lives among the unsettled places north of here, in a cabin down in a hollow. Though Leif will not admit it, it was she who took the curse off Eric's sword."

It seemed to Alwin that here at last was an opening. He said harshly: "I wonder if she would be wise enough to tell whom Leif will marry you to before the feasting is over?"

Helga stood still and looked at him. "What are you talking about?"

He stopped in front of her, with a fierce gesture, and in one angry burst told her all he had heard. He could not understand how she could listen so calmly, kicking the snow with the toe of her shoe.

When he had finished, she said quietly: "Yes, I know he has that intention in his mind. It is for that reason that every time I go to a feast he gives me costly ornaments, and makes me wear them. I have had great kindness from his hands. But do not let us speak of it further."

Alwin caught her roughly by her wrists, and shook her a little as he looked into her eyes. "You must not let him marry you to anyone. Do you hear? You _must_ not, _I_ love you."

Helga's look of resentment changed to one of pleased surprise, and she shook his hands heartily. "Do you truly, comrade? I am glad, for I like you very much indeed,—as much as I like Sigurd."

"Then swear by your knife that you will not let him marry you to anyone."

She pulled her hands away, a little impatiently. "Why do you ask that which is useless?"

"But you have just said that you liked me."

"I do; but what does that matter, since I cannot marry you?"

So light had the yoke of servitude grown on Alwin's shoulders that he had almost forgotten its existence. He opened his lips to ask, "Why?" Then it came back to him that he was a slave, a worthless, helpless dog of a slave. He closed his lips again and walked on without speaking, staring ahead of him with fierce, despairing eyes.

CHAPTER XVIII. THE WITCH'S DEN

```
Moderately wise
Should each one be,
But never over-wise:
His destiny let know
No man beforehand;
His mind will be freest from care.
     Ha'vama'l
```

Because it was Yule Eve, the long deserted temple on the plain was filled with light and sound. Fires blazed upon the floor; the row of gilded idols came out of the shadow and shone in all their splendor. The altars were reddened with the blood of slaughtered cattle; the tapestried walls had been spattered with it. The temple priest dipped a bunch of twigs into the brimming copper bowl, and sprinkled the sacrificial blood over the people who sat along the walls ... They raised the consecrated horns and drank the sacred toasts. To Odin! For victory and power. To Njord! To Frey! For peace and a good year ... Eric of Brattahlid laid his hands upon the atonement boar and made a solemn vow to render justice unto all men, whatsoever their transgressions. The others followed him in this, as in everything.

Because this was happening in the temple, Brattahlid, the source of light and good cheer, was dark and gloomy. In the great hall there was no illumination save the flickering firelight. Black shadows blotted out the corners and stretched across the ceiling. The long benches were emptied of all save Leif's followers and Thorhild's band of women. The men sat like a row of automatons, drinking steadily, in deep silence, with furtive glances toward their leader. Leif leaned back in his high-seat, neither speaking nor drinking, scowling down into the flames.

The Thrall of Leif the Lucky

"He is angry because Eric keeps up the heathen sacrifice," the women whispered in each other's ears. "He has all of Eric's temper when he is angered. It would be as much as one's life were worth to go near him now." Shivering with nervousness, they crouched on the bench beside their mistress's seat.

Thorhild leaned on the arm of her chair, shading her brow with her hand that she might gaze at Leif unseen. Sometimes her eyes dwelt on his face, and sometimes they rested on the silver crucifix that shone on his breast; and so great was her tenderness for the one, that she embraced the other also in a look of yearning love.

When the house—thralls had cleared away the tables, they crept into a corner and stayed there, fearing even to go forward and replenish the sinking fire, though gusts of bitter cold came through the broken window behind them.

Little as they guessed it, something besides cold was coming through the hole in the window. Even while they shivered and nodded beneath it, a pair of gray Saxon eyes were sending keen glances through it, searching every corner.

As the eyes turned back to the outer darkness, Alwin's voice whispered with a long breath of relief: "I am certain they have not noticed that we have gone out."

From the darkness, Sigurd's voice interrupted softly: "Is Kark there?"

"I think he is still in his comer. The light is bad, and the flames are leaping between, but it seems to me that I can make him out."

They emerged from the shadow into the moonlight, and it became evident that Sigurd was shaking his head dubiously.

"It seems to me also that I heard the door creak after us, and saw a shadow slip past as we turned this corner. He is always on the watch; it might easily be that our going out aroused his suspicions so that he is hiding somewhere to track us. More than anything else in the world, is he desirous to catch you in some disobedience."

Alwin tramped on doggedly. To all appearances, the court was as deserted as a graveyard at midnight. Not even the whinny of a horse broke the stillness. They passed into the shadow of a storehouse, and Alwin dived into, the recess under the steps and began to fumble for something hidden there. When he drew out a pair of skees and proceeded to put them on, Sigurd burst forth with increased vehemence.

"Alwin, I implore you to heed my advice. My mind tells me that nothing but evil can come of meddling with Skroppa. There will be no limit to Leif's anger if he—"

"I tell you he will not find out," Alwin answered over his shoulder. "His mind is so full of Eric's ill–doings, that he will not notice my absence before I am back again. And to–night is the only night when I am not in danger of being spied upon by Eric's men. It is my only chance."

"Yet Kark—"

"Kark may go into the hands of the Trolls!"

"It is not unlikely that you will accompany him. You are doing a great sin. Harald Fairhair burned his son alive for meddling with witchcraft."

Although his toes were thrust into the straps of the runner–like skees, Alwin stamped with exasperation. "You need not tell me that again. I know as well as you that it is a sin. But will not penance make it right?"

"You will dishonor Leif's holy mission."

"I shall not cause any quarrel, nor offend anyone. What harm can I do?"

Sigurd laid his hands on his friend's shoulders and tried to see his face in the dark. "Give it up, comrade; I beseech you to give it up. If you should be discovered, I tell you that though a priest might win you a pardon from Heaven, no power on earth could make your peace with Leif Ericsson."

Alwin said slowly: "If he discovers what I have done, I will endure any punishment he chooses, because I owe him some obedience while I eat his bread and wear his clothes. But I am not his born thrall, so I will have my own way first. Urge me no more, brother; my mind is fixed."

The Thrall of Leif the Lucky

Sigurd released him instantly. "I will say nothing further,—except that it is my intention to try my luck with you." Stooping into the recess, he drew out an-other pair of skees and began to fasten them on.

At the prospect of companionship, Alwin felt a rush of relief,—then a twinge of compunction.

"Sigurd, you must not do this thing. There is no reason why you should run this risk."

"There would be no reason why you should call me your friend if I did otherwise," Sigurd cut him short. "Do you think me a craven, to let you go alone where you might be tricked or murdered? Have you a weapon?"

"Leif will not allow me so much as a dagger, so to-night I borrowed from his table the old brass-hilted knife that Eric gave him in his boyhood. It is unlikely that he will miss that. I have it here." Throwing back his cloak, he showed it thrust through his girdle.

"Come, then," said Sigurd curtly. "And have a care for your skees. You are not over-skilful yet."

He caught up the long staff that acts something like a balance-pole in skeeing, and darted away. Alwin followed, with an occasional prod of his staff into a shadow that seemed thicker than it should be. By a side-gate, they left the courtyard and struck out across the fields, where the snow was packed as hard as a road-bed. Noiseless as birds, and almost as swift, they skimmed along over the snow-clad plains and half-frozen marshes.

As was to have been expected, the young Viking was an expert. To see him shoot down a hillside at lightning speed, his skees as firmly parallel as though they were of one piece, his graceful body bending, balancing, steering, was to see the next best thing to flying. Alwin's runners threw him more than once, lapping one over the other as he was zigzagging up a slope, so that he tripped and rolled until a snow-bank stopped him.

As he regained his feet after one of these interruptions, he made some angry remark; but beyond this there was little said. It was a dreary night to be on an uncanny errand, with a chill in the air that seemed to freeze the heart. A fitful, spiteful wind drove the clouds like frightened sheep, and strove to blow out the pale patient moon. Sometimes it seemed

111

almost to succeed; suddenly, when they most needed light to guide their six−foot runners between the great boulders, the light would go out like a torch in the water. The gusts lay in wait for them at the corners, to leap out and lash their faces with a shriek that chattered their teeth. The lulls between the gusts were even worse; it seemed as though the whole world were holding its breath in dread. They held theirs, darting uneasy glances at the glacier wall glittering far ahead of them.

When a long, low wail smote their ears, their hearts leaped into their throats. They were travelling along the edge of a black ravine. Halting, they stood with suspended breath, staring down into the darkness.

The cry came again, yet more piercing; then suddenly it split into a hissing sound like a kettle boiling over. Alwin broke into a nervous laugh. "Cats!" he said.

But Sigurd stiffened as quickly as he had relaxed. "One of Skroppa's! She swarms with them. See! Is not that a light down there?"

A sudden flicker there certainly was,—if it was not a ghost−fire. The last cloud scurried from before the face of the long−suffering moon; before the wind could bring up another fleecy flock, the pale light crept down into the hollow and revealed the dark outline of a cabin clinging among the rocks.

Alwin slipped out of his skees and made sure of his knife. "That, then, is her house. We will leave the skees here."

"Though you never were known to heed advice, I will offer you another piece," Sigurd answered. "We must go softly; and if we find the door unlocked, enter quickly and without knocking. Otherwise it is possible that we will stay outside and talk to the stones."

It was a tedious descent, yet somehow the time seemed plenty short enough before they stood at the threshold. The stillness at the bottom of the hollow was death−like; only the flickering light on the window spoke of life. Silently the door yielded to Alwin's touch.

Darkness and a dying fire were all that met their eyes. They thought the room empty, and took a step forward. Instantly the space was alive with the green eyes of countless cats.

The Thrall of Leif the Lucky

The air was split with yowlings and spittings and hissing. Soft furry bodies bounced against them and bit and clawed around their legs. From the farthest corner came the lisping voice of a toothless old woman.

"Who dares interrupt my sleep when the visions of things I wish to know are passing before me? Better would it be for him to put his hand into the mouth of the Fenriswolf."

Alwin said slowly, "It is the English thrall."

After a pause, the voice answered crossly, "I know no English thrall."

"How comes it, then, that more than a year ago you told something concerning him which made Egil Olafsson his mortal foe?"

Out of the darkness came a sudden cackling laugh. "That is true. I told the Black One that the maiden he loved would love an English thrall instead. And he wished to stick his sword through me!"

"Is that what you told him?" cried Alwin, in amazement.

Sigurd echoed the cry. Yet as their minds ran back over Egil's strange actions, they could not doubt that this was the key that unlocked their mystery.

From an invisible corner came a stir, a creak, and then the sound of feet lighting softly on the floor. A tiny figure appeared on the edge of the shadows beyond the dying fire. The light fell upon furry gray feet; and Alwin's first thought was that a monstrous cat had dropped down. Then the flames leaped higher, and showed a furry cloak and a furry hood, and from its fuzzy depths protruding, a sharp yellow beak for a nose, and a hairy yellow peak for a chin. Of eyes, one saw nothing at all.

Out of the fuzzy depths came a lisping voice. "When a thrall of Leif Ericsson, who is also a Christian, thinks it worth while to risk his life and his soul to consult me, I forgive it that I am wakened at midnight. It is a compliment to my powers that I do not take ill. Say what you wish to learn from me."

The Thrall of Leif the Lucky

Alwin felt Sigurd touch him reproachfully, and shame burned in his cheeks; but he had gone too far to retreat. He said bluntly: "I wish to know whether Helga, Gilli's daughter, is to be given to Egil. Each time he speaks across the floor to her, I am as though I were pricked with sharp knives. I have endured it through three feasts; but I look upon her with such eyes of love, that I can bear it no longer."

"I will dull those knives, even as Odin blunts the weapons of his enemies. Helga will not be given to Egil, because he is too haughty to ask for her since he knows that she loves you instead of him."

It had seemed to Alwin that if he could only know this, he would be satisfied; yet now his questions piled upon each other.

"Then do you promise that she will be given to me? How am I to save her? How am I to get my freedom? How long am I to wait?"

The Sibyl sank her head upon her breast so that her nose and chin quite disappeared, and she stood before them like some furry headless beast. There was a long pause. Alwin nervously followed the pairs of eyes, noiselessly appearing and disappearing, from floor to ceiling, in every part of the room. Sigurd set his back against the door and carried on a silent struggle with the heavy lumps, hanging by teeth and claws upon his cloak.

At last Skroppa raised her head and answered haltingly: "You ask too much, according to the time and the place. To know all that clearly, I should sit on a witches' platform and eat witches' broth, and have women stand about me and sing weird songs. Without music, spirits do not like to help. I can only see bits, vaguely as through a fog... I see your body lying on the ground I see a ship where never ship was seen before I see—I see Leif Ericsson standing upon earth where never man stood before. It seems to me that I read great luck in his face... And I see you standing beside him, though you do not look as you look now, for your hair is long and black. The light is so bright that I cannot... Yes, one thing more is open to my sight. I see that it is in this new land that it will be settled whether your luck is to be good or bad."

She stopped. They waited for her to go on; but soon it became evident that the foretelling was finished. With all his prudence, Sigurd began to laugh; and Alwin burst out in a passion of impatience: "For which, you gabbler? For which? I can make nothing of such

114

jargon. Tell me in plain words whether it will be for good or ill."

Skroppa answered just one word: "Jargon!"

Alwin stormed on unheeding, but Sigurd's laughter stopped: something in the tone of that one word chilled his blood and braced his muscles like a frost. He strained his eyes to pierce the shadow and make out what she was doing; and it seemed to him that he could no longer see her. She had disappeared,—where? In a sudden panic he groped behind him for the door; found it and flung it open. It was well that the moon was shining at that moment.

"Alwin!" he shouted. The yellow face was close to the thrall's unconscious shoulder; one evil claw–like hand was almost at his cheek. What she would have done, she alone knew.

While his cry was still in the air, Sigurd pulled his companion away and through the door. Up the steep they went like cats. Near the top, Alwin tripped, and his knife slipped from his belt and fell against a boulder. It lay there shining, but neither of them noticed it. Into their skees, and over the crusted plains they went,—reindeer could not have caught them.

CHAPTER XIX. TALES OF THE UNKNOWN WEST

```
Fire is needful
To him who is come in,
And whose knees are frozen;
Food and raiment
A man requires
Who o'er the fell has travelled.
    Ha'vama'l
```

"I tell you I must go over the track once more. It may have slipped out of my girdle at some of the places where I tripped."

Alwin's words rose in frosty cloud; for he was Leif's unheated sleeping–room, drawing on an extra pair of thick woollen stockings in preparation for his customary outing.

"It is foolishness. Four times already have you been over the ground without finding it. A long brass–halted knife could not have been overlooked if it had been there. I tell you that you lost it among the rocks of the hollow, and that you would be wise to give it up."

Sigurd's answer came in muffled though emphatic tones, for he was huddled almost out of sight among the furs on the chest, as he waited for his companion to complete his dressing. Now that genuine winter weather was upon them, the loft was necessarily abandoned as a sleeping apartment; but it still served as a dressing–room for such slight and speedy alterations as were attempted.

As he pulled on the big heelless skeeing–shoes, Alwin sighed anxiously. "I must find it. Any day Leif may miss it and ask."

"He is not likely to, since he has already gone a week without noticing its absence. And if he should, you have only to say that you borrowed it to protect yourself from wolves. That will not be much of a lie, Skroppa being nearer wolf than human. He will feel that he was wrong to have denied you a weapon, and he will only scold a little."

"It is true that he is in a good temper again," Alwin admitted. "Yesterday I heard Tyrker tell Valbrand that many more chiefs had asked concerning Christianity; and last night, after Eric had gone to sleep in his seat, I heard Leif say to Thorhild that if now he could only do some great deed to prove the power of his God, it was his opinion that half of Greenland would be ready to believe."

Sigurd crept out of the bearskins with a shiver. "I say nothing against that. But let us end this talk. My blood–drops are so frozen they rattle in my body."

He thumped down the steps as though rigid with cold, and jumped and danced and beat his breast before he could bring himself to stand still long enough to fasten on his skees.

"Where shall we go, then?" Alwin asked, as they glided out of the gate in the dim light of an Arctic winter day. "It may be that to go over that road again might become a misfortune. Once I saw Kark looking after us with a grin which I would have knocked off his face if I had not been in a hurry."

Sigurd instantly faced toward the snow–crusted hills that lay between them and Eric's Fiord. "Then to–day it will be useful to go in another direction, so that any suspicions he has may go to sleep again. If Thorhall had been at home, he would have overtaken you before this. His green eyes are well fitted for spying."

Perhaps it was this reference to green eyes that recalled to Alwin the scene of the foretelling. Perhaps it had never gone very far out of his mind.

After they had swung along a while in silent enjoyment of the swift motion and the answering tingle in their blood, he said abruptly: "It may be that there was some truth at her tongue-roots, after all."

Sigurd made a sly move with his staff, so that the other suddenly tripped and fell headlong; whereupon he said gravely: "Lo, I believe so too, for behold, already it has come true that 'I see your body lying on the ground.'"

Alwin consented to laugh, as he picked himself up and untangled his runners; but he was too much in earnest to be turned aside.

"I do not mean in regard to that," he said, when they were once more in motion. "I mean what she told concerning some new untrodden land."

Sigurd became instantly attentive, as though the reference had been much in his own mind also.

"It has occurred to me that perhaps she was speaking of that western land you told me of. It might he that this would be a way out of my difficulties. If I could escape to that land with Helga, so would I at once save her and gain my freedom."

Sigurd's eyes brightened, then gloomed again. "Yes,—but that 'if' is like a mile-wide rift in the ice. You can never get over it."

"It might be that I could get around it. I tell you I shall go out of my wits if I cannot see some trail to follow, no matter how faint it is. Tell me what else you know of this land."

They were starting down a slope at the speed of the wind, but Sigurd suddenly leaped into the air with a cheer; and cheered again as he landed, right-side up and unstaggered, at the bottom of the hill.

"By Michael, I will do better than that! I will take you to talk with one of Biorn's own men. One is visiting Aran Bow–Bender now, across the fiord. I heard Brand Knutsson say so last week."

"By my troth, Sigurd," Alwin cried eagerly, "when things come to one's hand like that, I believe it is a sign that he should try his luck with them! Would we have time to go there to–day?"

"Certainly; do you not see that the light is only just fading from the mountain tops? so it can be but a little past noon. The only difficulty is that the ice may not be in a condition for us to cross the fiord. A warm land–wind has been blowing for three days; and even in the North, where the seal–hunters go, the ice often breaks up under them. But now allow me to get my bearings. That is the smoke from Brattahlid, behind us; and yonder I see the roofs of Eric's ship–sheds. Here,—we will go in this direction until we come to a high point of the bank."

Across the white plain that stretched in that direction, they skimmed accordingly. Once they came upon a herd of Eric's reindeer, rooting under the snow for moss; but aside from that, they saw no living thing. Low–hanging gray clouds seemed to have shut out the world. Now and then, from far out in the open water came the grinding and crunching of huge ice–cakes, see–sawing past each other. Once there sounded the reverberating thunder of two icebergs in a duel.

"If there were any bears on that ice, they have found by this time that there can be even worse things than men with spears," Sigurd observed, as he listened.

It is doubtful whether Alwin had heard the noise at all. He answered, absently: "Yes,—and if we do not wish to come to the subject at once, we can say that we are cold and dropped in to warm ourselves."

"To say that we are cold will always be truthfully spoken," Sigurd assented, his teeth chattering like beads. "I do not believe that Stark–Otter was much chillier when he pulled off his clothes and sat in a snow–bank."

It turned out to be even more truthful than they imagined. They had little more than left the shore and ventured out upon the ice, when the gentle east wind developed into a gale, that presently wrapped them in the blinding folds of a snow–storm. The ice became invisible a step ahead of their feet. They had retained their staffs when they left their skees upon the bank; but even feeling their way step by step was by no means secure. It was not long before Alwin went through, up to his neck; and if he had been uncomfortable before, he was in wretched plight now, drenched to the skin with ice–water.

"If you also get in this condition, we shall both perish," he chattered, when he had managed to clamber out again by the fortunate accident of his staff's falling crosswise over the hole. "I will continue to go first; and do you hoard your strength to save us both when I get too stiff to move." It proved a wise precaution; for in a few minutes he broke through again, and it took all his companion's exertions to pull him out. Before they reached the opposite shore, he had been in four times, and was so benumbed with cold that Sigurd was obliged to drag him up the bank and into the hut of Aran Bow–Bender.

One low room was all there was of it, and that was smoky and dirty, the air thick with the smells of stale cooking and musty fur garments. Dogs were lying about, and there was a goat–pen in the corner; but a fire roared in the centre, a ring of steaming hot drinks stood around it, and behind them sat a circle of jovial–hearted sportsmen, who seemed to ask no greater pleasure than to pull off a stranger's drenched garments, rub him to a tingle, and pour him full of hot spicy liquids.

To return that night was out of the question. Alwin was too exhausted even to think of it,—beyond a sleepy wonder as to whether a scolding or a flogging would be the penalty of his involuntary truancy. He even forgot the existence of the man he had come to see, though the round, red–faced sailor dozed in a corner directly opposite him.

Sigurd, however, was less muddled; and he had, besides, a strong objection to returning the next morning, to be laughed at for his weather–foolishness.

"If we do not want to be made fun of, it would be advisable for us to take someone back with us to distract people's attention," he reasoned, and laid plans accordingly. The next day, as they began buckling up their various outer garments preparatory to departure, he suddenly struck into the conversation with a reference to the festivities at Brattahlid.

In a moment the sailor—man's eyes opened, like two round windows, above his fat cheeks.

The Silver—Tongue spoke on concerning the products of the Brattahlid kitchen, the fat beeves that were slaughtered each week, the gammons and flitches that were taken from the larder, and the barrels of ale that were tapped.

As he settled his boots with a final stamp, and stretched out his hand toward the door, Grettir the sailor arose in his corner.

"Hold on, Jarl's son," he said thickly. "If it is not against your wish, I will go with you." He made a propitiatory gesture to the group around the fire. "You will not take it ill, shipmates, if I leave you now, with many thanks for a good entertainment. The truth is that it has always been in my mind to visit this renowned Eric, if ever I should be in this part of Greenland; and now that some one is going that way to guide me, I think it would be unadvisable to lose the chance."

"The matter shall be as you have fixed it, Grettir," Sigurd said politely, "if you are able to run on skees with us."

Grettir laughed in a jovial roar, as he helped himself to a pair of runners that rested on antlers against the wall. "You have a sly wit, Sigurd Jarlsson. You think, because I am round, I am wont to roll like a barrel. I will show you."

And it proved that, for all his bulk, he was as light on his feet as either of them. In those days, when every landlubber could handle a boat like a seaman, every sailor knew at least something about farming, and could ride a horse like a jockey. All the way back, he kept them going at a pace that took their breath.

In the excitement of welcoming so renowned a character to Brattahlid, reprimands and curiosity were alike forgotten. By the time they had him anchored behind an ale—horn on the bench in the hail, he held the household's undivided attention. Good—natured with feasting, and roused by the babel around him, he began yarn—spinning at the first hint.

"The western shore? No man living can tell you more of the wonders of that than I,—not Biorn Herjulfsson himself!" he declared. And forthwith he related the whole adventure, from Biorn's rash setting out into unknown seas, to his final arrival on the Greenland coast.

To hear of these strange half—mythical shores from one who had seen them with his own eyes, was more than interesting. The jarls' sons listened breathlessly while he reeled out his tale between swallows.

"And the fair winds ceased, and northern winds with fog blew continually, so that for many days we did not know even in what direction we were sailing. Then the sun came into sight, and we could distinguish the quarters of heaven. We hoisted sail, and sailed all day before we saw land, but when we came to it we knew no more what it was than this horn here. Biorn said he did not think it was Greenland, but he wished to go near it. It had no mountains but low hills, and was forest—clad. We kept the land on our left and sailed for two days before we came to other land. This time it was flat and covered with woods. Biorn said that he did not think this was Greenland, for very large glaciers were said to be there. We wished to go ashore, as we lacked both wood and water, and the fair wind had fallen. There were some cross words when Biorn would not, but gave orders to turn the prow seaward. This time we sailed three days with a southwest wind, and more land came in view, which rose high with mountains and a glacier. Biorn said this had an inhospitable look, and he would not allow that we should land here either. But we sailed along the shore, and saw that it was an island. After this we had no more chances, for the fourth land we saw was Greenland."

A buzz of comment rose from all sides. "Is that all that you made of such a chance as that?"—"Certainly the gods waste their favors on such as Biorn Herjulfsson."—"Is he a coward, or what does he lack?" "He is as dull as a wooden sword."

Now whether or no all this coincided with the private opinion of Grettir the Fat, has nothing to do with the matter. Biorn Herjulfsson had been his chief. The sailor rose suddenly to his feet, with his hand on his knife and an angry look on his red face.

"Biorn Herjulfsson is no coward!" he shouted fiercely. "I will avenge it in blood on the head of him who says so."

Eric was not there to keep order; a dozen mouths opened to take up the challenge. But before any sound could come out of them, Leif had risen to his feet. "Are you such mannerless churls that I must remind you of what is due to a guest?" he said, sternly. "Learn to be quicker with your hospitality, and slower with your judgment of every act you cannot under–stand. Grettir, I invite you to sit here by me and tell me more concerning your chief's voyage."

When Grettir had gone proudly up to take his seat of honor, and the others had returned to their back–gammon and ale, Sigurd looked at Alwin with a comical grimace.

"Now I wonder if my cleverness in bringing this fellow here has happened to overshoot the mark! Leif is eager to get renown; suppose he takes it into his head to make this voyage himself?"

Alwin sank his voice to a whisper: "The idea came to me as soon as he called Grettir to him. But it was not your doing. Now the saying is proved true that 'things that are fated take place.' Do you remember the prophecy,—that when I stand on that ground I shall stand there by the side of Leif Ericsson?"

CHAPTER XX. ALWIN'S BANE

```
Much goes worse than is expected.
    Ha'vama'l
```

The light of the short day had faded, but the wind had not gone down with the sun. Powdery snow choked the air in a blinding storm. One could not distinguish a house, though it were within a foot of his eyes.

"If I do not come to the gate before long," Alwin observed to the shaggy little Norwegian pony along whose neck he was bending, "I shall believe that the fences have been snowed under."

He had been sent out to find another of Biorn's sailors who chanced to be visiting in the neighborhood, to invite him to come to Brattahlid and tell what else he might know concerning his chiefs voyage,—a subject in which Leif had become strangely interested. Alwin had accomplished his errand, and was returning half–frozen and with a ravenous appetite that made him doubly impatient over their slow progress.

The Thrall of Leif the Lucky

"If we do not get there before long," he repeated to the pony, with a dig into his flanks, "I shall get afraid that the drifts have covered the houses also, and that we are already riding over the roofs without knowing it."

But as he said it, a tall gate-post rose on either side of him; and the pony turned to the left and began groping his way across the courtyard to his stable.

The windows of the great hall glowed with light, and warmth and jovial voices and fragrant smells burst out upon the storm with every swing of the broad door. As soon as he had stabled his horse, Alwin hurried toward it eagerly, and, stamping and shaking off the snow, pushed his way in through the crowd of house-thralls, who were running to and from the pantry with bowls and trenchers and loads of food. He hoped that Leif was there, so that he should not have to go back across the snowy courtyard to the sleeping-loft to make his report. Stopping just inside the threshold, he looked about for him, blinking in the strong light and shaking back the wet fur of his collar.

It seemed as though every member of the house-hold except Leif were lounging along the benches, waiting for the evening meal. Eric leaned against one arm of his high-seat, talking jovially with Thorhall the steward, who had returned that morning from seal-hunting. Thorhild bent over the other arm, and gesticulated vigorously with her keys, as she gave her housekeeper some last directions regarding the food. Further along, Sigurd and Helga sat at draughts. Near at hand, a big fur ball, which was the outward and visible sign of Tyrker, was rolled up close to a chess-board. Only Leif's cushioned seat was empty.

With petulant force, Alwin jammed his bearskin cap down upon his head and turned to retrace his steps. Turning, his eye fell upon an object that Eric had just taken from the steward and held up to the light to examine. The flames caught at it eagerly, flashing and sparkling, so that even at that distance Alwin had no difficulty in recognizing the brass-hilted knife. Eric burst into a mighty roar of laughter. His voice, never greatly subdued, penetrated to every corner of the room. "I could stake my head that it is Leif's! I myself gave it to him for a name-fastening. And you found it in Skroppa's den? Oh, this is worth a hearing! Here is mirth! In Skroppa's den,—Leif the Christian! Ho, Flein, Asmund, Adils, comrades,—listen to this! No jester ever invented such a jest."

The Thrall of Leif the Lucky

He got on his feet and beckoned them with both arms, stamping with laughter. Catching sight of Alwin's white face at the door,—for it was ashen white,—he beckoned him also, with a fresh burst of malicious laughter.

"And you, you little priest-robed puppet, come nearer, so you shall not lose a word. Oh, it will be great fun for you! And for you, my Thorhild,—and the haughty-headed Helga! And gray old Tyrker too! Listen now, Graybeard, and learn, even with one foot in the grave. Saw you never such a game as this foster-son of yours has played with unchanging face!" He choked with his laughter, so that his face grew purple; and the household waited, leaning from the benches, nudging and whispering; the servants gaping over the dishes in their hands; Alwin standing by the door, motionless as the dead; Sigurd sitting, still as the dead, in his place.

Stamping and rocking himself back and forth, and banging on the arm of his seat, the Red One got his breath at last, and bellowed it out. "Leif the Christian in the den of Skroppa the Witch! His knife proves it; Thorhall found it among the rocks at her very door. Saw I never such slyness! Think of it, comrades; he is driven to ask help of Skroppa,—he who feigns to scowl at her very name!—he who would have us believe in a god that he does not trust in himself! Here is an unheard-of two-facedness! Never was such a fraud since Loki. Here is merriment for all!"

He continued to shout it over and over, roaring with mocking laughter; his men nudging each other, sniggering and grinning and calling gibes across the fire. Leif's men sprang up, burning with rage and shame,—then stood speechless, daring neither to deny nor resent it.

Alwin made a quick step forward to where the firelight revealed him to all in the room, and cried out hoarsely: "Here is falsehood! My hand, and no other, took Leif Ericsson's knife to the den of Skroppa the Witch."

Motion and sound stopped for a moment,—as though the icy blast, that came just then through the opening door, had frozen all the life in the room. Then a voice called out that the thrall was lying to cover his master; and Eric's laughter burst out anew, and the jeering redoubled.

The Thrall of Leif the Lucky

But Alwin's voice rose high above it. "Fools! Is it worth while for me to give my life for a lie? Ask Sigurd Haraldsson, if you will not believe me. He knows that I went there on Yule Eve, to ask concerning my freedom. The knife slipped from my belt as I was climbing the rocks. Leif knew of it no more than you. Ask Sigurd Haraldsson, if you will not believe me."

Sigurd rose and tried to speak, but his tongue had become like a withered leaf in his mouth, so that he could only bow his head.

Yet from him, that was enough. Such an uproar of delight broke from Leif's men as drowned all the jeering that had gone before, and made the rafters ring with exulting. Alwin knew that, whatever else he would have to bear, at least that lie was not upon him, and he drew a deep breath of relief. All the light did not die out of his face, even when Leif stepped out of the shadow of the door and stood before him.

She had not spoken falsely who had said that the fire of Eric burned in the veins of his son. In his white-hot anger, the guardsman's face was terrible. Death was in his stern-set mouth, and death blazed from his eyes. Rolf, Sigurd, Helga, even Valbrand, cried out for mercy; but Alwin read the look aright, and asked for nothing that was not there.

While their cries were still in the air, Leif's blade leaped from its scabbard, quivered in the light, and flashed down, biting through fur and hair and flesh and bone. Without a sound, Alwin fell forward heavily, and lay upon his face at his master's feet.

That all men might know whose hand had done the deed, Leif flung the dripping sword down beside its victim, and without speaking, strode out of the room.

Then a strange thing happened. Helga ran over to where the lifeless heap lay in a widening pool of blood, and raised the wounded head in her arms, and rained down upon the still white face such tears as no one had ever thought to see her shed. When Thorhild came to take her away, she cried out, so that every one could hear:

"Do you not understand?—I loved him. I did not find it out until now. I loved him with all my heart, and now he will never know! I—loved him."

CHAPTER XXI. THE HEART OF A SHIELD-MAIDEN

```
Cattle die,
Kindred die,
We ourselves also die;
But the fair fame
Never dies
Of him who has earned it.
    Ha'vama'l
```

Out of doors the stir of spring was in the air; snow melting on the hills, grass sprouting on the plains. Editha's troubled face brightened a little, as she turned up the lane against the sun and felt its warmth upon her cheek.

"It gives one the feeling that it will melt one's sorrows as it melts the snow," she told herself.

Then she passed through the gate into the budding courtyard, where her eye fell upon Leif's sleeping-loft, with Kark running briskly up the steps; and the brightness faded.

"But there is some ice the sun cannot melt," she sighed.

On the threshold of the great hall, Thorhild stood waiting for her. Inside, all was confusion,—men placing tables and bringing in straw; maids spreading the embroidered cloths and hanging the holiday tapestries. The matron's head-dress was awry; her cheeks were like poppies, and her keys were kept in a perpetual jingle by her bustling motions.

She cried out, as soon as Editha came within hearing distance: "How long you have been, you little good-for-nothing! I have looked out four times for you. Was Astrid away from home? Did you return by Eric's Fiord, and learn whose ship it is that is coming in?"

The little Saxon maid dropped her respectful curtsey. If at the same time she dropped her eyes with a touch of embarrassment, the matron was too preoccupied to observe it.

"I was hindered by necessity, lady. Astrid was not away from home, but she was uncertain whether her son would wish to sell any malt, so I was obliged to wait until he came in from the stables."

The Thrall of Leif the Lucky

"Humph," sniffed Thorhild; "Egil Olafsson has become of great importance since his father was mound–laid. This is the third time I have been kept waiting for his leave." She turned on the girl sharply. "By no means do I believe that to be the reason for your long absences. I believe you plead that as an excuse."

Editha caught at the door–post, and her face went from red to white and back to red again.

"Indeed, lady—" she began.

Thorhild shook a menacing finger at her. "One never needs to tell me! She keeps you there to gossip about my household. Though she is my friend, she is as great a gossip as ever wagged a tongue."

Even though the hand still threatened her ears, one would have said that Editha looked relieved. She said, with well–feigned reluctance: "It is true that we have sometimes spoken of Brattahlid while I waited. Astrid looks favorably upon my needlework. Once or twice she has said that she would like to buy me—"

This time Thorhild snorted. "She takes too much trouble! Helga will never sell you to anyone. You need get no such ideas into your head. Why do you talk such foolishness, and hinder me from my work? Can you not tell me shortly whether or not you got the malt?"

"I did, lady. Two thralls will bring it as soon as it can be weighed."

"I shall need it, if guests arrive. And what of the ship? Did you learn whose it is? It takes till pyre–and–fire to get anything out of you."

Editha's rosy face, usually as full of placid content as a kitten's, suddenly puckered with anxiety. "Lady, as I passed, it was still a long way down the fiord. I could only see that it was a large and fine trading–vessel. But one of the seamen on the shore told me it was his belief that it is the ship of Gilli of Trond–hjem."

The house–wife's keys clashed and clattered with her motion of surprise. "Gilli of Trondhjem! Then he has come to take Helga!"

127

The Thrall of Leif the Lucky

Editha nervously clasped and unclasped her hands. "I got afraid it might be so."

"Afraid, you simpleton?" The matron laughed excitedly, as she brushed all stray hairs out of her eyes and tightened her apron for action. "It will become a great boon to her. Since the Englishman's death, she has been no better than a crazy Brynhild. To take her out into the world and entertain her with new sights,—it will be the saving of her! Run quickly and tell her the tidings; and see to it that she puts on her most costly clothes. Tell her that if she will also put on the ornaments Leif has given her, I will give her leave to stop embroidering for the day."

Editha observed to herself, as she tripped away, that undoubtedly her mistress had already done that without waiting for permission. And it proved very shortly that she was right.

In the great work–room of the women's–house, among deserted looms and spindles and embroidery frames, Helga sat in dreamy idleness. The whirlwind of excitement that had swept her companions away at the news of approaching guests, had passed over her without so much as ruffling a hair. Her golden head rested heavily against the wall behind her; her hands lay listlessly upon her lap. Her face was as white as the unmelted snow in the valleys, and the spring sun–shine had brought no sparkle to relieve the shadow in her eyes.

Without looking around, she said dreamily: "It was one year ago to–day that I came into the trader's booth in Norway and saw him sitting there among the thralls."

Editha stole over to her and lifted one of her hands out of her lap and kissed it. "Lady, do not all the time thinking of him. You will break your heart, and to no purpose. Besides, I have news of great importance for you. I have seen the ship that is coming up the fiord, and men say it is the vessel of your father, Gilli of Trondhjem."

With something of her old fire, Helga snatched her hand away and started up. "Do you know this for certain? And do you believe that Thorhild will give me up to him?"

"Worse than that, lady,—she is even anxious that he shall take you, thinking it will be to your advantage."

For awhile Helga sat staring before her, with expressions of anger and despair flickering over her face. Then, gradually, they died down like flames into ashes. She sank back against the wall, and her eyes faded dull and absent again.

"After all, what does it matter?" she said, listlessly. "I shall not find it any worse there than here. Nothing matters now."

Editha made a little moan, like one in sudden pain; hut it seemed as though she did not dare to interrupt the other's revery. She stood, softly wringing her hands. It was Helga who finally broke the silence. Suddenly she turned, an angry gleam replacing the dulness in her eyes.

"Did the ship bring more tidings of the battle? Is it certain that King Olaf Trygvasson is slain?"

Editha answered, in some surprise: "It had not come to land when I was there, lady. I am unable to tell you anything new. But the men who came last week, and first told us of the battle, say that Eric Jarl is now the King over Norway, and there is no doubt that Olaf Trygvasson is dead."

Helga laughed, a hateful laugh that made her pretty mouth as cruel as a wolf's. "It gladdens me that he is dead. I am well content that Leif's heart should be black with mourning. He killed the man I loved, and now the King he loved is slain,—and he was not there to fight for him. It is a just punishment upon him. I am glad that he should suffer a little of all that he has made me suffer."

Editha moaned again, and flung out her hands with a gesture of entreaty. "Dearest lady, if only you would not allow yourself to suffer so! If only you would bear it calmly, as I have begged of you! Even though you died, it would not help. It is wasting your grief—" She stopped, for her mistress was looking at her fixedly.

"I do not understand you," Helga said, slowly. "Is it wasting grief to mourn the death of Alwin of England, than whom God never made a nobler or higher–minded man?" She rose out of her seat, and Editha shrank away from her. "I do not understand you,—you who pretend to have loved him since he was a child. Is it indeed your wish that I should act as though I cared nothing for him? Did you really care nothing for him yourself? Your

129

face has grown no paler since his death–day; you are as fat as ever; you have seldom shed a tear. Was all your loyalty to him a lie? By the edge of my knife, if I thought so I would give you cause to weep! I would drive the blood from your deceitful face forever!"

She caught the Saxon girl by the wrist and forced her upon her knees; her beautiful eyes were as awful as the eyes of a Valkyria in battle. The bondmaid screamed at the sight of them, and threw up an arm to shield herself.

"No, no! Listen, and I will tell you the truth! Though they kill me, I will tell yon. Put down your head,—I dare not say it aloud. Listen!"

Mechanically, Helga bent her head and received into her ear three whispered words. She loosed her hold upon the other's wrists and stood staring at her, at first in anger, and then with a sort of dawning pity.

"Poor creature! grief has gotten you out of your wits," she said. "And I was harsh with you because I thought you did not care!" She put out a hand to raise her, but Editha caught it in both of hers, fondling it and clinging to it.

"Sweetest lady, I am not out of my wits. It is the truth, the blessed truth. Mine own eyes have proved it. Four times has Thorhild sent me on errands to Egil's house, and each time have I seen—"

"Yet said nothing to me! You have let me suffer!"

"No, no, spare me your reproaches! How was it possible for me to do otherwise? If you had known, all would have suspected; 'A woman's eyes cannot hide it when she loves.' Sigurd Haraldsson bound me firmly. I was told only because it was necessary that I should carry their messages. It has torn my heart to let you grieve. Only love for him could have kept me to it. Believe it, and forgive me. Say that you forgive me!"

Helga flung her arms open wide. "Forgive? I forgive everyone in the whole world—everything!" She threw herself, sobbing, upon Editha's breast, and they clung together like sisters.

While they were still mingling their tears and rejoicings, the old housekeeper looked in with a message from Thorhild.

"Sniffling, as I had expected! Have the wits left both of you? Even now Gilli of Trondhjem is coming up the lane. It is the command of Thorhild that you be dressed and ready to hand him his ale the moment he has taken off his outer garments. If you have any sense left, make haste."

When the door had closed on the wrinkled old visage, Editha sent a doubtful glance at her mistress. But the shield—maiden leaped up with a laugh like a joyful chime of bells.

"Gladly will I put on the finest clothes I own, and feast the whole night through! Nothing matters now. So long as he is alive, things must come out right some way. Nothing matters now!"

CHAPTER XXII. IN THE SHADOW OF THE SWORD

```
It is better to live,
Even to live miserably;
. . . . . . . . . .
The halt can ride on horseback;
The one-handed, drive cattle;
The deaf, fight and be useful;
To be blind is better
Than to be burnt;
No one gets good from a corpse.
    Ha'vama'l
```

"Egil! Egil Olafsson!" It was Helga's voice, with a note of happiness thrilling through it like the trill in a canary's song.

Egil turned from the field in which his men were and came slowly to where she stood leaning over the fence that separated the field from the lane. He guessed from her voice that they had told her the secret, and when he came near enough to see, he knew it from her face; it was like a rose—garden burst into bloom. His lowering brow scowled itself into a harder knot. With the death of his father, he had thrown aside the scarlet clothes of Leif's men, and wore the brown homespun of a farmer. From his neck downward,

131

everything spoke of thrift and industry and peace. But his fierce dark face looked the harsher for the contrast.

Helga stretched her hand across the fence. "I am going to see Alwin, for the first time after all these months. They told me two days ago, but this is the first chance I could find. But even before I saw him, I thought it right to see you and thank you for your wondrous goodness. Sigurd has told me how they carried Alwin to you in the night, and you received him and sheltered him, and—"

Egil silenced her with a rough gesture. "I kept my oath of friendship; speak no further of it. Do you know where he is hidden?"

"Sigurd told me he is in the cabin of your old foster–mother, Solveig. I do not remember whether that is to the left or the right of the lane. But it is a most ingenious hiding–place. No one ever goes there, and Solveig is the most accomplished of nurses."

"Since you do not remember where it is, I will walk with you, if it is not against your wish." He shouted some final directions to the men in the field, then leaped over the fence and strode along beside her.

He appeared to have nothing to say, after they were once started, and they went through lane and pasture and field in silence. But as soon as she broke out with fresh praise for his kindness, he found his tongue in all its curt vigor.

"Enough has been said about that. I have been wishing to speak to you of something that happened at the feast the other night. Do you know that my kinswoman Astrid told Gilli of her wish to buy your bondwoman, and—"

For a moment there was something wolfish about Helga's white teeth. She struck in quickly: "Yes, I know. Gilli agreed to sell Editha to her, the day we sail. It is exactly what I expected of him. If Astrid should offer a little more, he would be apt to sell me. He is the lowest–minded—Bah!" It seemed as though words failed her. She threw her hands apart in a gesture of utter detestation. The glow was gone out of her face.

"What I wanted to say is, that if it is your wish, I will persuade my mother to withdraw her offer."

After a while Helga shook her head. "No. He would only sell her to some one else. It would trouble me to think of her among strangers, and your mother would treat her kindly." She paused, at the top of the stile they were climbing over, to look down at him earnestly. "I should be thankful if you would promise me that, Egil. You are master now, and can have your will about everything. Promise me you will see that she is well treated."

"I promise you." Helga threw a grateful look after him, as he went along before her. "Your word is like a rock, Egil. One could hold on to it though everything else should roll away."

The cloud was passing from her face. By the time she gained his side, the rose—garden was once more radiant in sunlight.

"After all, I do not feel that I have a right to let anything grieve me much, since God has given Alwin back from the dead. I set my mind to thinking of that, and then everything else seems small and easily remedied. Even Gilli's coming it is possible to turn to profit. I have a fine plan—"

She broke off abruptly as, through a clump of white—birch trees, she caught sight of a tiny cabin nestled in their green shelter.

"That is Solveig's house; now I remember it! How is it possible that it has held such a secret for four months, and still looks just as usual? Let us hurry!" She seized his arm to pull him along. Only when he wrenched away and came to a dead stop, did she slacken her pace to stare at him over her shoulder.

"Do you wish to drive me crazy?" he shouted.

She thought him already so, and drew back.

He waited to take a fresh grip on his self—control. When he spoke at last, it was with labored slowness: "Every week for four months I have come to this door and asked the Englishman how he fared; and he has not wished for anything that I have not given it to him. The night they left him with me, I could have put my fingers around his throat and killed him; and no one would have known. But I held my hands behind me, and allowed

133

him to live. So far, I have kept my oath of friendship. Do you wish me to go in with you and break it now?"

Before she could gather her wits together to answer him, he was gone.

Standing where he had left her, she stared after him, open−mouthed, until her eye fell upon the cabin among the bushes, when she forgot everything else in the world. She ran toward it and threw open the door.

The low room was smoky and badly lighted. Before she could distinguish her lover in the dimness, he was upon her, calling her name over and over, crushing her hands in his. She cried out, and lifted her face, and his lips met hers, warm and living. It was the same as though nothing had happened since last she saw him.

No, not quite the same; she saw that, the instant she drew back. Alwin was very thin, and in the half−light his face showed white and haggard. An ugly scar stretched half across his forehead. At the sight of it her eyes flashed, and she reached up and touched with her lips the fiery mark.

"How I hate Leif for that!" Then she saw the greatest change of all in him, the quiet grimness that had come upon him out of his nights of pain and days of solitude.

"That is unfairly spoken, sweetheart. I have but paid the price I agreed to pay if luck went against me. Leif has dealt with me only according to justice; that I will maintain, though I die under his sword at the last."

She drew a quick, sharp breath. In the joy of recovery, she had let herself forget that he is only half alive who lives under the shadow of a death sentence. She set her teeth over her lip to stop its trembling, and stiffened herself to the iron composure of a shield−maiden.

"It is true that you are yet in great danger. His anger has not yet departed from him, for not once has your name passed his lips. Sit down here and tell me what you think of your case."

Alwin recalled the weeping and fainting of his mother's waiting−women, in that far−off time of trouble, and pressed her hand gratefully as he took his seat by her side upon the bench. "You are my brave comrade as well as my best friend. I can talk with you as I would with Sigurd."

Just for a moment she laid her cheek against his shoulder. "It gladdens me that you are content with me as I am, instead of wishing me to be like Bertha of Trondhjem and other women," she whispered.

Then the memory linked with that name caused her to straighten again and look at him doubtfully. "Has Solveig told you all the latest tidings?"

"She has told me nothing for a week. She is up at the hall just now, helping with the spinning; but Editha was here two days ago. Is it of King Olaf that you are thinking? She told me of the battle; and I am full of sorrow for Leif. She told me that his room was draped in black, and that he stopped preparing for his exploring voyage and shut himself up for four days and four nights, without eating or speaking."

"He has begun his preparations again. His sorrow is not worth considering. Or, rather, I shall grieve with him when he grieves for you. The tidings that I mean concern Gilli of Trondhjem. Do you know that he has come to take me away?"

She wanted to see the despair in his face, that she might feel how much he cared; then she hastened to reassure him. "But do not trouble yourself over that. Even though I go with him, it will do no harm. If he tries to marry me to anyone, I will pretend that I think the marriage beneath me. I will work upon his greediness, and so trick him into waiting; and in a year you will come and rescue me."

"If I am alive!" Alwin interrupted her sharply. He sprang up and began to pace the floor, clenching his fists and knocking them together. "If I am alive I will come. But it is by no means unlikely that Leif will carry out his intention. Then you will be left in Gilli's power forever."

She laughed as she went to him and brought him back and pushed him down upon the bench.

"See how love makes a coward of a man as well as of a woman! But do not trouble yourself over that, either. Have you never heard the love–tale of Hagberth and Signe?

135

How, the same moment in which she saw him hanged upon the gallows, she set fire to her house and strangled herself with her ribbons, so that their two souls met on the threshold of Paradise and went in together? If you die, I will die too; and that will arrange everything." She clung to him for a moment, and he feared that she was about to dishonor her shield by a burst of tears.

But in an instant she looked up at him with her brave smile. "We will end this talk about dying, however. Remember the old saying, 'If a man's time has not come, something is sure to aid him.' There is another fate in store for you than to lose your life in this matter, or you would have died when Leif struck you down. I love the cap that saved you! We will not talk about dying, but only of our hopes. I have planned how Gilli may be made useful, so that on his vessel you can escape to Norway."

She put her hand over his mouth as he would have spoken. "No, listen to me before you say anything against it. Gilli will sail next week. At that time Leif will be absent on a visit to Biorn Herjulfsson, who has just returned to Greenland from Norway. With Leif, Kark will go, so that we shall not have his prying eyes to fear. What would prevent you from stealing down to the shore, the night before we sail, and swimming out to the ship and hiding yourself in one of the great chests in the foreroom? The steersman will not hinder you, for I have spoken so many fine words to him, with this deed in view, that he is ready to chop off his head at my bidding. Thus will you get far out at sea before they discover you. Gilli will not know that he has ever seen you before, you are so white and changed; and when he has taken away all the property you have on you, he will say nothing further about the matter. So will you be brought to Norway,—and thence it is not far to your England, though I do not know if that is of any importance. But if you say that this plan is otherwise than ingenious, I shall be angry with you."

Alwin vented a short laugh. "It is most ingenious, comrade. The only trouble with it is that I have no ambition to go either to Norway or to England."

This time it was he who sealed her lips, as her amazement was about to burst through them.

"Give me a hearing and you will understand. I do not wish to go to England because I could do nothing there to improve my credit in any way. My kin have disappeared like withered grass, and the Danes are all-powerful. I do not wish to go to Norway because there I could never be more than a runaway slave; and though I strove to my uttermost, it is unlikely that I could ever acquire either wealth or influence,—and without both how would it ever be possible to win you? See how the North has conquered me! First it was only my body that was bound; and I was sure that, if ever I got my freedom, I should enter the service of some English lord and die fighting against the Danes. And now a Norse maiden has conquered my heart, so that I would not take my liberty if it were offered me! No, no, sweetheart; I have thought of it, night and day, until at last I see the truth. The only chance I have is with Leif."

Helga wrung her hands violently. "You must be crazy if you think so! He would strike you down the instant his eyes—"

"It is not my intention that he shall know me until he has had cause to soften toward me. Do you not remember Skroppa's prophecy? has not Sigurd told you of it?—that it is in this new untrodden country that my fate is to be decided? I will disguise myself in some way, and go on this exploring expedition among his following. I shall have many chances to be of service to him."

"But suppose they should not come soon enough? Suppose your disguise should be too shallow? His eyes are like arrows that pierce everything they are aimed at. Suppose he should recognize you at once?"

The new grimness again squared Alwin's mouth. "Then one of two things will happen. Either he will pardon me, for the sake of what I have already endured; or else he will keep to his first intention, and kill me. In neither case will we be worse off than we were four months ago."

Such logic admitted of no reply, and Helga gave way to it. But so much anguish was betrayed in her face, that Alwin gave another short laugh and asked her:

"Who is it now that love is making a coward of?"

She shook her head gravely. "I am no coward. It gladdens me to have you face death in this way, and to know that you will not murmur even if luck goes against you. But I do not wish you to throw your life away; and you know no prudence. Let us speak of this disguise. What have you fixed upon?"

137

"I acknowledge that I have accomplished very little. Solveig has told me of a bark whose juice is such that with it I can turn my skin brown like that of the Southerners. And I have decided to make believe that I am a Frankish man. I know not a little of their tongue, which will help to disguise my speech. But how I am to cover up my short hair, or account for my appearance in Greenland—" He shrugged his shoulders, and dropped his chin upon his fist.

Helga clasped her hands around her knee and stared at him thoughtfully. "I have heard Sigurd tell of a strange wonder he saw in France,—I do not know what you call it,—like a hood made of people's hair. A girl who had lost her hair through sickness was wont to wear it; and Sigurd did not even suspect that it was rootless, until one day she caught the ends in her cloak, and pulled it off. If you could get one of those—"

"If!" Alwin murmured. But Helga did not hear him. Suddenly, in the dim perspective of her mind, she had caught a glimpse of a plan. As she darted at it, it eluded her; but she chased it to and fro, seeing it more clearly at each turn. Finally she caught it. She leaped up and opened her mouth to shout it forth, when an impulse of Editha's caution touched her, and instead, she threw her arms around his neck and laughed it into his ear.

He drew back and gazed at her with dawning appreciation. She nodded excitedly.

"Is it not well fitted to succeed? You can escape to Norway as I planned, and after that you can easily reach Normandy. All that you lack is gold, and Leif and Gilli have covered me with that."

His face kindled as he mused on it. "It sounds possible. Sigurd's friends would receive me well for his sake; and after I had got everything for my disguise, I would have yet many good chances to return to Nidaros and board the ship of Arnor Gunnarsson, who comes here each summer on a trading voyage. Coming that way, who could suspect me?—particularly when it is everyone's belief that I am dead."

"No one!" Helga cried joyously. "No one! It is perfect!"

In a sudden burst of gratitude, he caught her hands and kissed them. "All is due to you, then. It is an unheard-of cleverness! You must be a Valkyria! Only a great hero is worthy of a maid like you."

Laughing with pleasure, she hid her face on his breast. And it must be that her plan possessed some of the advantages she claimed for it, for it came to pass that, on the same day that Gilli and his daughter set sail for Norway, a fair-skinned thrall with a shaven head disappeared from Greenland so completely that even Kark's keen eyes would have found it impossible to trace him.

CHAPTER XXIII. A FAMILIAR BLADE IN A STRANGE SHEATH

"Now it is related that Bjarni Herjulfsson came from Greenland to Eirek Jarl, who received him well. Bjarni described his voyage and the lands that he had seen. People thought he had shown a lack of interest as he had nothing to tell about them, and he was somewhat blamed for it. He became the Jarl's hirdman and went to Greenland the following summer, Now there was much talk about land discoveries." —FLATEYJARBO'K.

The week after Gilli's departure for Norway, Leif returned from his visit to Herjulf's Cape, and made public his intention to take Biorn's barren beginning and carry it out to a definite finish. He brought with him three of the men of Biorn's old crew, and also the same stanch little trading-vessel in which Herjulfsson had made his journey. The ship-sheds upon the shore became at once the scene of endless overhauling and repairing. Thorhild's women laid aside their embroidering for the task of sail-making. There began a ransacking of every hut on the commons and every fishing-station along the coast, for the latest improved hunting-gear and fishing-tackle; and day after day Tyrker rode among the farms, purchasing stores of grain and smoked meats.

As the old saga says: "Now there was much talk about land discoveries." The Lucky One became the hero of the hour. With all its stubbornness, Eric's pride could not but be gratified. He began to show signs of relenting. Gradually he ceased to avert his face. One day, he even worked himself up to making a gruff inquiry into their plans.

"If we return with great fame, it is likely his pleasure will reconcile him entirely," Leif's men chuckled to each other.

The Thrall of Leif the Lucky

The diplomatic guardsman was quick to understand the change, but as usual, he went a step beyond their expectations. The day after his father made this first advance, he invited him to inspect the exploring ship and advise them concerning her equipment. While they stood upon the shore, admiring the coat of scarlet paint that was being laid upon her hull, he suddenly offered the Red One the leadership of the expedition.

Eric's eyes caught fire, and his wiry old frame straightened and swelled with eagerness. Then, though his eyes still sparkled, his chest sank like a pierced bladder.

"It is not possible for me to go. I am too old, and less able to bear hardship than formerly."

Rolf and the steersman, who had overheard the offer, exchanged glances of relief, and allowed themselves to breathe again. But to their consternation, Leif did not take advantage of this loop-hole. He argued and urged, until Eric drew in another long breath of excitement, until his aged muscles tingled and twitched with a spasm of youthful ardor, until at last, in a burst of almost hysterical enthusiasm, he accepted the offer. In the warmth of his pleasure, he grasped his son's hand and publicly received him back into his affections. But at the moment, this was cold comfort for Leif's followers. They turned from their painting and hammering and polishing, to stare at their lord in amazed disapproval. The instant the two chiefs had gone up from the shore, complaints broke out like explosions.

"That old heathen at the steering-oar! All the bad luck in the world may be expected!"—" Nowhere lives a man more domineering than Eric the Red." "What is to become of Leif's renown, if the glory is to go to that old pagan?"—"Skroppa has turned a curse against the Lucky One. He has been deprived of his mind."

"It is in my mind that part of that is true," Rolf said thoughtfully, leaning on the spear-shaft he was sharpening. "I believe the Saxon Saints' Book has bewitched his reason. From that, I have heard the Englishman read of men who gave up honor lest it might make them vain. I believe Leif Ericsson is humbling his pride, like some beaten monk."

He was interrupted by a chorus of disgust. "Yah! If he has become such a woman as that !"—"A man who fears bad luck."—"A brave man bears the result of his action, whatever it is."—" The Saints' Book is befitting old men who have lost their teeth."—"Christianity is a religion for women."

Sigurd struck in for the first time. Although he had been frowning with vexation, some touch of compunction had held him silent. "I will not allow you to say that, nor should you wish to speak so." He hesitated, rubbing his chin perplexedly. "I acknowledge that I experience the same disgust that you do; yet I am not altogether certain that we are right. I remember hearing my father say that what these saints did was more difficult than any achievement of Thor. And I have heard King Olaf Trygvasson read out of the Holy Book that a man who controls his own passions is more to be admired than a man who conquers a city."

For perhaps two or three minutes there was a lull in the grumbling. But it was not to be expected, in that brutal age, that moral strength should find a keen appreciation. Indeed, Sigurd's words were far from ringing with his own conviction. Little by little, the discontent broke out again. At last it grew so near to mutiny, that the steersman felt called upon to exercise his authority.

"All this is foolishly spoken, concerning something you know nothing of. Undoubtedly Leif has an excellent reason for what he does. It may be that he considers it of the greatest importance to secure Eric's friendship. Or it may be that he intends to lead him into some uninhabited place, that he may kill him and get rid of his ill—temper. It is certain that he has some good reason. Go back to your work, and make your minds easy that now, as always, some good will result from his actions."

The men still growled as they obeyed him; but however right or wrong he was regarding Leif's motives, he was proved correct in his prophecy. Out of that moment on shore, came the good of a complete reconciliation with Eric. No more were there cold shoulders, and half—veiled gibes, and long evenings of gloomy restraint. No longer were Leif's followers obliged to sit with teeth on their tongues and hands on their swords. The warmth of gratification that had melted the ice of Eric's displeasure seemed to have set free torrents of generosity and good—will. His ruddy face beamed above the board like a harvest moon; if Leif would have accepted it, he would have presented him with the entire contents of Brattahlid. Following their chief's example, his retainers locked arms with their former enemies and swore them eternal brotherhood. Night after night they drank out of the same horns, and strengthened their bonds in lauding their chiefs. Never had the great hall seen a time of such radiant good cheer.

By the last week of Leif's preparations, interest and enthusiasm had spread into every corner of inhabited Greenland. Strings of people began to make pilgrimages to stare at the exploring vessel that had once been within sight of the "wonder–shores" and now seemed destined actually to touch them. Men came from ail parts of the country in the hope of joining her crew, and were furious with disappointment when told that her equipment was limited to thirty–five, and that that number had already been made up from among Leif's own followers. Warriors thronged to visit the Lucky One, until the hall benches were filled, and the courtyard was so crowded with attendants that there was barely room for the servants to run between the horses with the ale horns. Outside the fence there was nearly always a mob of children and paupers and thralls lying in wait, like a wolf–pack, to tear information out of any member of the household who should venture beyond the gates.

Usually it was only vague rumor and meagre report that fell to the share of these outsiders; but the day before Leif's departure it happened that they got a bit of excitement first–hand.

Late that afternoon word went around that the trading–ship of Arnor Gunnarsson was coming up Eric's Fiord. The arrival of that merchant was one of the events of the year. Not only did it occasion great feasting among the rich, which meant additional alms among the poor, but besides a chance to feast one's stomach, it meant an opportunity to feast one's eyes on beautiful garments and wonderful weapons; and in addition to all else, it meant such a budget of news and gossip and thrilling yarns as should supply local conversation with a year's stock of topics,—a stock always run low and rather shopworn towards the end of the long winters. At the first hint of the "Eastman's" approach, a crowd of idlers was gathered out of nowhere as quickly as buzzards are drawn out of empty space.

As the heavy dun–colored merchantman came slowly to its berth and the anchor fell with a rattle and a splash, the motley crowd cheered shrilly. When the ruddy gold–bearded trader appeared at the side, ready to clamber into the boat his men were lowering, they cheered again. And they regarded it as an appropriate tribute to the importance of the occasion when one of their number came running over the sand to announce breathlessly that Leif Ericsson himself was riding down to greet the arrivals, accompanied by no less a person than his high–born foster–son.

"Although it is no great wonder that the Lucky One feels interest," they told each other. "The last time that Eric the Red came to meet traders, they returned his greeting with a sweep of their arms toward their ships, and an invitation to take whatever of its contents best pleased him."

"The strange wonder to me," mumbled one old man, "is that it is always to those who have sufficient wealth to purchase them that presents are given. It may be that Odin knows why gifts are seldom given to the poor: certainly I think one needs to be all–wise to understand it."

His companions clapped their hands over his mouth, and pointed at the approaching boat.

"Look!"—"Look there!"—"It is a king's son!" they cried. And then it was that their hungry teeth closed upon their morsel of excitement.

In the bow of the boat, shining like a jewel against the dark background of the trader's dun mantle, stood a most splendidly arrayed young warrior. The fading sunbeams that played on his gilded helm revealed shining armor and a golden cross embossed upon a gold–rimmed shield. Still nearer, and it could be seen that his cloak was of crimson velvet lined with sables, and that gold–embroideries and jewelled clasps flashed with every motion.

Buzzing with curiosity, they crowded down to the water's edge to meet him. The keel bit the sand; he stepped ashore into their very midst, and even that close scrutiny did not lessen his attractions. His olive–tinted face was haughtily handsome; his fine black hair fell upon his shoulders in long silken curls; he was tall and straight and supple, and his bearing was bold and proud as an eagle's.

"He is well fitted to be a king's son," they repeated one to another. And those in front respectfully gave way before him, while those behind fell over one another to get near in case he should speak,—and Leif himself paused in his greeting of Arnor Gunnarsson to look at the stranger curiously.

The Thrall of Leif the Lucky

The youth stood running his eyes over the faces of those around him, until his gaze fell upon Sigurd Haraldsson. He uttered a loud exclamation, and sprang forward with outstretched hand.

Sigurd's cheeks, which had been looking rather pale, suddenly became very red; and he leaped from his horse and started forward. Then he wavered, stopped, and hesitated, staring.

"_Mon_ami_!" said the stranger, in some odd heathen tongue very different from good plain Norse. "_Mon_ami_!" He took another step forward, and this time their palms met.

The spectators who were watching Sigurd Haraidsson, whispered that the young warrior must be the last man on earth that he expected to see in Greenland, and also the man that he loved the best of all his sworn brothers. The fair–haired jarl's son and he of the raven locks stood grasping each other's hands and looking into each other's eyes as though they had forgotten there was anyone else in the world.

"He looks to be a man to be bold in the presence of chiefs, does he not?" the trader observed to Leif Ericsson, regarding the pair benevolently as he stood twisting his long yellow mustache. "He said to me that the jarl's son was his friend; it is great luck that he should find him so soon. He is somewhat haughty–minded, as is the wont of Normans, but he is free with his gold." And the thrifty merchant patted his money–bag absently.

The crowd circulated the news in excited whispers. "He is a friend of Sigurd Haraldsson."—"He is a Norman."—"That accounts for the swarthiness of his skin."—"Is it in the Norman tongue that they are speaking?"—" Normandy? Is that the land Rolf the Ganger laid under his sword?"—"Hush! Sigurd is leading him to the chief."—"Now we shall learn what his errand is."

And the boldest of them pushed almost within whip–range of the pair.

But there was no difficulty about hearing, for Sigurd spoke out in a loud clear voice: "Foster–father, I wish to make known to you my friend and comrade who has just now arrived on the Eastman's vessel. He is called Robert Sans–Peur, because his courage is such as is seldom found. I got great kindness from his kin when I was in Normandy."

The Thrall of Leif the Lucky

The Norman said nothing, but he did what the bystanders considered rather surprising in a knee-crooking Frenchman. Neither bending his body nor doffing his helmet, he folded his arms across his breast and looked straight into the Lucky One's eyes.

"As though," one fellow muttered, "as though he would read in the chief's very face whether or not it was his intention to be friendly!"

"Hush!" his neighbor interrupted him. "Leif is drawing off his glove. It may be that he is going to honor him for his boldness."

And so indeed it proved. In another moment, the chief had extended his bare hand to the haughty Southerner.

"I have an honorable greeting for all brave men, even though they be friendless," he said, with lofty courtesy. "How much warmer then is the state of my feelings toward one who is also a friend of Sigurd Haraldsson? Be welcome, Robert Sans-Peur. The best that Brattahlid has to offer shall not be thought too good for you."

Whether or not he could speak it, it was evident that the Fearless One understood the Northern tongue. His haughtiness passed from him like a shadow. Uncovering his raven locks, he bowed low,—and would have set his lips to the extended hand if the chief, foreseeing his danger, had not saved himself by dexterously withdrawing it.

Sigurd, still flushed and nervous, spoke again: "You have taken this so well, foster-father, that it is in my mind to ask of you a boon which I should be thankful if you would grant. As far off as Normandy, my friend has heard tidings of this exploring-journey of yours; and he has come all this way in the hope of being allowed to join your following. He has the matter much at heart. If my wishes are at all powerful with you, you will not deny him."

A murmur of delight ran through the crowd. That this splendid personage should have come to do homage to their hero, was the final dramatic touch which their imaginations craved. It was with difficulty that they repressed a cheer.

But the guardsman looked puzzled to the point of incredulity.

The Thrall of Leif the Lucky

"Heard the tidings as far as Normandy?" he repeated. "A matter of so little importance to anyone? How is that likely?" Straightening in his saddle, he looked at the Norman for a moment with eyes that were more keen than courteous.

"He would be liable to disaster who should try to put a trick upon Leif Ericsson," the thrall–born whispered.

Robert Sans–Peur was in no wise disconcerted. Meeting the keen eyes, he answered in plain if halting Norse: "The renowned chief has forgotten that early this season a trading–ship went from here to Trondhjem. Not a few of her shipmates went further than Nidaros. One of them, who was called Gudbrand–wi'–the–Scar, travelled even so far as Rouen, where it was my good fortune to encounter him."

"It is true that I had forgotten that," the chief said, slowly. He lowered his gaze to his horse's ears and sat for a while lost in thought. Then once more he extended his hand to the Southerner.

"It appears to me that you are a man of energy and resource," he said, with a return of his former cordiality. "Since wind and wave have not hindered you from your desire, it would be unheard–of churlishness for me to refuse you. Get now into my saddle and allow your friend to conduct you to the hall. It is necessary that I oversee the storing of these wares, but after the night–meal we will speak further of the matter." To forestall any further attempts at hand–kissing, he sprang from his horse and strode over to the trader.

With an air of grave ceremony that was swallowed open–mouthed by the onlookers, Sigurd held his friend's stirrup; then, quickly remounting his own steed, the pair rode off.

This time the mob would not be restrained, but burst into a roar of delight.

"Here at last is a great happening that we have seen with our own eyes!" they told each other, as they settled down at a safe distance to watch Leif and the merchant turning over the bales of goods which the sailors were engaged in bringing to shore. "This will be something to relate in time to come,—a great event concerning which we understand everything."

The Thrall of Leif the Lucky

"'Concerning which we understand everything!'" Sigurd, overhearing them, repeated laughingly to his friend as they galloped up the lane.

Robert the Fearless laughed too, with a vibration of uneasiness in the peal.

"Few there are who are capable of making that boast," he answered. "Even you, comrade, are unequal to it. Here now is something that is worth a hearing." Leaning from his saddle, he poured into Sigurd's ear a stream of low-toned words that caused the Silver-Tongued to stop short and stare at him incredulously, and then look back at the anchored ship and pound his knee in a fury of exasperation.

The cloud rested on Sigurd's sunny face for the rest of the evening. Thorhild, enchanted at the tribute to her idolized son, plied the stranger with every attention; and Kark himself, for all his foxy eyes, removed the gilded helm from the smooth black locks without a thought to try whether or no they were indigenous to the scalp from which they sprang,—but Sigurd's brow did not lighten.

As they put a final polish upon their shields and hung them for the last time upon the wall behind their seats, Rolf said to him with a searching glance: "It is bidden from me why you look so black, comrade. If it were not for the drawback of old Eric at the steering-oar, certainly every circumstance would be as favorable as could be expected."

Sigurd arose and pulled his cloak down from its peg with a vicious jerk.

"There are other witless people besides Eric the Red who thrust themselves where they are not wanted," he retorted grimly. Then, turning abruptly, he strode out into the darkness; and none of the household saw him again until morning.

The sun rose upon a perfect day, warm and bright, with the wind in the right quarter, steady and strong. And as if to make sure that not even one thing should mar so auspicious a beginning, Leif's luck swept away the only drawback that Rolf had been able to name.

Down in the lane, midway between the foot where it opened upon the shore and the head where it ended at the fence, there lay a bit of a rock. A small stone or a big pebble was all it was, but in the hands of Leif's luck it took on the importance of a boulder.

When the moment of departure arrived, and the cavalcade poured out of the courtyard gates, with a clanking of armor and a flapping of gorgeous new mantles, warmed by the horns of parting ale that had steamed down their throats, singing and boasting and laughing, and cheered by the rabble that ran alongside, their way down to the shore lay directly over the head of this insignificant pebble. Who would have thought of avoiding it? Yet, though a score of children's feet danced over it unharmed, and sixty pairs of horses' hoofs pranced over it unhindered, when Eric reached it his good bay mare stumbled against it and fell, so that her rider was thrown from his saddle and rolled in the dust.

There were no bones broken; he was no more than shaken; he was up before they could reach him; but his face was gray with disappointment, and his frame had shrunk like a withered leaf.

"It is a warning from the gods that I am on the wrong road," he said hoarsely. "It is a sign that it cannot be my fate to be the discoverer of any other land than the one on which we now live. My luck go with you, my son; but I cannot."

Before they could remonstrate, he had wheeled his horse and left them, riding with the bent head and drooping shoulders of an old, old man.

A stern sign from Valbrand restrained Leif's men from venting the cheers they were bursting with; but the looks they darted at their leader, and then at each other, said as plainly as words: "It is his never-failing luck. Why did we ever doubt him? We would follow him into the Sea of Worms and believe that it would end favorably."

In this promising frame of mind they left their friendly haven and sailed away into an unknown world.

CHAPTER XXIV. FOR DEAR LOVE'S SAKE

```
He alone knows,
Who wanders wide
And has much experienced,
By what disposition
Each man is ruled
Who common sense possesses.
```

The Thrall of Leif the Lucky

```
Ha'vama'l
```

The first night out was a moonless night, that shut down on the world of waters and blotted out even the clouds and the waves that been company for the solitary vessel. The little ship became a speck of light in a gulf of darkness, an atom of life floating in empty space. Under the tent roofs, by the light of flaring torches, the crew drank and sang and amused themselves with games; but beyond that circle, there was only blackness and emptiness and silence.

Sigurd gazed out over the vessel's side, with a yawn and a shiver combined. "It feels as though the air were full of ghosts, and we were the only living beings in the whole world," he muttered.

A tow-headed giant known as Long Lodin overheard him, and laughed noisily, jerking his thumb over his shoulder toward the deck where Leif's eagle face showed high above their heads.

"_His_ luck could carry us safe through even the world of the dead," he reassured him.

But Rolf paused in his chess game to throw his friend a keen glance. "The Silver-Tongue has been one not apt to speak womanish words," he said, gravely. "Something there is on your mind which disturbs you, comrade."

Sigurd pulled himself together with an attempt at his usual careless laugh. "Is it your opinion that I am the only person who is thinking of ghosts to-night?" he parried. "Look yonder at Kark, how he fears to turn his back on the shadows, lest the Evil One overtake him! It is my belief that he would like it better to die than to venture into the dark of the foreroom."

Following his glance, they beheld the bowerman, leaning against the mast with a face as pale as a toadstool. When a sailor threw a piece of dried fish at him, he jumped as though he had been struck by a stone. Rolf's gentle smile expanded into a broad grin, and he let himself be turned thus easily from his object.

"Now that is true; I had not observed him before. He appears as if the goddess Ran already had hold of his feet to pull him down under the water. Let us have a little fun with him. I will send him to the foreroom on an errand."

Robert of Normandy set down his drinking—horn with a sharp motion, and Sigurd leaned forward hastily; but the Wrestler's soft voice was already speeding his command.

"Ho there, valiant Kark—with—the—white—cheeks! Get you into the foreroom and bring my bag of chess—men from the brass—bound box."

Kark heard the order without a motion except an angry scowl, and Sigurd drew back with something like a breath of relief. But Rolf made a sudden move as though to rise to his feet, and the effect was magical.

"I am going as soon as is necessary," the thrall growled. "You said nothing of being in haste." And he shuffled over to one of the torches to light a splinter in its flame, and pushed his way forward with dragging feet.

Sigurd and the Norman both sprang after him.

"I tell you, Rolf, I have something against this!" Sigurd stormed, as the Wrestler's iron hand closed upon his cloak. "My—my—my valuables are in the same chest. I will not have him pawing them over. Let me go, I say!" He managed to slide out of his cloak and dodge under Rolf's arm.

A spark of something very like anger kindled the Wrestler's usually mild eyes; he caught the Norman around the waist, as the latter tried to pass him, and swung him bodily into the air. For an instant it seemed possible that he might hurl him over the ship's side into the ocean. But he finally threw him lightly upon a pile of skin sleeping—bags, and turned and hastened after the jarl's son.

Guessing that some friendly squabble was in progress, the sailors made way for him good—humoredly, and he reached the forecastle only a moment behind Sigurd. Kark's taper was just disappearing among the shadows beneath the deck.

Before the pursuers could speak, the bowerman leaped back upon them with a shriek that cut the air.

The Thrall of Leif the Lucky

"Ran is in there! I saw her hair hanging over a barrel. It was long and yellow. It is Ran herself! We shall drown—"

Sigurd Haraldsson dealt him a cuff that felled him like a log.

"The simpleton is not able to tell a piece of yellow fox-fur from a woman's hair," he said, contemptuously. "Since you are here, Rolf, hold the light for me, and I will get the chess-bag myself." He spoke loudly enough so that the men on the benches heard, laughed, and turned back to their amusements. Then he drew Rolf further into the room, laid a hand over his mouth, and pointed to the farthest corner, where barrels and piled-up bales made a screen half-way across the bow.

Hair long and yellow there was, as the simpleton had said; but it was not the vengeful Ran who looked out from under it. Tumbled and dishevelled, paling and flushing, short-kirtled and desperate-eyed, Helga the Fair stood before them.

"Behold how a prudent shield-maiden helps matters that are already in a snarl," the jarl's son said, dryly.

The Wrestler started back in consternation.

Helga dropped her eyes guiltily. "I cannot blame you for being angry," she murmured. "I have become a great hindrance to you."

"It is an unheard-of misfortune!" gasped Rolf. "In flying from Gilli you have broken the Norwegian law; and by causing Leif to aid you in your flight you have made him an accomplice. A bad result is certain."

Helga's head bent lower. Then suddenly she flung out her hands in passionate entreaty.

"Yet I could not help it, comrades! As I live, I could not help it! How could I have the heart to remain in safety, without knowing whether Alwin lived or died? How could I spend my days decking myself in fine clothes, while my best friend fought for his life? Was it to be expected that I could help coming?" She spoke softly, half-crouching in her hiding-place, but her heart was in every word.

151

Her judges could not stand against her. Rolf swore that she would have been unworthy the name of shield–maiden had she acted otherwise. And Sigurd pressed her hand with brotherly tenderness.

"You should know that I am not blaming you in earnest, my foster–sister, because I grumble a little when I cannot see my way out of the tangle." He bent over Kark to make sure that he was really as unconscious as he seemed; then he lowered his voice nervously. "What makes it a great mishap is that your presence doubles Alwin's risk, and because one can never be altogether sure to what lengths Eric's son will go,—even with one whom he loves as well as he loves you. If I could find some good way in which to break the news to him before he sees you,—"

Helga sprang out of her niche, and stood, straight and rigid, before them. "You shall not endanger yourself to shield me. You will feel it enough for what you have already done. The first burst of his anger I will bear myself, as is my right."

Before they had even guessed her intention, she slipped past them, leaped lightly over Kark's motionless body, and delivered herself into the light of the torches. In another instant, a roar of amazement and delight had gone up from the benches; and the men were dropping their games and knocking over their goblets to crowd around her.

"She has got out of her wits," Rolf said, wonderingly.

"He will kill her," Sigurd answered, between his teeth. "For half as much cause, Olaf Trygvasson struck a queen in the face."

They followed her aft, like men walking in a dream; but between the rings of broad shoulders they soon lost sight of her. All they could see was the Norman's dark face, as he stepped upon a bench and silently watched the approaching apparition.

"The Troll take him! If he cannot keep that look out of his eyes, why does he not shut them?" Sigurd muttered, irritably.

Perhaps it was that look which Helga encountered, as she made the last step that brought her face to face with the chief. At that moment, a great change came over her. When the guardsman pushed back to the extreme limits of his chair to regard her in a sort of incredulous horror, she did not fall at his feet as everyone expected her to, and as she herself had thought to do. Instead, she flung up her head with a spirit that sent the long locks flying. Even when anger began to distort his face,—anger headlong and terrible as Eric's,—her glance crossed his like a sword–blade.

"You need not look at me like that, kinsman," she said, fiercely. "It is your own fault for giving me into the power of a mean–minded brute,—you who brought me up to be a free Norse shield–maiden!"

If the planks of the deck had risen against them, the men could not have looked at each other more aghast. Her boldness seemed to paralyze even Leif. Or was it the grain of truth in the reproach that stayed him? He let moment after moment pass without replying. He sat plainly struggling to hold back his fury, gripping his chair–arms until the knuckles on his fists gleamed white.

After peering at him curiously for awhile, as though trying to divine his wishes, his shrewd old foster–father put aside the chess–board on which they had been playing, and hobbled over and laid a soothing hand on the girl's arm.

"Speak you of Gilli?" he inquired. "Tell to us how he has ill–treated you."

It was only very slightly that the pause had cooled Helga's valor.

"He has treated me like a horse that traders deck out in costly things, and parade up and down for men to see and offer money for," she answered hotly.

Though they knew Gilli's conduct was entirely within the law, and there was not a man there who might not have done the same thing, they all grunted contemptuously. Tyrker stroked his beard, with an–other sidelong glance at his foster–son, as he said, cautiously:

"So? _Aber_,—how have you managed it from him to escape?"

"Little was there to manage. As I told you, he loaded me with precious things; after which he left me to sit at home with his weak–minded wife, while he went on a trading voyage, as was his wont. A horse brought me to Nidaros; gold bought me a passage with Arnor Gunnarsson, and his ship brought me into Eric's Fiord."

153

The Thrall of Leif the Lucky

Then, for the first time, Leif spoke. His words leaped out like wolves eager for a victim.

"Do not stop there! Tell how you passed from his ship into mine. Tell whom you found in Eric's Fiord who became a traitor for your gold."

She answered him bravely: "No one, kinsman. No one received so much as a ring from me. May the Giant take me if I lie! I swam the distance between the ships under the cover of darkness, and—"

His voice crashed through hers like a thunder–peal: "Who kept the watch on board, last night?"

Half a dozen men started in sudden consternation; but they were spared the peril of a reply, for Sigurd Haraldsson stepped out of the throng and stood at Helga's side.

"I kept the watch last night, foster–father," he said, quietly. "Let none of your men suffer in life or limb. It was I who received her on board, while it was the others' turn to sleep; and I alone who hid her in the foreroom."

Those who had hoped that Leif's love for his foster–son might outweigh his anger, gauged but poorly the force of the resentment he had been holding back. At this offer of a victim which it was free to accept, his anger could no more be restrained than an unchained torrent. It burst out in a stream of denunciation that bent Sigurd's handsome head and lashed the blood into his cheeks. Coward and traitor were the mildest of its reproaches; contempt and eternal displeasure were the least of its dooms. Though Helga besought with eyes and hands, the torrent thundered on with a fury that even the ire of Eric had never surpassed.

Only a lack of breath brought it finally to an end. The chief dashed himself back into his chair, and leaned there, panting and darting fiery glances from under his scowling brows,—now at Rolf and the Norman, now at Helga, and again at the motionless figure of Sigurd Haraldsson, silently awaiting his pleasure. When he spoke again, it was with the suddenness of a blow.

"Nor do I altogether believe that it was to escape from Gilli that she took this venture upon herself. By her own story, Gilli had gone away for the season and left her free. It is my opinion that it took something of more importance to steal the wits out of her."

Helga blanched. If he was going to pry into her motives, what might not the next words bring out? Under the Norman's silken tunic, an English heart leaped, and then stood still. There was a pause in which no one seemed to breathe. But the next words were as unexpected as the last.

Of a sudden, Leif started up with a gesture of impatience. "Have I nothing to think of besides your follies? Trouble me no longer with the sight of you. Tyrker, take the girl below and see to it that she is cared for." While the culprits stared at him, scarcely daring to credit their ears, he still further signified that the incident was closed, by turning his back upon them and inviting Robert Sans–Peur to take the German's place at the chess–board.

In a daze of bewilderment, Sigurd let Rolf lead him away. "What can he mean by such an ending?" he marvelled, as soon as it was safe to voice his thoughts. "How comes it that he will stop before he has found out her real motive? It cannot be that he will drop it thus. Did you not see the black look he gave me as I left?" He raised his eyes to Rolf's face, and drew back resentfully. "What are you smiling at?" he demanded.

"At your stupidity," Rolf laughed into his ear. "Do you not see that he believes he has found out her real motive?" As Sigurd continued to stare, the Wrestler shook him to arouse his slumbering faculties. "Simpleton! He thinks it was for love of you that Helga fled from Norway!"

"_Nom_du_diable_!" breathed Sigurd. Yet the longer he thought of it, the more clearly he saw it. By and by, he drew a breath of relief that ended in a laugh. "And he thinks to make me envious by putting my Norman friend before me! Do you see? He in–tends it as a punishment. By Saint Michael, it seems almost too amusing to be true!"

CHAPTER XXV. "WHERE NEVER MAN STOOD BEFORE"

```
Wit is needful
To him who travels far:
At home all is easy.
    Ha'vama'l
```

The Thrall of Leif the Lucky

Four days of threading fog–thickets and ploughing over watery wastes, and the stanch little vessel pushed her way into sight of the first of the unknown lands. It towered up ahead like a storm–cloud, bleak and barren–looking as Greenland itself. From its inhospitable heights and glaciers gleaming coldly in the sunshine, they knew it at once for the last–seen land of Biorn's narrative.

"It looks to me like a good omen that we are to begin where Biorn left off," Rolf observed to one of the men engaged in lowering the ship's boat.

The fellow was a stalwart Icelander who had every current superstition at his tongue's end, and was even accredited with the gift of second sight. He hunched his shoulders sceptically, as he bent over the ropes.

"It is my opinion that good omens have little to do with this land," he returned. "It bears every resemblance to the Giant Country which Thor visited."

"I believe it is Helheim itself," quavered Kark.

The Wrestler glanced at the thrall's blanching cheeks and laughed a long soft laugh. Such a display was one of the few things that moved him to mirth. Suddenly he caught up the bowerman as one picks up a kitten, and, leaning out over the side, dropped him sprawling into the long–boat.

"Here, then, is your chance to enter the world of the dead in good company," he laughed. He stood guard over the gunwale until Leif and the other ten men of the boat's crew were ready to go down; pounding the poor wretch's fingers when he attempted to climb back, while a row of grinning faces mocked him over the side.

The unpromising aspect of the shore did not lessen as the explorers approached it. If they had not made an easy landing, on a gravelly strip between two rocky points, they would have felt that their labor had been wasted. From the sea to the ice–tipped mountains there stretched a plain of nothing but broad flat stones. They looked in vain for any signs of life. Not a tree nor a shrub, nor even so much as a grass–blade, relieved the dead emptiness. When they caught sight of a fox, whisking from one rocky den to another, it startled them into crossing themselves.

156

The Thrall of Leif the Lucky

"It is over such wastes as this that the dead like to call to each other," Valbrand muttered in his heard.

And his neighbor mumbled uneasily, "I think it likely that this is one of the plains on which the Women who Ride at Night hold their meetings. If it were not for the Lucky One's luck, I would prefer swallowing hot irons to coming here."

Then both became silent, for Leif had faced about and was awaiting their full attention before announcing the next move. "I dislike to see brave men disgrace their beards with bondmaids' gabble," he said sternly. "Fix in your minds the shame that was spoken of Biorn Herjulfsson because of his lack of enterprise. The same shall not be said of us. Rolf Erlingsson and Ottar the Red and three others shall follow me; and we will walk inland until the light has entirely faded from the highest mountain peak yonder, and the next point below is yellow as a golden fir–cone. The others of you shall follow Valbrand for the same length of time, but walk southward along the shore, since it may be that something of interest is hidden behind these points—"

A howl from Kark interrupted him. "I will not go! By Thor, I will not go! Spirits are hidden behind those points. Who knows what would jump out at us? I will not stir away from the Lucky One. I will not! I will not!" Gibbering with terror, he clutched Leif's cloak and clung there like a cat.

For a moment the chief hesitated, looking down at him with disgust unutterable. Then he quietly loosened the golden clasp on his shoulder, flung the mantle off with a sweep that sent the thrall staggering backward, and marched away at the head of his men.

Valbrand had handled rebellious slaves before.

Shaking the fellow until he no longer had any breath to howl with, the steersman said briefly, "It is very unlikely that we shall see any ghosts, but it is altogether certain that your hide will feel my belt if you do not end this fuss."

Kark made his choice with admirable swiftness. He got what comfort he could, poor wretch, out of a carefully selected position. As between two shields, he crept between the mystic Icelander and the dauntless Norman warrior. Valbrand led the way, his flint face set to withstand the Devil and all his angels; and three strapping Swedes brought up the

157

rear, with drawn swords and thumping hearts.

If only the way could have lain straight and open before them, even though it bristled with beasts and foes! But for the whole distance it screwed itself into a succession of crescent–shaped beaches, each one lying between rocky spurs of the beetling crags.

Each point they rounded disclosed nothing more alarming than lichened boulders and pebbly shore, with here a dead fish, and there a heap of shining snaky kelp, and yonder a flock of startled gulls,—but who could tell what the next projection might be hiding? They walked with their fists gripped hard around their weapons, their eyes shifting, their ears strained, while the waves hissed around their feet and the gulls screamed over their heads.

Slowly the light faded from the mountain top and lay upon the next peak, a golden cone against the blue. At last, even Valbrand's sense of duty was satisfied. "We will turn back now," he announced, halting them. "But first I will climb up the cliff, here where it is lowest, and try to see a little way ahead, that we may have as much news as possible to report to the chief."

As he spoke, he gave a great spring upward on to a shelving ledge, and pulled himself up to the next projection; a rattling shower of sand and pebbles continued to mark his ascent. Robert the Fearless walked on to look around the rock they had almost reached; but the rest remained where they were, following their leader's movements with anxious eyes.

They were so intent that they jumped like startled horses at an exclamation from the Icelander. He was pointing to the strip of beach which lay between Kark and the Norman.

"Look there!" he cried. "Look there!"

Their alarm was in no way diminished when they had looked and seen that the space was empty. The cold drops came out on their bodies, and the hair rose on their heads.

Robert of Normandy, who had caught the cry but not the words, came walking back, inquiring the cause of the excitement; and at that the Icelander cried out louder than before:

The Thrall of Leif the Lucky

"Have a care where you go! Do you not see it? You will get blood upon your fine cloak. It is at your feet."

In blank amazement, the Norman stared first at the ground and then at the seer.

"Have the wits been stolen out of you? There is not even so much as a devil–fish where you are pointing."

The Icelander took off his cap, and commenced wiping the great beads from his forehead. "You begin to listen after the song is sung," he answered, peevishly. "The thing ran away as soon as you approached. It was a fox that was bloody all over."

A yell of terror distended Kark's throat.

"A fox!" he screeched. "My guardian spirit follows me in that shape; a foreknowing woman told me so. It is my death–omen! I am death–fated!" His knees gave way under him so that he sank to the ground and cowered there, wringing his hands.

The Icelander shot a look of triumph at the sceptical stranger. "They have no call to hold their chins high who hear of strange wonders for the first time," he said, severely. "It is as certain that men have guardian spirits as that they have bodies. Yours, Robert of Normandy, goes doubtless in the shape of a wolf because of your warrior nature; and I advise you now, that when you see a bloody wolf before you it will be time for you to draw on your Hel–shoes. The animal ran nearest the thrall—"

Kark's lamentations merged into a shriek of hope. "That is untrue! It lay at the Norman's feet; you told him so!"

While the seer turned to look rather resentfully at him, he climbed up this slender life–line, like a man whom sharks are pursuing.

"It was not a fox that you saw, at all; it was a wolf! So excited were you that your eyes were deceitful. It was a wolf, and it was nearest the Norman. A blind man could see what that means."

159

The Thrall of Leif the Lucky

The Icelander pulled off his cap again, but this time it was to scratch his head doubtfully. "It was when the stranger approached it, that it was nearest to him," he persisted. "While this may signify that he will seek death, I am unable to say that it proves that he will overtake it. Yet I will not swear that it was not a wolf. The sun was in my eyes—"

Robert the Fearless burst into a scornful laugh. "Oh, call it a wolf, and let us end this talk!" he said, contemptuously. "I shall not die until my death-day comes, though you see a pack of them. Call it a wolf, craven serf, if that will stay your tongue."

There was no chance for more, for at that moment Valbrand joined them. "There is naught to be seen which is different from what we have already experienced," he said shortly; and they began the return march.

They reached the landing-place first; but it was not long before the heads of their companions appeared above a rocky ridge. This party, it was evident, had had better sport. Several men carried hats filled with sea-birds' eggs. Another explorer had under his arm a fat little bear cub that he had picked up somewhere. Rolf's deftness at stone-throwing had secured him a bushy yellow fox-tail for a trophy.

The party had gone inland far enough to discover that creeping bushes grew on the hills, and rushes on the bogs; that it was an island, as Biorn had stated, and that forests equal in size to those of Greenland grew in sheltered places. But they had seen nothing to alter their unflattering first opinion. Vikings though they were, warriors who would have been flayed alive without flinching, relief was manifest on every face when the leader finally gave the word to embark.

Probably it was because he understood the danger of pushing their fidelity too far, that the chief gave the order to return so soon. For his own part, he did not seem to be entirely satisfied. With one foot on the stern of the boat, and one still on the rocks, he lingered uncertainly.

"Yet we have not acted with this land like Biorn, who did not come ashore," he muttered. Rolf displayed the fox-tail with a flourish.

"We have accomplished more than Eric after he had been in Greenland an equally short time, chief. We have taken tribute from the inhabitants." Leif deigned to smile slightly.

The Thrall of Leif the Lucky

He stepped into his place, and from the stern he swept a long critical look over the barren coast,—from the fox-dens up to the high-peaked mountains, and back again to the sea.

"We will give as well as take," he said at last. "I will give a name to the land, and call it Helluland, for it is indeed an icy plain."

They were welcomed on board with a hubbub of curiosity. Almost every article of value upon the ship was offered in exchange for the cub and the fox-tail. The uncanny accounts of the place were swallowed with open-mouthed greediness; so greedily that it was little wonder that at each repetition the narratives grew longer and fuller. Told by torchlight, at a safe distance from Leif, each boulder took on the form of a squatting dwarf; and the faint squeaking of foxes became the shrieking of spirits. The tale of the death-omen swelled to such proportions that Kark would have been terrified out of his wits if he had not rested secure in the conviction that the vision had been a wolf. The explorers who had gotten little pleasure out of their adventure at the time of its occurrence, came to regard it as their most precious possession. The fire of exploration waxed hot in every vein. Every man constituted himself a special look-out to watch for any dawning speck upon the horizon.

With Fortune's fondness for surprising mankind, the next of the "wonder-shores" crept upon them in the night. The sun, which had set upon an empty ocean, rose upon a low level coast lying less than twenty miles away. In the glowing light, bluffs of sand shone like cliffs of molten silver; and more trees were massed upon one point than the whole of Greenland had ever produced. Even Leif was moved to exclaim at the sight.

"Certainly this is a land which names itself!" he declared. "You need not wait long for what I shall fix upon. It shall be called Markland, after its woods."

Sigurd's enthusiasm mounted to rashness. "I will have a share in this landing, if I have to plead with Leif for the privilege," he vowed. And when, for the second time, Rolf was told off for a place in the boat, and for the second time his claims were slighted, he was as reckless as his word.

"Has not my credit improved at ail, after all this time, foster-father?" he demanded, waylaying the chief on his descent from the forecastle. "I ask you to consider the shame it will bring upon me if I am obliged to return to Norway without having so much as set foot upon the new–found lands."

For awhile Leif's gaze rested upon him absently, as though the press of other matters had entirely swept him out of mind. Presently, however, his brows began to knit themselves above his hawk nose.

"Tell those who ask, that you were kept on board because a strong–minded and faithful watchman was needed there," he answered curtly, and turned his back upon him.

Robert the Fearless was standing at the side, gazing eagerly toward the shore. As though suddenly reminded of his existence, the chief stopped behind him and touched him on the shoulder.

"The Norman is as much too modest as his friend is too bold," he said, with a note of his occasional courtliness. "A man who has thought it worth while to travel so far is certainly entitled to a share in every experience. Let Robert Sans–Peur go down and take the place that is his right."

As the boat bounded away with the Fearless One on the last bench, Sigurd's face was a study. Between mortification and amusement, it was so convulsed that Rolf, who shared the Norman's seat, could not restrain his soft laughter.

"Whether or not the Silver–Tongued has given his luck to you, it is seen that he has none left for himself," he laughed into his companion's ear.

The Norman bent to his oar with a petulant force that drove it deep into the water and far out of stroke.

"Whether or not he has any left for himself, it is certain that he has given none of it to me," he muttered. "Here are we at our second landing, and no chance have I had yet to endanger my life for the chief. Nor do I see any reason for expecting favorable prospects in this tame–appearing land. Is it of any use to hope for wild beasts here?"

The Wrestler regarded him over his shoulder with amused eyes. "Is it your opinion that Leif Ericsson needs your protection against wild beasts?" he inquired.

The Thrall of Leif the Lucky

Under the Norman's swarthy complexion, Alwin of England suddenly flushed. When a wish is rooted in one's very heart, it is difficult to get far enough away to see it in its true proportions.

The cliffs of gleaming silver faded, on the boat's approach, into gullied bluffs of weather–beaten sand; but the white beach that met the water, and the green thickets that covered the heights, remained fair and inviting. No fear of dark omens along that shining sand; no danger of evil spirits in that sunlit wood. All was pure and bright and fresh from the hand of God. In place of a spur, the explorers needed a rein,—and a tight one. But for the chief's authority, they would have spread themselves over the place like birds'–nesting boys.

"Ye know no more moderation than swine," Leif said sternly, checking their rush to obey the beckoning of the myriad of leafy hands. "And ye are as witless as children, besides. Have ye not learned yet that cold steel often lies hid under a fair tunic? We will divide into two bands, as we did at our first landing; and I forbid that any man shall separate himself from his party, for any reason whatsoever."

Then he proceeded to single out those who were to follow him; and to the great joy of Robert of Normandy, he was included in that favored number.

Valbrand's men crashed away through bush and bramble; and the chief's following threw themselves, like jubilant swimmers, into the sea of undergrowth. Now, waist–high in thorny bushes, they tore their way through by sheer force of strength. Now they stepped high over a network of low–lying vines, ankle–bonds tougher than walrus hide. Again, imitating the four–footed pioneer that had worn the faint approach to a trail, they crawled on their hands and knees. Every nest they chanced upon, and each berry bush, paid a heavy toll; but they gave the briers a liberal return in the way of cloth and hair and flesh.

"I think it likely that I could retrace my steps by no other means than the hair that I have left on the thorns," Eyvind the Icelander observed ruefully, when at last they had paused to draw breath in one of the few open spaces.

The Fearless One overheard him and laughed. "When I found that my locks were liable to be pulled off my head entirely, I disposed of them in this manner," he said. He was leaning forward from his seat on a fallen oak to shew how his black curls were tucked snugly inside his collar, when a shriek of pain from the thicket behind them brought every man to his feet.

The chief ran his eye over the little group. "It is Lodin that is missing," he said. "Probably he lingered at those last berry bushes." Knife in hand, he plunged into the jungle.

While a rustling green curtain still hid the tragedy, the rescuers learned the nature of their companion's peril; for suddenly, above the cries for help and the crash of trampled brush, there rose the roar of an infuriated bear.

Alwin's heart leaped in his breast, and his nostrils widened with such a fierce joy as won him the undying respect of the sportsmen around him. Pushing past his comrades, he tore his way through the tangle of twining willowy arms and gained the side of the chief.

Leif pushed aside the last overhanging bough, and the conflict was before them.

Locked in the embrace of as big a bear as it had ever been their luck to see, stood Lodin the Berry−Eater. That the beast had come upon him from the rear was evident, for the chisel−like claws of one huge paw had torn mantle and tunic and flesh into ribbons; but in some way the Viking must have managed to turn and grapple with his foe, for now his distorted face was close to the dripping jaws. Two bloody mangled spots upon either arm showed where the brute's teeth had been; but if the bear's paws were gripping the man's shoulders, still the man's hands were locked about the bear's ears. That the pair had been down once, leaves and dirt in hair and fur were witness; and now they went down again, ploughing up the earth, screaming and panting, growling and roaring; one of the brute's hind legs drawing up and striking down in a motion of terrible meaning.

It was too ghastly a thing to watch inactive. Already every man's knife was in his hand, and three men were crouching for a spring, when the chief swept them back with a stern gesture.

"Attacking thus, you can reach no vital part," he reminded them. And he shouted to the struggling man, "Feign death! you can do nothing without your weapon. Feign death."

It appeared to Alwin that to do this would require greater courage than to struggle; but while the words were still in the air, the man obeyed. His hands relaxed their hold; his head fell backward on the ground; and he lay under the shaggy body like a dead thing. The black muzzle poked curiously about his face, but he did not stir.

After a suspicious sniff, the victor appeared to accept the truth of his conquest. Exactly as though he said, "Come! Here is one good job done; what next?" he got up with a grunt, and, rising to his hind feet, stood growling and rolling his fiery little eyes from one to another of the intruders in the brush.

"If now one could only hurl a spear at his heart!" murmured the sailor at Alwin's shoulder. But the difficulties of path-finding through an unbroken thicket had kept the men from cumbering themselves with weapons so unwieldy.

Leif spoke up quickly, "There is no way but to trust to our knives. Since I am superior to any in strength, I will grapple with him first. If I fail, which I do not expect, I will preserve my life as Lodin is doing; and the Fearless One here shall take his turn."

Alwin was too wild with delight to remember any–thing else. "For that, I thank you as for a crown!" he gasped.

Even as he stepped out to meet the foe, Leif smiled ironically. "Certainly you are better called the Fearless than the Courteous," he said. "It would have been no more than polite for you to have wished me luck."

Anything further was drowned in the bear's roar, as he took a swift waddling step forward and threw out his terrible paws. Even Leif's huge frame could not withstand the shock of the meeting. His left hand caught the beast by the throat and, with sinews of iron, held off his foaming jaws; hut the shock of the grappling lost him his footing. They fell, clenched, and rolled over and over on the ground; those terrible hind feet drawing up and striking down with surer and surer aim.

Alwin could endure it no longer. "Let me have him now!" he implored. "It is time to leave him to me. The next stroke, he will tear you to pieces. I claim my turn."

It is doubtful if anyone heard him: at that moment, swaying and staggering, the wrestlers got to their feet. In rising, Leif's hold on the bear's throat slipped and the shaggy head shot sideways and fastened its jaws on his naked arm, with a horrible snarling sound. But at the same moment, the man's right arm, knife in hand, shot toward the mark it had been seeking. Into the exposed body it drove the blade up to its hilt, then swerved to the left and went upward. The stroke which the chisel–shod paws had tried for in vain, the little strip of steel achieved. A roar that echoed and re–echoed between the low hills, a convulsive movement of the mighty limbs, and then the beast's muscles relaxed, stiffening while they straightened; and the huge body swayed backward, dead.

From the chief came much the same kind of a grunt as had come from the bear at the fall of his foe. Glancing with only a kind of contemptuous curiosity at his wounded arm, he stepped quickly to the side of his prostrate follower and bent over him.

"You have got what you deserve for breaking my orders," he said, grimly. "Yet turn over that I may attend to your wounds before you bleed to death."

In the activity which followed, Robert of Normandy took no part. He leaned against a tree with his arms folded upon his breast, his eyes upon the slain bear which half of the party were hastily converting into steaks and hide. The men muttered to each other that the Southerner was in a rage because he had lost his chance, but that was only a part of the truth. His fixed eyes no longer saw the bear; his ears were deaf to the voices around him. He saw again a shadowy room, lit by leaping flames and shifting eyes; and once more a lisping voice hissed its "jargon" into his ear.

"I see Leif Ericsson standing upon earth where never man stood before; and I see you standing by his side, though you do not look as you look now, for your hair is long and black... I see that it is in this new land that it will be settled whether your luck is to be good or bad..."

He said slowly to himself, like a man talking in his sleep, "It has been settled, and it is to be bad."

Then the room passed from his vision. He saw in its place Rolf's derisive smile, and heard again his mocking query: "Is it your opinion that Leif Ericsson needs your protection against wild beasts?"

Of a sudden he flung back his head and burst into a loud laugh that jarred on the ear like grating steel.

166

The Thrall of Leif the Lucky

When at last Lodin's wounds were dressed so that he could be helped along between two of his comrades, the party began a slow return. By the time they came out on to the shining white beach again, they were a battered-looking lot. There was not a mantle among them but what hung in tatters, nor a scratched face that did not mingle blood with berry juice. But at their head, the huge bear skin was borne like a captured banner. At the sight of it, their waiting comrades burst into shouts of admiration and envy that reached as far as the anchored ship.

"Never was such sport heard of!"—"A better land is nowhere to be found!" they clamored. "In one month we could secure enough skins to make us wealthy for the rest of our lives!"

And then some muttered asides were added: "It is a great pity to leave such a place."—"It is folly to give up certain wealth for vague possibilities." And though the dissatisfaction rose no louder than a murmur, it spread on every hand like fire in brush.

Now there was one man among the explorers who had been a member of Biorn Herjulfsson's crew, and was brimful of conceit and the ambition to be a leader among his fellows. When the command to embark swelled the murmurs almost to an outspoken grumbling, he thought he saw a chance to push into prominence, and swaggered boldly forward.

"If it is not your intention to come back and profit by this discovery, chief, I must tell you that we will not willingly return to the ship. Certainly not until we have secured at least one bear apiece. We are free men, Leif Ericsson, and it is not to our minds to be led altogether by the—"

Whether or not he had meant to say "nose," no one ever knew. At that moment the chief wheeled and looked at him, with a glance so different from Biorn Herjulfsson's mild gaze that the word stuck in the fellow's throat, and instinctively he leaped backward.

Leif turned from him disdainfully, and addressed the men of his old crew. "Ye are free men," he said; "but I am the chief to whom, of your own free wills, you have sworn allegiance on the edge of your swords. Do you think it improves your honor that a stranger should dare to insult your chosen leader in your presence?"

The Thrall of Leif the Lucky

"No!" bellowed Valbrand, in a voice of thunder.

And Lodin shook his wounded arm at the mutineer. "If my hand could close over a sword, I would split you open with it," he cried.

The other men's slumbering pride awoke. Loyalty seldom took more than cat—naps in those days, in spite of all the hard work that was put upon her.

"Duck him!"—"Souse him!"—"Dip him in the ocean!" they shouted. And so energetically that the ringleader, cursing the fickleness of rebels, found it all at once advisable to whip out his sword and fall into a posture of defence.

But again Leif's hand was stretched forth.

"Let him be," he said. "He is a stranger among us, and your own words are responsible for his mistake. Let him be, and show your loyalty to your leader by carrying out his orders with no more unseemly delay."

They obeyed him silently, if reluctantly; and it was not long before those who had remained on ship—board were thrown into a second fever of envious excitement.

They were not pleasant, however, the days that followed. In the flesh of those who had missed the sport, the bear—fight was as a rankling thorn. The watches, during which a northeast gale kept them scudding through empty seas with little to do and much time to gossip, were golden hours for the growth of the serpent of discontent. Though the creature did not dare to strike again, its hiss could be heard in the distance, and the gleam of its fangs showed in dark corners. If Leif had had Biorn's bad fortune, to begin at the wrong end of his journey, so that a barren Helluland was the climax that now lay before him, the hidden snake might have swelled, like Thora Borga Hiort's serpent—pet, into a devastating dragon.

Was it not Leif's luck that the land which was revealed to them, on the third morning, should be as much fairer than their vaunted Markland as that spot was pleasanter than Greenland's wastes?—a land where, as the old books tell, vines grew wild upon the hills, and wheat upon the plains; where the rivers teemed with fish, and the thickets rustled with game, and the islands were covered with innumerable wild fowl; where even the dew upon the grass was honey–sweet!

As they gazed upon the blooming banks and woods and low hills, warm and green with sunlight, cries of admiration burst from every throat.

Valbrand made bold to warn his chief, "Though I do not dispute your will in this, any more than in anything else, I will say that difficulties are to be expected if men are to be parted from such a land without at least tasting of its good things."

Even for those who had been longest with him, the Lucky One was full of surprises.

"It has never been my intention to continue sailing after we had accomplished the three landings," he answered quietly. "Ungrateful to God would we be, were we to fail in showing honor to the good things He has led us to. I expect to stay over winter in this place."

CHAPTER XXVI. VINLAND THE GOOD

"... They sailed toward this land, and came to an island lying north of it, and went ashore in fine weather and looked round. They found dew on the grass, and touched it with their hands, and put it to their mouths, and it seemed to them that they had never tasted anything so sweet as this dew. Then they went on hoard and sailed into the channel, which was between the island and the cape which ran north from the mainland. They passed the cape, sailing in a westerly direction. There the water was very shallow, and their ship went aground, and at ebb-tide the sea was far out from the ship. But they were so anxious to get ashore that they could not wait till the high-water reached their ship, and ran out on the beach where a river flowed from a lake. When the high-water set their ship afloat they took their boat and rowed to the ship and towed it up the river into the lake. There they cast anchor, and took their leather-bags ashore, and there built booths."—FLATEYJARBO'K.

The Thrall of Leif the Lucky

It was October, and it was the new camp, and it was Helga the Fair tripping across the green background with a skirtful of red and yellow thorn–berries and a wreath of fiery autumn leaves upon her sunny head.

Where a tongue of land ran out between a lake–like bay and a river that hurried down to throw herself into its arms, there lay the new settlement. Facing seaward, the five newly–built huts stood on the edge of a grove that crowned the river bluffs. Behind them stretched some hundred yards of wooded highland, ending in a steep descent to the river, which served as a sort of back stairway to the stronghold. Before them, green plains and sandy flats sloped away to the white shore of the bay that rocked their anchored ship upon its bosom. Over their lowly roofs, stately oaks and elms and maples murmured ceaseless lullabies,—like women long–childless, granted after a weary waiting the listening ears to be soothed by their crooning.

"I have a feeling that this land has always been watching for us; and that now that we are come, it is glad," Helga said, happily, as she paused where the jarl's son leaned in a doorway, watching Kark's cook–fires leap and wave their arms of blue smoke. "Is it not a wonderful thought, Sigurd, that it was in God's mind so long ago that we should some day want to come here?"

"It is a fair land," Sigurd agreed, absently. And then for the first time Helga noticed the frown on his face, and some of the brightness faded from her own.

"Alas, comrade, you are brooding over the disfavor I have brought upon you!" she said, laying an affectionate hand upon his arm. "I act in a thoughtless way when I forget it."

Sigurd made a good–natured attempt to arouse himself. "Do not let that trouble you, _ma_mie_," he said, lightly. "When ill luck has it in her mind to reach a man, she will come in through a window if the door be closed. It is a matter of little importance."

He patted the hand on his arm and his smile became even mischievous. "Still, I will not say anything against it if you wish to pay some forfeit," he added. "See,—yonder Leif sits, playing with the bear cub while he waits for his breakfast. Now, as he turns his eyes upon us, do you reach up and give me such an affectionate kiss as shall convince him forever that it was for love of me that you fled from Norway."

170

The Thrall of Leif the Lucky

A vigorous box on the ear was his answer; yet even before her cheeks cooled, Helga relented and turned back.

"Even your French foolishness I will overlook, for the sake of the misfortune I have been to you. Take now a handful of these berries, and make the excuse that you wish to give them to the bear. While you do so, speak to Leif strongly and tell him your wish. That he is playing with the cub is a sign that he is in a good humor."

Sigurd's eyes wandered wistfully beyond the cook—fires and the storehouses to the last hut in the line, before which a dozen men were buckling on cloaks and arming themselves, in a bustle of joyful anticipation. He thrust out his palm with sudden resolve.

"By Saint Michael, I will! I had sworn that I would never entreat his leave again, but this time there is no one near enough to witness my shame if he refuses me. There—that is sufficient! It is needful that I make haste: yonder come Eyvind and Odd with the fish; Kark will not be long in cooking it."

Carefully careless, he strolled past the open shed in which the new—found wheat was being stored, past the sleeping—house and a group of fellows mending nets, and came to the great maple—tree under which a rough bench had been placed. There, like a Giant Thrym and his greyhounds, Leif sat stroking his mustache thoughtfully, while with his free hand he tousled the head of the camp pet.

Scenting dainties, the bear deserted his friend and shambled forward to meet the newcomer. The chief raised his eyes and regarded his foster—son over his hand, seemingly with less sternness than usual. Yet he did not look to be so blinded by good—nature that he would be unable to see through manoeuvring. Sigurd decided to strike straight from the shoulder.

The cub, finding that the treat was not to be had in one delicious gulp, rose upon his haunches and threw open his jaws invitingly. While he tossed the berries, one by one, between the white teeth, Sigurd spoke his mind.

"It is two weeks now, foster—father, since the winter booths were finished and you began the practice of sending out exploring parties. In all those days you have but once permitted me to share the sport. I ask you to tell me how long I shall have to endure

171

this?"

It appeared that the hand which stroked the chief's mustache also hid a dry smile.

"You grasp your weapon by the wrong end, foster–son," he retorted. "You forget that each time I have chosen an exploring party to go out, I have also chosen a party to remain at home and guard the goods. How is it possible that I could spare from their number a man who has shown himself so superior in good sense and firm–mindedness—"

Sigurd's foot came down in an unmistakable stamp; and the remaining berries were crushed in his clenching fist.

"Enough jests have been strung on that thread! I have submitted to you patiently because it appeared to me that your anger was not without cause, yet it is no more than just for you to remember that I was helpless in the matter. Since the girl was already so far, it would have been dastardly for me to have refused her aid. It is not as though I had enticed her from Norway—"

A confusing recollection brought him suddenly to a halt, the blood tingling in his cheeks. He knew that the eyes above the brown hand had become piercing, but there were many reasons why he did not care to meet them. After a moment's hesitation, he frankly abandoned that tack and tried a new one. Dropping on one knee to wipe his berry–stained hand in the grass, he looked up with his gay smile. "There is yet another reason why you should allow me my way, foster–father. Upon the one occasion when I did accompany the party, the discovery was made of those fields of self–sown wheat which you prize so highly. Since then I have remained at home, and nothing of value has come to light. Who knows what you might not find this time, if you would but take my luck along with you?"

Leif pushed the cub aside and rose to his feet, the strengthening savor of broiled salmon announcing the imminent approach of the morning meal.

"Although I cannot say that I consider that an argument which would win you a case before a law–man," he observed, "yet I will not be so stark as to punish you further. Take your chance with the rovers if you will; though it is not likely that you will have time both to eat your food and to make yourself ready."

The Thrall of Leif the Lucky

Sigurd was already gone on a bound.

"It will not take me long to choose between the two," he called back joyously, over his shoulder.

While the rest feasted noisily at the long table before the provision sheds, the Silver-Tongued hurried between sleeping house and store-room, rummaging out his heaviest boots, his stoutest tunic, his oldest mantle. At the last moment, the edge on his knife was found to be unsatisfactory, and he went and sat down by one of the cook-fires and fell to work with a sharpening stone.

On the other side of the fire Kark sat cross-legged upon the ground, skinning rabbits from a heap that had just been brought in by the trappers. He looked up with an impudent grin.

"It is a good thing if your fortunes have mended at last, Sigurd Jarlsson. It did not appear that the Norman brought you much luck in return for your support." He glanced toward that part of the table where the black locks of Robert the Fearless shone, sleek as a blackbird's wing, in the morning sun. "The Southerner has an overbearing face," he added. "It reminds me of someone I hate, though I cannot think who."

Sigurd's fiery impulse to cuff him was cooled by a sudden frost. He said as carelessly as possible: "You are a churlish fool; but it is likely you have seen Robert Sans-Peur in Nidaros. He was there shortly before we came away."

The thrall assented with a nod, but his interest seemed to have taken another turn, for after a while he said absently: "You will call me fool again when I tell you who the Norman made me think of at first. No other than that pig-headed English thrall that Leif killed last winter,—if it were not that one is black and the other was white, and one is living and the other dead."

He commenced to grin over his work, a veritable image of malice, quite unconscious that Sigurd's eyes were blazing down upon his head. By and by he broke into a discordant roar.

The Thrall of Leif the Lucky

"Too great fun is it to keep silent over! What can it matter, now that Hot–Head is dead? Ah, that was a fine revenge!" He squinted boldly up into Sigurd's face, though he did not raise his voice to be heard beyond. "Did you know that it was not Thorhall the steward who found the knife that betrayed the English–man? Did you dream of that, Jarl's son? Did you know that it was I who followed you out of the hall that night, and listened to you from the shadows, and followed your trail the next sunrise, until I came upon the knife at Skroppa's very door? You never suspected that, Jarl's son. I was too cunning to let you put your teeth into me. Thorhall you could do no harm—"

"Wretched spy! Do you boast of your deed?" the young Viking interrupted hotly. "What is to hinder my biting now?" He had leaped the flames, and his hand was on the other's throat before he finished speaking.

But the thrall fought him off with unusual boldness.

"It is unadvisable for you to injure Leif's property, Sigurd Haraldsson," he panted. "My life is of value to him now. You are not yet out of disgrace. It would be unadvisable for you to offend him again."

However contemptible its present mouthpiece, that was the truth. Sigurd paused, even while his fingers twitched with passion. While he hesitated, a shout of summons from Valbrand decided the matter. Loosening his hold, the young warrior vented his rage in one savage kick and hastened to join his comrades.

Twelve brawny Vikings with twelve short swords at their sides and twelve long knives in their belts, they stood forth, headed by Valbrand of the Flint–Face and—by Tyrker! The little German had left off the longest of his fur tunics; a very long knife indeed garnished his waist, and he used a spear for a staff. Yet none of these preparations made him appear very formidable. Sigurd stared at him in amazement.

"Tyrker! My eyes cannot believe that you have the intention to undertake such a march! Before a hundred steps, it will become such an exertion to you that you will lie down upon a rock in a swoon."

The old man blinked at him with his little twinkling eyes.

The Thrall of Leif the Lucky

"So?" he said, chuckling. "Then will we a bargain together make; for me shall you be legs, while I be brains for you. Then shall we neither be left behind for wild beasts to eat, nor yet shall our wits like beer–foam off–blown be, if so it happens that a beautiful maiden crosses our path."

Sigurd swore an unholy French oath, as the laughter arose. Would those jests never grow stale on their tongues? he wondered. He sent a half–resentful glance to where Robert Sans–Peur stood, calm and lofty, watching the departure. Whatever else threatened Alwin of England, he had none of this nonsense to endure. Over his shoulder, as he marched away, the Silver–Tongued made a sly face at his friend.

The Norman caught the grimace, but no answering smile curved the bitter line of his lips. Smiles had been strangers to his gaunt dark face for many weeks now.

The sailors said of him, "Since the Southerner lost his chance at the bear, he has had the appearance of a man who has lost his hope of Heaven."

When the noise of the departing explorers sank into the distance, Robert Sans–Peur strolled away from the busy groups and stretched himself in the shade of a certain old elm–tree. The chief stripped off his mantle and upper tunic, and betook himself to the woods with an axe over his shoulder. The hammers of the carpenters made merry music as they built the bunks in the new sleeping–house. Out in the sunshine, fishers and trappers came and went; harvesters staggered in under golden sheaves; and a group of bathers shouted and splashed in the lake. But the Norman neither saw nor heard anything of the pleasant stir. Through the long golden hours he lay without sound or motion, staring absently at the green turf and the dying leaves that floated down to him with every breeze.

A meal at midday was not a Brattahlid custom; but when the noon–hour came, there was a lull in the activity while Kark carried around bread and meat and ale. Combining prudence with a saving of labor, the thrall made no attempt to approach the brooding stranger; nor did the latter give any sign of noticing the slight. But the chief's keen eyes saw it, as they saw everything.

From his seat under the maple–tree, he called out with the voice of authority: "Hardy bear–fighters are not made by abstaining from food; nor are wits sharpened by sulking. I

175

invite the Norman to sit with me, while he drinks his ale and tells me what lies heavy on his mind."

It was with more embarrassment than gratification that Robert Sans—Peur responded to this invitation.

"It may well be that my head is drowsy because I have had too much ale," he made excuse, as he took his seat.

Over the chunk of bread he was raising to his mouth, the chief regarded his guest critically.

"There is an old saying," he observed, "that when it happens to a man that his head is sleepy in the day—time, it is because his mind is not in his body but wanders out in the world in another shape. In what land, and in what form, do the Norman's thoughts travel?"

After a moment, Robert the Fearless rose to his feet and bowed low. "They have returned to rest contentedly in an unnamed land," he answered; "and they wear the shape of thanks to Leif Ericsson for his many favors. I drink to the Lucky One's health, and to his undying fame! Skoal!"

As he set down his horn after the toast, the Norman's glance happened to encounter a glance from the shield—maiden, who was passing. Taking another horn from the thrall, he bowed again, with proverbial French gallantry; then quaffed off the second measure of ale to the honor of Helga the Fair.

Leif turned in time to catch a rather unusual expression on the maiden's face, though her courtesy was a model of formality. He held out his hand peremptorily.

"Come hither, kinswoman, and tell me how matters go with you," he commanded. "It is to be hoped that Tyrker has not lost you out of his mind, as I have done during these last weeks. How are you entertaining yourself this morning, while he is absent?"

Helga sped a guilty thought to a certain green nook on the river bluff; and winged heavenward a prayer of thanks that she had put off until afternoon her daily pilgrimage to the beloved shrine.

She answered readily, "I have entertained myself very poorly so far, kinsman, for I have been doing such woman's-work as Thorhild commends. I have been in your sleeping-house, sewing upon the skin curtains that are to make the fourth wall of my chamber."

Leif glanced at the Norman with a dry smile. "Chamber!" he commented. "Learn from this, Robert of Normandy, how a Norse maiden regards a stall! Yet, whatever hostile thing attacks us, a Norman lady in her bower would be no safer. Tyrker's sleeping-place, and mine and Valbrand's, lie between the house-door and the chamber of Helga, Gilli's daughter." He freed the girl's hand, though he still held her with his eyes. "Whither do you betake yourself now?" he demanded. "Long rambles are unsafe in an unknown country."

In her perfect composure, Helga even laughed; a silvery peal that sent a thrill of pleasure through the brooding old trees.

"By my knife, kinsman, you take your responsibility heavily, now that you have remembered it at all!" she retorted. "I do not go far; only a little way up the river, where grow the rushes of which I wish to make baskets."

The chief released her then; and soon she disappeared among the trees.

One by one, the men finished their meal and drifted back to their various employments. The hammers began again their merry tattoo; and the wrangling voices of dice-throwers replaced the shouts of the bathers. Except for these, however, the place was still. The sun shone hotly, and the trees appeared to nap in the drowsy air.

Perhaps because he preferred asking questions to answering them, Robert Sans-Peur began an earnest conversation, concerning the harvest, the traps, and the fishing. But as the hour grew, the gaps between his inquiries stretched wider. As the tree-heads ceased even their nodding and hung motionless, the chief's answers became briefer and slower. At last the moment arrived when no response at all was forthcoming. Glancing up, the Norman found his host tilted back against the maple trunk in placid slumber.

The Thrall of Leif the Lucky

The young man let something like a sigh of relief escape him. Still, watching the sleeping face warily, he tried the effect of another question. Oblivion. He rose to his feet with a daring flourish of yawns and stretching, and awaited the result of that test. The deep breathing never faltered.

Then Alwin the Lover hesitated no longer. Quietly and directly, as one who treads a familiar path, he walked around the corner of the last hut and disappeared among the trees.

Many feet had worn a distinct trail through the woods to the edge of the bluff, and down the steep to the water; but only two pair of feet had ever turned aside, midway the descent, and found the path to Eden. Like a rosy curtain, a tall sumach bush hid the trail's beginning; the overhanging bluffs concealed it from above; the tangle of shrubs and vines which covered the bank from the water's edge screened it from below. Hardly more than a rabbit track, a narrow shelf against the wall of the steep, it ran along for a dozen yards to stop where a ledge of moss−covered rock thrust itself from the soil.

When Alwin pushed aside the leafy sprays, Helga stood awaiting him with outstretched hands. "You have been long in coming, comrade. I dare not hope that it is because Leif delayed you with some new friendliness?"

Her lover shook his head, as he bent to kiss her hands.

"Do not hope anything, sweetheart," he said, wearily. "That is the one way not to be disappointed." He threw himself down on the rock at her feet, unaware that her smooth brows had suddenly drawn themselves into a troubled frown.

She said with grave slowness, "I do not like to hear you speak like that. You are foremost among men in courage, yet to hear you now, one would almost imagine you to be faint−hearted."

Alwin's mouth bent into a bitter smile, as his eyes stared away at the river. "Courage?" he repeated, half to himself. "Yes, I have that. Once I thought it so precious a thing that I could stake honor and life upon it, and win on the turn of the wheel. But I know now what it is worth. Courage, the boldness of the devil himself, who of the North but has that? It is cheaper than the dirt of the road. If I have not been a coward, at least I have been a fool."

All at once, Helga shook out her flying locks like so many golden war banners, and turned to face him resolutely. "You shall not speak, nor think like that," she said; "for I see now that it is not good sense. Before, though my heart told me you were wrong, I did not understand why; but now I have turned it over in my mind until I see clearly. The failure of your first attempt to win Leif's favor is a thing by itself; at least it does not prove that you have not yet many good chances. I will not deny that we may have expected too many opportunities for valiant deeds, yet are there no other ways in which to serve? Was it by a feat of arms that you won your first honor with the chief? It was nothing more heroic than the ability to read runes which, in five days, got you more favor than Rolf Erlingsson's strength had gained him in five years. Are your accomplishments so limited to your weapons that when you cannot use your sword you must lie idle? Many little services will count as much as one big one, when the time of reckoning comes. Shake the sleep–thorn out of your ear, my comrade, and be your brave strong–minded self again. Without courage, never would Robert Sans–Peur have come to Greenland, nor Helga, Gilli's daughter, have followed him to Norway. Despise it not, but mate it with your good sense, and the two shall yet draw us to victory."

It was a long time before Alwin answered. The river splashed and murmured below; birds rustled in the bushes around them, or dived into the green depths with a soft whir of wings. A rabbit paused to look at them, and two squirrels quarrelled over a nut, within reach of their hands,—so still were they. But when at last Alwin raised his eyes to hers, their gaze reassured her.

"The sleep–thorn is out, sweetheart," he said, slowly. "Now is the whole of my folly clear to me for the first time. Never again shall you have cause to shame my manhood with such words."

"Shame! Shame you, who are the best and bravest in the world!" she cried, passionately, and threw herself on her knees by his side, entreating.

But he silenced her lips with kisses, and put her gently back upon the rock.

"Do not let us speak further of it, dear one. I have thought so much and done so little. After this you shall see how I will bear myself... But let us forget it now, and rest awhile.

The Thrall of Leif the Lucky

Let us forget everything in the world except that we are together. Lay your hand in mine and turn your face where I can look into it; and so shall we be sure of this happiness, whatever lies beyond."

A vague fear laid its icy finger, for an instant, on Helga's brave heart; but she shook it off fiercely. Locking her hand fast in her comrade's, she let all the love of her soul well up and shine from her beautiful eyes. So they sat, hand in hand, while the hours slipped by and the shadows lengthened about them, and the light on the river grew red.

With the sunset, came the sound of distant voices. Helga started up with a finger on her lips.

"It is the exploring party, returning! It is possible that one of them might blunder in here. Do you think we can climb the bluff before they turn the bend and see us?"

The voices were becoming very distinct now. Alwin shook his head.

"I think it better to remain where we are. Sigurd knows that we are likely to be here. He will turn them aside, if need be. See; yonder is his blue cloak now, at the—"

He broke off and slowly rose to his feet, a look upon his face that made Helga whirl instinctively and glance over her shoulder. She did not turn back again, but sat as though frozen in the act; for behind the sumach bush Leif stood, watching them.

How long he had been there they had no idea, but his eyes were full upon them; and they realized that at last he knew truly for whom it was that Helga, Gilli's daughter, had fled from home. His lips were drawn into a straight line, and his brows into a black frown.

The voices came nearer and nearer,—until Sigurd's blue cloak fluttered at the very foot of the trail. When he saw the chief's scarlet mantle mingling with the scarlet of the sumach leaves, the jarl's son gave a great leap forward. It was no longer than the drawing of a breath, however, before he recovered himself.

His clear voice rose like a bugle call, "_Diable_! foster-father! I have just made a very different discovery from the one I promised you,—Tyrker has been left behind."

The Thrall of Leif the Lucky

The chief was down the bank in three long leaps, shooting a volley of fierce questions. Each member of the party instantly raised his voice to defend himself and blame his neighbor. The remainder of the camp, brought to the spot by the noise, rent the air with upbraiding and alarms. When the shield–maiden suddenly sprang from nowhere and stood in their midst, the men did not even notice her; nor did the appearance of the Norman attract more attention. As an accident, it was incredibly fortunate; as a diversion, it was a master–stroke.

Yet it did not take the chief long to quell the up–roar, when at last he had made up his mind what course to pursue. Seizing a shield from a man at his side, he hammered upon it with his sword until every other sound was drowned in the clangor.

"Silence!" he shouted. "Silence, fools! Would you save him by deafening each other? We must reach him before wild beasts do: he would be as a child in their clutches. Ten of you who are fresh–footed, get weapons and follow me. The least crazy of you who accompanied him, shall guide us back."

Only as he was turning away and ran bodily into him, did he appear to remember the Norman's existence. His eyes gave out an ominous flash.

"You also follow," he commanded.

As the little column moved over the hills in the fading light, Helga looked after them, half dazed.

"What is the meaning of that?" she murmured to the jarl's son at her side. "It is certain that Leif recognized him; yet he chooses him to accompany them. I do not understand it."

Nothing could have been sturdier than Sigurd's manner; she did not think to look at his face.

"That may easily be," he returned. "Since it angered the chief to find you two together, it would be no more than natural that he should wish to make sure of your separation."

Helga did not appear to hear him. She stood transfixed with the horror of a sudden conviction.

"It is to kill him!" she gasped. "That is why he has taken him away, that he may kill him quietly and without interference. I will go after them... By running, I can catch up—let me go, Sigurd!"

The fact that his foreboding was quite as black as hers did not prevent Sigurd from tightening his grasp, almost to roughness.

He said sternly, "Be still. You have done harm enough by such crazy actions. If by any chance he is not discovered, you would be certain to betray him. You can do nothing but harm in any case."

As he felt her yield to his grasp, he added, less harshly, "More likely than not, nothing of any importance will happen; if Tyrker is found unharmed, Leif's joy will be too great to allow him to injure anyone, whatever his offence."

She interrupted him with a low cry of anguish. "But if Tyrker is not found, Sigurd! If Tyrker is not found, Leif will vent his rage upon the nearest excuse. A Norseman in grief is like a bear with a wound: it matters not whom he bites."

Burying her face in her hands, she sank upon the ground and rocked herself back and forth. Out from the bower of long hair that streamed over her, came pitiful moans.

"He will slay him and leave him out there in the darkness... I shall not be by to raise his head and weep over him, as I did before .... Oh, thou God, if there is help in Thee—! I shall not be with him... Leif will slay him and leave him out in the darkness, alone..."

Sigurd's face grew white as he watched her, and he clenched his hands so that the nails sank deep in the flesh.

"There is nothing to do but to wait," he said, briefly. "If Tyrker is found, all will be well." He paced to and fro before her, his ear set toward the river.

Over in front of the cook–house, Kark's fires began to twinkle out like altars of good cheer. Like votaries hurrying to worship at them, the hungry men went and threw themselves on the grass in a circle; with dice and stories and jests they whiled away the time pleasantly enough.

182

The Thrall of Leif the Lucky

For the pair in the shadow, the moments dragged on lead-shod feet. Time after time, Sigurd thought he heard the sounds he longed to hear, and started toward the river,—only to come slowly back, tricked. An owl began to call in the tree above them; and ever after, Helga connected that sound with death and despair, and shuddered at it.

When at last the distant hum of voices crept upon them, they would not believe it; but sat with eyes glued to the ground, though their ears were strained. But when one of the approaching voices broke into a rollicking drinking-song, which was caught up by the group around the fire and tossed joyously back and forth, there could no longer be any doubt of the matter.

Sigurd leaped up and pulled his companion to her feet, with a cheer. "They would not sing like that if they bore heavy tidings," he assured her. "Do not spoil matters now by a lack of caution. Stay here while I run forward to meet them."

Then, for the first time since the failing of the blow, Helga recalled with a flush of shame that she was a dauntless shield-maiden; and she took hold of her composure with both hands.

Singing and shouting, the rescuers came out of the woods at last and into the circle of firelight. On the shoulders of the two leaders sat Tyrker, his little eyes dancing with excitement, his thin voice squeaking comically in his attempts to pipe a German drinking-song, as he beat time with some little dark object which he was flourishing. The chief walked behind him with a face that was not only clear but almost radiant. Still further back came Robert Sans-Peur, quite un-harmed and vigorous. In the name of wonder, what had happened to them?

"It is the strangest thing that ever occurred."—"It is a miracle of God!"—"Growing as thick as crow-berries." —" Such juice will make the finest wine in the world!"—"Biorn Herjulfsson will dash out his brains with envy."—" Was ever such luck as the Lucky One's?" were the disjointed phrases that passed between them.

Waving the dark object over his head, Tyrker struggled down from his perch. "Wunderschoen! As in the Fatherland growing! And I went not much further than you,—only a step, and there—like snakes in the trees gecoiled! So solid the bunches, that them your fingers you cannot between pry. The beautiful grapes! Foster-son, for this day's work I ask you to name this country Vine–land. Such a miracle requires that. Ach, it makes of me a child again!"

He tossed the fruit into their eager hands and began all at once to wipe his eyes industriously upon the skirt of his robe. Swiftly the bunch passed from hand to hand. Each time a juicy ball found its way down a thirsty throat a great murmur of wonder and delight arose.

"There is more where this came from? Plenty, you say?" they inquired, anxiously. And on being assured that hillside after hillside was covered with bending wreaths of purple clusters, their rapture knew no bounds.

Ale was all well enough; but wine—! Not only would they live like kings through the winter, but in the spring they would take back such a treasure as would make their home–people stare even more than at the timber and the wheat.

"You need have no fear concerning Leif's temper," Sigurd whispered in Helga's ear. "This discovery makes his mission as sure of success as though it were already accomplished. No man's nose rises at timber, but two such miracles as wheat and grapes, planted without hands and growing without care,—these can be nothing less than tokens of divine favor! The Lucky One would spare his deadliest foe tonight."

"That sounds possible," Helga admitted, studying the chief's face anxiously. As she looked, Leif's gaze suddenly met hers, and she had the discomfort of seeing a recollection of their last encounter waken in his eyes. Yet they did not darken to the blackness that had lowered from them at the cliff. They took on more of an expression of quiet sarcasm. Turning where the Norman stood, a silent witness of the scene, the chief beckoned to him.

"A while ago, Robert Sans–Peur, I had it in my mind to run a sword through you," he said, dryly. "But I have since bethought myself that you are a guest on my hands; and also that it is right to take your French breeding into account. Yet, though it may easily be a Norman habit to look upon every fair woman with eyes of love, it is equally contrary to Norse custom to permit it. Give yourself no further trouble concerning my kinswoman, Robert of Normandy. Attach yourself to my person and reserve your eloquence for my ear,—and my ear only."

184

CHAPTER XXVII. MIGHTIER THAN THE SWORD

```
Middling wise
Should every man be,
Never too wise;
Happiest live
Those men
Who know many things well.
    Ha'vama'l
```

They must have missed a great deal of enjoyment, to whom a new world meant only a new source of gold and slaves. To these men from the frozen north, the new world was an earthly paradise. A long clear day under a warm sun was alone a gift to be thankful for. To plunge unstinted hands into the hoarded wealth of ages, to be the first to hunt in a game—stocked forest and the first to cast hook in a fish—teeming river,—to have the first skimming of nature's cream—pans, as it were,—was a delight so keen that, saving war and love, they could imagine nothing to equal it. Like children upon honey, they fell upon the gift that had tumbled latest out of nature's horn of plenty, and swept through the vineyard in a devastating army. Snuffing the sweet scent of the sun—heated grapes, they ate and sang and jested as they gathered, in the most innocent carousal of their lives. Shouting and singing, they brought in their burdens at night,—litters of purple slain that bent even their stout backs. The roofs were covered with the drying fruit, which was to be doctored into raisins, and cask after cask of sour tangy wine was rolled into the provision shed beside the garnered grain.

"The King of Norway does not live better than this," they congratulated each other. "We have found the way into the provision house of the world."

Their delight knew no bounds when they found that the arrival of winter would not interfere with sport. Winter at Brattahlid meant icebergs and blizzards, weeks of unbroken twilight and days of idling within doors. Winter in this new land,—why, it was not winter at all!

"It is nothing worse than a second autumn," Helga said, wonderingly. "They have patched on a second autumn to reach till spring."

The Thrall of Leif the Lucky

The woods continued to be full of game, and the grass on the plains remained almost unwithered. There was only enough frost in the air to make breathing it a tonic, a tingling delight. Not even a crust formed over the placid bay; and the waters of the river went leaping and dancing through the sunshine in airy defiance of the ice–king's fetters.

On the last day of December, autumn employments were still in full swing. The last rays that the setting sun sent to the bay through the leafless branches, fell upon a group of fishermen returning with a load of shining fish hanging from their spears. From the grove came the ringing music of axes, the rending shriek of a doomed tree, the crackling, crashing thunder of its fall. Down at the foot of the bluff a boat was thrusting its snout into the soft bank, that an exploring party might land after a three days' journey along the winding highway of the river.

In the bow stood the chief, and behind him were Sigurd Haraldsson and Rolf; and behind them, Robert the Norman.

With a great racket of joyous hallooing for the benefit of their camp–mates, the crew leaped ashore. While some stayed to load themselves with the skins and game stowed under the seats, the rest began to climb the trail, laughing and talking noisily.

Sigurd leaped along between Rolf and the Norman, a hand on the shoulder of each, shaking them when their sentiments were unsatisfactory.

"How long am I to wait for you to have a free half–day?" he demanded of his friend from Normandy. "It was over a week before we left that I found those bear tracks, and still am I putting off the sport that you may have a share in it. Is it Leif's intention to keep you dangling at his heels forever, like a tassel on an apron? Certainly he cannot think that there is danger of your talking love to Helga while you are fighting bears."

"Though once I would have said that wooing a shield–maiden was a very similar sport," Rolf added, pleasantly.

Whereupon Sigurd shook them both, with an energy that sent all three sprawling on their faces, to the huge amusement of those who came after.

186

The Thrall of Leif the Lucky

They scrambled to their feet in front of a tall sumach bush that grew half—way up the slope. Alwin's eyes fell upon a narrow ledge—like path that showed plainly between the bare branches, and he nodded toward it with a smile.

"Missing bear—fights is certainly undesirable," he said. "But it was not long ago—and on this same bank—that I anticipated a worse fate than that."

"Nevertheless, I have never seen so much service exacted from a king's page," Sigurd growled, as he bent to brush the dirt from his knees.

But Rolf shook his head with quiet decision.

"One need never tell me that it is only to keep you from saying fine things to Helga that the chief demands your constant presence. It is because he has come to take comfort in your superior intelligence, and to value your attendance above ours. There, he is calling you now! I foretell that you will not fight bears to—morrow either." He gave the broad back a hearty slap that was at the same time a friendly shove forward.

The chief's voice had even taken on an impatient accent by the time the young squire reached his side.

"I should like much to know what is the cause of your deafness! Are you dead or moonstruck that I must shout twenty times before you answer? If your wits go sleep—walking, then may we as well give up, for I have depended upon them as upon crutches. I want you to keep it in mind for me that it is after the river's second bend to the right, but its fourth bend to the left, that the trees stand which I wish to mark. And the spring—the spring is—"

"And the spring is beyond the third turning to the right," the young man finished readily. "The chief need give himself no uneasiness. It is written on my brain as on parchment."

Leif turned from him with something like an angry sigh.

"It needs to be more than written," he said. "It needs to be carved as with knives."

On the crest of the bluff he paused suddenly to shake his fists in a passion of impotence.

The Thrall of Leif the Lucky

"A man who has no more than a trained body is of less account than a beast!" he cried. "My brain is near bursting with the details which I have sought to remember concerning these discoveries, and yet what assurance have I that I have got even half of them correct? That I have not remembered what was of least importance, and confused this place with that, and garbled it all so that the next man who comes after me shall call me a liar and laugh at my pretensions? And even though I relate every fact as truly as the Holy Book itself, what will there be left of it by the time it has passed through a hundred sottish brains in Greenland yonder? I tell you, this stained rag of a cloak I wear is nearer to what it was first, than that tale will be after swinish mouths have chewed upon it a day. It is the curse of the old gods upon the heathen. And I fling my curse back at them, for the chains they have hung upon my free hands and the beast–dumbness with which they have gagged my man's mouth."

In an abandonment of fury, he shook both fists high over his head at the scattered star faces that were peering out of the pale sky.

Not till he had turned and stamped away over the snapping twigs, did his men come out of their trance of bewilderment.

As they resumed their climbing, Eyvind the Ice–lander observed sagely, "Never saw I any one whose speech reminded me so strongly of the hot springs we have at home. All of a sudden, without warning or cause, the words shoot up into the air, boiling hot; and it would be as much as one's life is worth to try to stop them. It is incomprehensible."

Passing amused comments, they gained the crest and vanished over it, without noticing that the Norman still stood where the chief had left him, with every appearance of being equally bereft of his senses.

With parted lips, and hands nervously opening and shutting by his side, he stood staring away into the dusk before him, until the voices of those who were coming after with the spoils fell on his ear and aroused him. Then he raised to the stars a face that was fairly convulsed with excitement, and took the rest of the climb in three wild leaps.

"It is open to my sight at last!" he muttered over and over, as he hurried through the darkness toward the lighted booths. "Heaven be thanked, it is open to my sight at last!"

The Thrall of Leif the Lucky

As he reached the end of the largest hut and was turning the corner in eager haste, an arm reached quickly out of the shadow and touched his cloak. Instinctively his hand went to his knife; but it fell away the next instant in a very different gesture, as Helga's voice whispered in his ear:

"Alwin,—it is I! I have waited for you since the first noise of the landing. I have a—hush, you must not do that! I have need of my lips to speak with No, no! Listen; I wish to warn you—"

"And I must tell you what has just occurred." Alwin's excitement bore down her caution. "I have guessed the riddle of what my service is to be,—or, to tell it truthfully, luck has guessed it for me, owl that I am! Here has it—"

But Helga's hand fell softly over his mouth. "Dumb as well as blind shall you be, till I have finished! Already I have stayed out long enough to excite suspicion. Listen to my warning; Kark suspects that your complexion is shallow. Yesterday I overheard him put the question to Tyrker, whether or not it were possible that a paint could color a man's skin dark so that it would not wear off."

"Devil take the—"

"Hush, that is not all! I have never thought it worth while to tell you, in the few words we have had together; but now I know that the creature has suspected us ever since the day when Leif came upon us on the bluff. The day after that, Kark dared to say to me, 'Is a shield—maiden as fickle as other women, for all her steel shirt? In Greenland, Helga, Gilli's daughter, loved an Englishman.' I beat him soundly for it, yet I could not uproot the thought from his mind; and now—"

"And now I tell you that it is of no consequence what he thinks," Alwin interrupted her, eagerly. "I have to-night found out a means by which I am as certain to win favor as—"

But he could not finish. Crackling steps in the grove behind them made Helga spring away from him like a startled bird. He had only time to whisper after her, "To-night,—watch me across the fire!" before she had vanished among the shadows, like one of them.

The Thrall of Leif the Lucky

After a moment the young man went his way around the corner of the cabin and came in through the open doorway, where his companions sat at supper.

The hall, which was also the larger of the sleeping–houses, was not an unworthy off–shoot of the splendors of Brattahlid. Here, as there, the rough walls were lined with gleaming weapons and shields that shone like suns in the ruddy glow of the fire. And in lieu of tapestries, there was a noble medley of bears' claws, fish nets, glistening birds' wings, drying hides, branching antlers, and squirrels' tails. The bunk–like beds, built against the walls, displayed a fortune in the skin covers that were spread over them; fox skins covered the benches, and wolf skins lay under foot. The chief's seat no longer boasted carven pillars or embroidered pillows, but it missed none of these when the great bear skin had been flung over the cushions of fragrant pine–needles. And if the table–service was not so fine as the gilded vessels on Eric's board, yet the fish and flesh and fowl that piled the trenchers, and the purple juice that brimmed the horns, had never been equalled in Greenland.

"Only to get such wine, the journey would be worth while," Rolf murmured to the shield–maiden, beside whom he sat, when at last the business of eating was over and the pleasure of drinking had begun. As he spoke he tilted his head back, with closed eyes and a beatific smile, and let the contents of his horn run slowly down his throat.

Even a woman might have had the sense to leave him undisturbed at such a moment; yet Helga bent forward and jogged his arm without compunction.

"Are you going to be forever swallowing?" she whispered, sharply. "Look across the fire and tell me what Alwin is doing with his hands. He has turned aside so that I cannot see."

It was with a distinct bang that the Wrestler set down his empty cup, and in a distinct snarl that his answer came over his shoulder. "Not a few men have been slain for such rudeness as that. Why should I care what the Norman is doing? Is it a time to be riding horseback or catching fish? Since there is no babbling woman at his elbow, it is likely that he is drinking."

But Helga's hand did not loosen its hold upon his arm.

The Thrall of Leif the Lucky

"Hush!" she entreated him. "Something really is going to happen; he warned me of it. Something of great importance. You will act with no more than good will if you look and tell me what you see."

Excitement is infectious; even through his sulks Rolf caught it, and leaning forward, he peered curiously over the flames. The Norman sat in his usual place at the chief's left hand. It was evident that his thoughts were far away, for his drinking–horn stood forgotten at his elbow and he was humming absently as he worked. His fingers were busy with a long splinter and a tuft of fox–hairs, that he was pulling carefully from the rug on which he sat.

Rolf's eyes widened into positive alarm as he watched. "He has the appearance of a crazy man!" he reported. "Or it may be that he is making a charm and that is the weird song which he is mumbling. See,—he has finally drawn Leif's attention upon him!"

"He is not acting without a purpose," Helga persisted. "He told me to watch him. Look! What is he doing now?"

Still humming, and with the leisurely air of one who works to please himself alone, the Norman completed his task and held the result up critically to the light. It was nothing more nor less than a clumsy little fox–hair brush. Leaning back on the bear skin the chief continued to gaze at it curiously. But the pair across the fire suddenly turned to each other with a gasp of comprehension.

The Norman, still humming carelessly, drew his horn nearer with one hand, and with the other pushed a bowl out of his way. Then dipping his brush in the purple wine, he began to paint strange–looking runes on the fair new boards before him.

"It has come to my mind to try whether I can remember the words of that French song which we heard together in Rouen," he said lightly to Sigurd Haraldsson who sat by him. "Was it not thus that the first line ran?"

Almost with the weight of a blow, Leif's hand fell upon his shoulder.

"Runes!" he cried, in a voice that brought every man to his feet, even those who had fallen asleep over their drinking. "Runes? Is it possible that you have the accomplishment

191

of writing them?"

His hold upon the shoulder tightened, of a sudden, to such a pressure that the young man was fain to drop his brush with a gasp of agony, and catch at the crushing hand. "You have had this power all these months that you have known of my great need? How comes it that you have never put forth a hand to help me?" he thundered.

Across the fire, Helga, Gilli's daughter, held herself down upon the bench with both hands. But though his lips were twisted with pain, the rune-writer met Leif's gaze unflinchingly.

"Help you, chief?" he repeated, wonderingly. "How was I to know that Norman writing would be of assistance to you? When did you ever tell me of your need?"

Though his gaze continued to hold the Norman for awhile, Leif's grip on his shoulder slowly relaxed. Then, gradually, his eyes also loosened their hold. Finally he burst into a loud laugh and slapped him on the back.

"By the edge of my sword, your wit is as nimble as a rabbit!" he swore. "I cannot blame you for this. At least you lost little time in coming to my support as soon as I had told my need. By the Mass, Robert Sans-Peur, you could not have brought your accomplishment to a better market! I tell you frankly that it is of more value to me than any warrior's skill in the world, and I am not too stingy to pay what it is worth."

Unclasping the gold chain from his neck, he threw it over the Norman's head.

"Take this to begin with, Robert of Normandy," he said, with grave courtesy. "And I promise you that, if your help proves to be as great as I expect, there will be little that you can ask that I shall not be glad to give."

Decked in the shining gold of his triumph, the masquerading thrall stood with bent head, a look that was almost shame-stricken stealing over his face. But it is probable that the chief feared that he meditated another attempt at hand kissing, for that brusque commander began to speak quickly and curtly of purely unsentimental matters.

The Thrall of Leif the Lucky

"I have none of the kid–skin of which your Southern books are made. Yet will not a roll of fresh white vadmal offer a fair substitute? And certainly there is enough wine—"

There certainly was enough, and more; yet at this suggestion an indignant murmur could not be suppressed.

"Though I never dispute your wisdom in anything, that appears to me to be little better than desecration," Valbrand declared, frankly.

With an effort the Norman roused himself. "It will not be necessary," he said, absently. "I know how to make a liquid out of barks that will have a dark color and suffer no damage from water."

He did not notice the expression that flared up in Kark's eyes; nor did he hear Helga's gasp, nor feel Sigurd's foot. His gaze fell again to the floor in moody abstraction.

The chief answered briefly to the murmurs: "It is unadvisable to oppose my whim for writing in wine; who knows but I might exchange it for a fancy to write in blood? Bring hither the vadmal, thrall, and we will lose no more precious moments."

Was ever monkish work begun in more unchurch–like surroundings? Alwin wondered, a festal board for a desk and a wine–cup for an ink–horn! The brawling crew along the benches drank and sang and rattled dice in their nightly carousal; and, in a corner, Lodin wrestled with the well–grown bear–cub before a circle of cheering spectators. The firelight flickered over the trophy–laden walls, picking out now a severed paw and now a grinning skull, until the whole place seemed a ghastly shrine of savagery.

The warrior–scribe wrote with painful slowness; and more than once, in trying to catch some of Helga's chatter across the fire, he wrote such twisted sentences that it was impossible to unravel them when he came to retranslate. Yet he did write. Ploddingly, haltingly, clumsily, he still caught the fleeting thoughts as they sped, and fastened them down, in purple and white, to last so long as one thread should lie beside another. No longer need anyone torture his brain to remember whether the tallest maple–trees stood beyond the river's second bend to the left or its fourth to the right, or between the third turning to the right and the fifth to the left. The little fox–hair brush sprang upon the fact and pinioned it, a prisoner for the remainder of time.

The Thrall of Leif the Lucky

The chief's pleasure was almost too great to be controlled. He went at the work as a starving man goes at food, and he hung over it as a drunkard hangs over his dram. Tyrker rose with considerable bustle to take his departure for the other house; and Vaibrand stamped about noisily as he renewed the torches on the walls; but the monotonous steadiness of the dictation never faltered. One by one, the men about Leif dropped off, snoring; and he heeded it no more than he did the soughing of the wind through the grove. By and by, even the fresh torches began to snore, in angry sputters; and the fire, which had long since begun to wink drowsily, shut its last red eye and lay in total oblivion.

Leif sat up reluctantly, and stretched his arms over his head with a regretful sigh. "My mind comes out of it as stubbornly as Sigmund's sword came out of the tree trunk. We will return to it the first thing in the morning. You have done me a service which I shall never forget while my mind lives in me."

Leaning back against the bear skin to stretch his arms again and yawn, he added thoughtfully, "Your accomplishments have remedied my misfortune that last winter I was obliged to kill a youth who was of great value to me."

The scribe sat thrusting his legs out before him and working the fingers of his cramped hand, in a stupor of weariness. He awoke suddenly and, through the flickering light of the one remaining torch, shot a stealthy glance at the chief's face.

After a while he said carelessly, "Obliged, chief? How came that? Could not his value outweigh his crime?"

Smothering a yawn, Leif rose to his feet and stood looking down at his follower, while he buckled his cloak around him. "Yes," he said, slowly; "yes, his value might have outweighed his crime,—but not his deceit. It was not only because he broke my strictest orders that I slew him; it was because, while pretending to submit to me, he was in truth scheming to get the better of me. And because he and his hot-headed friend, Sigurd Haraldsson, had the ambition to penetrate the state of my feelings and handle me as you handle your writing-brush there. Is it to be expected that a man would take it well to be fooled by a pair of boys?"

The Norman sat for a long time staring at a huge furry skin that hung on the wall in front of him. It shook sometimes in the draught; and when the light flickered over it, it looked like some quivering shapeless animal, crouching to spring upon him out of the shadow. After a while, he laughed harshly.

"If he was simple enough to expect that he could play with you and then survive the discovery of his trick, he deserved to die, for nothing more than his folly," he said, bitterly.

He straightened himself suddenly and drew a long breath as though to speak further. But at that moment the chief turned and left the booth.

While the Southerner stood looking after him, a sound like a smothered laugh came from the corner where Kark slept. Alwin wheeled toward it; but before he could take a step, Rolf's arm stretched out from his bunk by the high seat and caught his friend's belt in a vise.

"It is unnecessary to soil your hands with snake's blood, just now," he said, gently. "Besides serpent's fangs, the thrall has also serpent's cunning in his ugly head. He knows that Leif will not, for any reason tongue can name, injure the man who is writing down his history. Wait until the records are finished; then it will be time to act."

He pulled his comrade clown on the bunk beside him, and held him there until the sleep of utter weariness had taken him into its safe–keeping.

CHAPTER XXVIII. "THINGS THAT ARE FATED"

```
The fir withers
That stands on a fenced field;
Neither bark nor foliage shelters it;
Thus is a man
Whom no one loves;
Why should he live long?
    Ha'vama'l
```

In a chain of lengthening golden days and softening silver nights, the spring came.

The Thrall of Leif the Lucky

The instinct which brings animals out of their dens to roam in the sunlight, awoke in the Norsemen's breasts and made them restless in the midst of plenty. The instinct which sets birds to nest–building amid the young green, turned the rovers' hearts toward their ice–bound home.

With glad applause, they hailed Leif's proclamation from under the budding maple–tree:

"Four weeks from to–day, if the season continues to be a forward one, it is likely that the pack–ice around the mouth of Eric's Fiord will be sufficiently broken to let us through. Four weeks from to–day, God willing, we will set sail for Greenland."

The camp entered upon a period of bustling activity. Carpenters fell to work on the re–furnishing of the ship, until all the quiet bay echoed with their pounding. With infinite labor, the great logs were floated down the river and hauled on board. Porters toiled to and from the shore with loads of grain–sacks and wine–kegs. The packers in the store–houses buzzed over the wealth of fruit like so many bees. Even Kark the Indolent caught the infection, and clashed his pots and kettles with joyful energy.

"A little time more, and the death–wolf shall claim his due," he sang over his work. "Only a little time more, and the death–wolf shall claim his due!"

On the morning of the last day in Vinland, Robert the Norman wrote the last word in the grotesque exploring record and laid down the brush forever.

"That ends the matter, chief," he said slowly.

They sat in the larger of the sleeping–houses, as they had sat on that December night when the work was begun. But now a flood of yellow sunlight fell through the open door, and a flowering pink bush flattened its sweet face against the window.

Leif regarded him with dull, absent eyes. "Yes, it is ended," he said, reluctantly; and was silent for so long that the young man looked up in surprise.

An odd expression of something like regret was on the chief's face. As he met his companion's glance, he laughed a short harsh laugh that had in it less of mirth than of scorn.

196

"It is ended," he repeated. "And though I know no better than yourself why it is that I am such a fool, yet I find myself full of sorrow because it is finished. I feel that I have lost out of my life something that was dear to me." He relapsed into another frowning silence; when he came out of it, it was only to motion toward the door. "No sense is in this," he said, savagely; "yet the mood has me, hand and foot. I am in no temper to talk of anything. To–night we will speak of your reward. Go now and spend the rest of the day as best pleases you."

He did not look up as his follower obeyed: he sat brooding over the great white roll as though it were the dead body of some one whom he had loved.

Out in the blithe spring sunshine, the men stood around in little groups, making hilarious plans for the day's sport. The preparations for the departure being completed, a day of untrammelled freedom lay before them; and what pastime is so dull that it is not given a zest and a relish by the thought that it is engaged in for the last time? In uproarious good spirits, they whetted their knives for a last hunt, and called friendly challenges across to each other. Inviting them to a wrestling bout, Rolf's voice rose loudest of all; but though much laughter and some gibing came in response, there were no acceptances.

When the Norman came out of the booth, the Wrestler ceased his proclamations and strolled to meet his friend with a welcoming smile. "Now I think Leif has behaved well," he said, heartily, "to remember that the last day in such a place as Vinland the Good is far too precious to be wasted on monkish tasks. Sigurd will get angry with himself that he did not wait longer for your coming."

A shade of disappointment fell over the Norman's face.

"Where has Sigurd gone?" he asked. "He swam out to an island in the bay where he has a favorite fishing–place he cannot bear to leave without another visit."

"And Helga? Where is she?"

The Wrestler looked at him in surprise. "She has gone into the woods somewhere, with Tyrker; but surely you would not be so mad as to accost her, even were she before you."

Alwin answered with an odd smile. "A man who is about to die will do many things that would be madness in a man who has life before him," he said. His eyes gazed into his friend's eyes with sombre meaning. "I finished the records this morning."

"You finished the records this morning?" Rolf repeated incredulously.

A note of impatience sharpened the other's voice. "I fail to understand what there is in that which surprises you. Certainly you must have heard Leif say, last night, that a hundred words more would end the work. And it was your own judgment that Kark would wait no longer than its completion—"

Rolf struck the tree they leaned against, with sudden vehemence. "The snake!" he cried. "That, then, is why he showed his fangs at me this morning in such a jeering smile. Yet, how could I believe that a man of your wit would allow such a thing to come to pass? With a mouthful of words you could have persuaded Leif that there was a host of things which he had forgotten. You could have prolonged the task—"

Alwin shook his head with stern though quiet decision.

"No, I have had enough of lying," he said. "Not for my life, nor for Helga's love, will I carry this deceit further. Such a smothering fog has it become around me, that I can neither see nor breathe through its choking folds... But let us leave off this talk. Since it is likely that my limbs will have a long rest after to—night, let us spend to—day roving about in search of what sport we can find. If I may not pass my last day with the man and woman that I hold dearest, still you are next in my love; you will accompany me, will you not?"

"Wherever you choose," Rolf assented.

They set forth as silently as on that spring morning, two years before, when they had set out from the Norwegian camp to witness Thorgrim Svensson's horse—fight. Now, as then, the air was golden with spring sunshine, and the whole world seemed a—throb with the pure joy of living. There was gladness in the chirp of the birds, and content in the drone of the insects; and all the squirrels in the place seemed to be gadding on joyful errands, for one could not turn a corner that a group of them did not scatter from before his feet. So common a thing as a dewdrop caught in a cobweb became more beautiful than jewel—spangled lace. The rustling of the quail in the brush, even the glimpse of a coiled snake basking on a sunny spot of earth, was fraught with interest because it spoke of life, glad and fearless and free.

They visited the nook on the bluff, screened once more in fragrant, rustling greenness; then descended to the river and walked along its bank, mile after mile. Here and there, they turned aside and threaded their way through the thicket to take a last look at the scene of some fondly recollected hunt, or to inspect some of the traps which they remembered to be there. But when in one snare they found a wretched little rabbit, still alive but frantic with terror, Alwin laid a detaining hand on Rolf's knife.

"Let him go," he said, shortly. "You have no need of him, and his life is all he has. Let him keep it,—for my sake."

He did not stay to watch the white dot of a tall go bobbing away over the ferns. He hurried on rather shamefaced; and when Rolf overtook him, they walked another mile without speaking.

Along in the middle of the forenoon they reached a point on the river where the banks no longer rose in bluffs but lay in grassy slopes, fringed with drooping trees. The sun was hot overhead, and their clothes were heavy upon their backs. Rolf suggested that they stop long enough for a swim.

"That will do as well as anything," Alwin assented. But when the delicious coolness of the water had closed about him, and he felt its velvet softness on his dusty skin, he decided that it was the best thing they could have done. The lounge upon the grassy bank, while they dried themselves in the sun, was dreamily pleasant. Even after he had gathered sufficient energy to get into his clothes again, Alwin lingered lazily, waiting for his companion to make the first move toward departure.

"This is a restful spot," he said, gazing up at the sky through the network of interlacing branches. "It gives one the feeling that it is so far away that no human foot has ever trod it before, and that none will ever come again when we have left."

From the ant—hill which he was idly spearing with grass—blades, Rolf looked up to smile. "Then your feelings are not to be trusted, comrade," he said; "for there are few spots on

199

the river which our men have more frequented. Even that lazy hound of a thrall comes here almost daily to look at the quail–traps in yonder thicket, that being the one food which he likes well enough to make an exertion for. Would that he would visit them to–day!"

Alwin did not seem to hear him. His eyes were still intent on the swaying tree–tops. "It is a fair land to be alive in," he said, dreamily; "yet, I cannot help wondering how it will be to be dead here. Does it not seem to you that if my spirit comes out of its grave at night and finds none but wolves and bears to call to, it will experience a loneliness far worse than the pangs of death? Think of it! In this whole land, not one human spirit! To wander through the grove and the camp, and find only emptiness and silence forever!"

His body stiffened suddenly, and he flung his arms high above his head and clenched his hands in agony.

"God!" he cried. "What have I done to make me deserving of such a doom? Why could I not have died when Leif cut me down? Why could I not have been buried where human feet would pass over me, and human voices fall on my ear at night?" He flung himself over on his face and lay there motionless.

Rolf laid a hand on his comrade's shoulder, and for once his voice was honestly kind. "It is hard to know what to say to you, Alwin, my friend. You who have borne trials so manfully have a right to a better fate. There is only one thing which I can offer you: choose what man you will—so long as he be no one with whom I have sworn friendship—and I promise you that before we sail to–morrow, I will pick a quarrel with him and slay him; so that, if worst comes, your spirit shall have at least one ghost for company. I—"

He did not finish his sentence. Suddenly his touch upon Alwin's arm became an iron grip, that dragged the Saxon to his feet.

"Look!" the Wrestler gasped, as he pulled him behind the great oak in whose shelter they had been lying. "Look! Are those ghosts, or devils?"

Half–dazed, Alwin could do no more than stare along the pointing finger. On the opposite bank, some hundred yards below their point of observation, stood two long–haired, skin–clad men. Another pair had already plunged into the river and were nearly half–way across. And as the white men gazed, four more beings crashed out of the underbrush and joined their companions.

"Praise the Saint who hung leaves upon the trees as thick as curtains!" Rolf breathed in his comrade's ear. "Up with you, for your life! And make no rustling about it either."

With the agility of cats they went up the great bole, and the kind leaves closed behind them.

"Is it your opinion that they are ghosts, or devils?" Alwin asked, when each had stretched himself along a branching limb and begun a curious peering through chinks in the enveloping foliage. "It has always been in my mind that ghosts were white and devils black, while these creatures appear to be of the color of bronze."

"We shall see more of them before the game is over," Rolf returned. "The first ones are even now coming to land."

As he spoke, the two shaggy swimmers clambered out of the water, like dripping spaniels, on the very spot that the white men's bodies had pressed less than an hour before.

"I am glad that we are not now lying there without our clothes," Alwin murmured.

And Rolf ejaculated under his breath, "Now it is certain that I would rather be the only human being in the land than be in company with such as these, granting them to be human. For by Thor's hammer, they have more the appearance of dwarfs than of men!"

They were not imposing, certainly, from all that could be seen of them through the leaves. Two of their lean arms would not have made one of the Wrestler's magnificent white limbs, and the tallest among them could not have reached above Alwin's shoulders. Skins were their only coverings; and the coarseness of their bristling black locks could have been equalled only in the mane of a wild horse. Though two of the eight were furnished with bows and arrows, the rest carried only rudely–shaped stone hatchets, stuck in their belts. When they began talking together, it was in a succession of grunts and growls and guttural sounds that bore more resemblance to animal noises than to human speech.

Rolf sniffed with contempt. "Pah! Vermin! I think we could put the whole swarm to flight only by drawing our knives."

But at that moment one of the number below raised his face so that Alwin caught a glimpse of the fierce beast–mouth and the small tricky eyes in the great sockets. The Saxon lifted his eyebrows dubiously.

"I am far from certain how that attempt would end," he answered. "Though it is likely that it will have to be tried, if their intention is to settle here for the day, as it appears to be."

The men of the stone hatchets had indeed settled themselves with every look of remaining. Though one of the bowmen continued to pace the bank like a sentinel, his fellows sprawled themselves upon the turf in comfortable attitudes, carrying on their uncouth conversation with deep earnestness.

"We shall certainly have to stay here all day if we do not do something," Rolf bent from his branch to whisper to his companion. Alwin did not answer, for at that moment the harsh voices below ceased abruptly, and there ensued a hush of listening silence.

Up in the tree, Saxon gray eyes and Norse blue ones asked each other an anxious question; then answered it with decided head–shakes. It was impossible that their whispers could have carried so far, or have penetrated the growl of those voices. It must have been some noise from beyond. They strained their ears, anxiously intent.

There was no trouble in hearing it this time; it rose shrill and piercing on the drowsy noon air, a man's whistle, rapidly approaching from the direction of the Norse camp.

While Alwin listened with dilated eyes, Rolf's lips shaped just one word: "Kark!"

Almost without breathing they lay peering out between the leaves. At the first sound, the men below had leaped to their feet and grasped their weapons. Now, after a muttered word together, they drew apart noiselessly as shadows and vanished among the bushes, without so much as the snapping of a twig. Smiling innocently in the sunlight, the little nook lay as peaceful and empty as before.

Nearer and nearer came the whistler; until the crunching of his feet could be heard upon the dead leaves. Rolf pushed the hair out of his eyes, and settled himself to watch with a sigh of almost child–like pleasure.

"Here is sport! Here is a chess game where the pieces are not of ivory. I would not have missed this for a gold chain!" he told his companion. "Imagine Kark's face when they spring out upon him! So intent is his mind upon your death, that he could walk into a pit with open eyes. You can never be sufficiently thankful, Alwin of England, that the Fate which destroys your enemy, gives you also the privilege of sitting by and watching the fun."

Uncertainty was on Alwin's face, as he gazed down through the branches and saw the thrall's white tunic suddenly appear among the green bushes.

He said slowly, "I do not dispute that it looks like the hand of fate—and it is true that he is my enemy—that it is his life or mine—"

A wild yell of alarm cut him short. One by one the lean brown men were gliding out of the bushes and forming in a silent circle around the thrall. They offered him no harm; they did not even touch him; yet the apparition of their shrivelled bodies in their animal–hides, with their beast–faces looking out from under their bristling black locks, was enough to try stouter nerves than Kark's. Shriek after shriek of maddest terror rent the air.

Rolf smiled gently as he heard it. "About this time our friend below is beginning to distinguish between death–wolves and death–foxes," he observed.

Glancing at his comrade for a response to his amusement, his expression changed. "What is it your intention to do?" he demanded sharply.

Alwin had drawn himself into a sitting posture; and with one hand was tugging at the handle of his knife. He flushed shamefacedly at the question, nor did he look up as he answered it.

The Thrall of Leif the Lucky

"I am going down to help the beast," he said. "I cannot remedy it if I am a fool. I do not deny that Kark is a cur; yet he is white, as we are; and alone. I cannot watch his murder."

He brought his knife out with a jerk; and putting it between his teeth, prepared to turn and descend.

Before he could make the move, Rolf had swung down from the limb above and landed beside him. Under his weight the boughs creaked so loudly that, but for the cover of Kark's cries, the pair must surely have been discovered.

The Wrestler spoke without drawling or gentleness: "Either you are a child or a silly fool. Do you understand that it is your enemy that they are ridding you of? What is it to you if he is chopped to pieces? You shall not stir one finger to aid him."

Forgetful of the dagger between his teeth, Alwin opened his mouth angrily. The weapon slipped from his lips and fell, a shining streak along the tree-trunk, and buried itself noiselessly in the soft sod between the roots. The next instant, a scarf from Rolf's neck was wound around the Saxon's jaws; one of the Wrestler's iron arms reached about him and gathered him up against the broad chest; one of the Wrestler's great hands closed around his wrists like fetters of iron; and a muscular leg bent itself backward over his legs like a hoop of steel. As well fight against steel or iron!

Again Rolf's voice became fairly caressing in its gentleness. "Willingly will I endure your struggles if it pleases you to employ your strength that way, comrade; yet I tell you that it would be wiser for you to spare yourself. I shall not let you go, whatever you do; whereas if you lie quietly, I will permit you to move where you can see what is going on. It looks as though it would become interesting."

It did indeed. At that moment, wearying perhaps of the howls, the brown men began to make experiments with a view toward changing the tune. Closing in upon the thrall, they commenced to feel of his clothing and his shaven head, and to pinch him tentatively between their lean fingers.

A redoubling of his outcries caused a spasm of frantic writhing in Alwin's fettered body, but Rolf's manner was as serene as before.

204

The Thrall of Leif the Lucky

"See now what you are missing by your head-strongness," he reproved his captive. "It is seldom that men have the opportunity to sit, as we sit, and learn from the experience of another what would have been their fate had their fortune been equally bad. Such great luck is it that I get almost afraid for your ingratitude. It will be a great mercy if some god does not punish you for your thanklessness... By Thor! In his terror the fool has attacked them... Ah!"

From below came a sudden snarl, a sudden savage yell, the noise of struggling bodies, and then a shriek of another kind from Kark, no longer a cry of mere apprehension, but a sharp piercing scream of bodily agony.

"Let me go!" Alwin panted through his muffled jaws. "It is a nithing deed for us—to permit the death of one of our number—so. Let me go, Rolf—he is a human being. Let me go!"

A man of wood could not have been more relentless than Rolf; a man of stone could hardly have been less moved.

He argued the matter amiably: "It is true that by some mistake or other Kark wears a man's shape," he admitted; "yet it is easily seen that in every other respect he is a dog. Indeed I think there are few dogs that have less of courage and loyalty. Take the matter sensibly, comrade. If you cannot rejoice in the death of your enemy, at least consider what interest it is thus to study the habits of dwarfs. The cur who was useless during his life, will be honored by serving a good purpose in his death. Leif will think it of great importance to learn how these creatures are disposed toward white men. They have the most unusual methods of amusing themselves. Now they are doing things to his ears—" Renewed shrieks for help and mercy drowned the remainder of his words, and called forth fresh exertions from Alwin.

But when at last the Fearless One ceased, and lay spent and panting against the brawny chest, he became aware that the cries were growing fainter.

"Though they have in no way hurried the matter, I believe that he is almost dead now," Rolf comforted his captive.

Even as he spoke, the last faint cry ended in a gurgling choke,—and there was silence.

Instantly the scarf was slipped from Alwin's mouth, and the living fetters unclasped themselves from his limbs.

"Thanks to me—" Rolf was beginning.

The brief interval of silence was shattered by a cry from the sentinel on the river bank, followed either by an echo or an answering whoop from the opposite shore. Rolf stretched himself along the branch, just in time to see the men below scatter in wildest confusion and plunge headlong into the thicket.

"In the Troll's name!" he ejaculated. "When dwarfs run like that, giants must be coming!"

Alwin had clambered to his feet, and stood with his head thrust up through the leafy roof.

"It is more out of the same nest!" he gasped. "They are coming from the other bank, swarms of them ....There! Some of them have landed..."

Rolf laughed his peculiar soft laugh of quiet enjoyment. "By Thor, was there ever such a game!" he exclaimed. "I can see them now; they are after the first lot like wolves after sheep—No, Kark was the sheep! These are the hunters after the wolves. Hear them howl!"

"The last ones have climbed out of the water," Alwin bent to report. "Do they also follow?"

"As dogs follow deer. Saw I never such sport! When we can no longer hear them, it will be time for us to run a race of our own."

Alwin made no answer, and they waited in silence. Gradually distance drew soft folds over the sharp cries and muffled them, as women throw their cloaks over the sharp swords of brawlers in the hall. Once again the drone and the chirping became audible about them, and the smile of the sunshine became visible in the air. It occurred to Alwin that the peacefulness of nature was like the gentleness of the Wrestler; and there floated through his head the saying of a wrinkled old nurse of his childhood, "The English can die without flinching; the French can die with laughs on their lips; but only the Northmen can smile as they kill." When the last smothered shout was unmistakably dead, Rolf swung himself down from the bough; hung there for an instant, stretching himself comfortably and shaking the cramps out of his limbs, then let himself down to the ground; and Alwin followed.

The soft sod lay trampled and gashed by the grinding heels; and the lengthening shadows pointed dark fingers at the middle of the nook, where a shapeless thing of white and red was lying.

Rolf bent over it curiously.

"It must be that these people love killing for its own sake, to go to so much trouble over it," he commented. "Evidently it is not the excitement of fighting which they enjoy, but the pleasure of torturing. I will not be sure but what they are trolls after all."

"It was a devils' deed," Alwin said hoarsely. He looked down at the ghastly heap with a shudder of loathing. "And we are not without guilt who have permitted it. It is of no consequence what sort of a man he was; he was a human being and of our kind,—and they were fiends. You need not tell me that we could not help it," he added in fierce forestalling. "Had he been Sigurd, we would have helped it or we would both have lain like that."

Rolf shrugged his shoulders resignedly as they turned away. "Have it as you choose," he assented. "At least you cannot deny that you were helpless; let that console you. May the gallows take my body if you are not the most thankless man ever I met! Here are you rid of your enemy, and at the moment when he was most a hindrance to you, and not only do you reap the reward of the deed, but you bear no dangerous responsibility—"

He was checked by a glimpse of the face Alwin turned toward him. Pride and loathing, passion and sternness, were all mingled in its expression.

The Saxon said slowly, "Heaven's mercy on the soul that reaps the reward of this deed! Easier would it be to suffer these tortures a hundredfold increased. Profit by such a deed, Rolf Erlingsson! Do you think that I would live a life that sprang from such a death? To cleanse my hand from the stain of such a murder, though the blood had but spattered on it, I would hew it off at the wrist."

CHAPTER XXIX. THE BATTLE TO THE STRONG

```
He is happy
Who gets for himself
Praise and good-will.
    Ha'vama'l
```

It was a picture of sylvan revelry that the sunset light reddened, as it bade farewell to the Norse camp on the river bluff. On the green before the huts, two of the fair-haired were striving against other in a rousing tug-of-war. Now the hide was stretched motionless between them; now it was drawn a foot to the right, amid a volley of jeers; and now it was jerked back a foot to the left, with an answering chorus of cheers. The chief sat under the spreading maple-tree, watching the sport critically, with an occasional gesture of applause. Over the head of the bear-cub she was fondling, Helga watched it also, with unseeing eyes. Those who had come in from hunting and fishing sprawled at their ease on the turf, and shouted jovial comments over their wine-cups.

They welcomed Rolf and the Norman with a shout, when the pair appeared on the edge of the grove.

"Hail, comrades!"—"It was in our minds to give you up for lost!" "Your coming we will take as an omen that Kark will also return some time."—"Yes, return and cook us some food."—"We are becoming hollow as bubbles."

Rolf accepted their greetings with an easy flourish.

"You will become also as thin as bubbles if you wait for Kark to cook your food," he answered, lightly. "I bring the chief the bad tidings that he has lost his thrall." Pushing his companion gently aside, he walked over to where the Lucky One sat. "It will sound like an old woman's tale to you, chief," he warned him; "yet this is nothing but the truth."

While the skin-pullers abandoned their contest and dropped cross-legged upon the hide to listen, and the outlying circle picked up its drinking horns and crept closer, he related the whole experience, simply and quite truthfully, from beginning to end.

From all sides, exclamations of amazement and horror broke out when he had finished. Only the chief sat regarding him in silence, a skeptical pucker lifting the corner of his mouth.

Leif said finally, "Truth came from your mouth when you foretold that this would appear to me as strange as the tales old women tell. Until within the last month we have passed through that district almost daily; and never yet have we found aught betokening the presence of human beings. That they should thus appear to you—"

"They came like the monsters in a dream, and vanished like them," Rolf declared.

"Saving in the fact that dream monsters do not leave mangled bodies behind them," Leif reminded him; and his eyes narrowed with an unpleasant shrewdness. "Rolf Erlingsson," he advised, "confess that they are the dreams you liken them to. That Kark was no favorite with you or your friend"—he nodded toward the Norman—"was seen by everybody. Confess that it was by the sword of one of you that the thrall met his death."

For once the Wrestler's face lost its gentleness. His huge frame stiffened haughtily, as he drew himself up.

"Leif Ericsson," he returned, fiercely, "when—for love of good or fear of ill—have you ever known me to lie?"

The chief looked at him incredulously.

"You will swear to the truth of the tale?"

"I will swear to its truth by my knife, by my soul, by the crucifix you wear on your breast."

After a moment, Leif arose and extended his hand. "In that case, I would believe a statement that was twice as unlikely," he said, with honorable frankness. And a sound of applause went around as their hands clasped.

From the spot where the Norman had halted when his companion pushed forward, there came the rustle of a slight disturbance. Sigurd had caught his friend by his cloak and was pleading with him in a passionate undertone, growing more and more desperate at each resolute shake of the black head. The instant Leif resumed his seat, the Fearless One wrenched himself free and strode forward. Rolf strove to bar his way, but Robert Sans-Peur evaded him also, and took up his stand before the bench under the maple-tree.

"The Fates appear to be balancing their scales to-night, chief," he said, grimly. "For the dead man whom you believed to be alive, you see here a living man whom you thought to be dead. For the thrall that you have lost, I present to you another."

Winding his hand in his long black locks, he tore them from his head and revealed the crisp waves of his own fair hair.

From either hand there arose a buzz of amazement and incredulity mingled with grunts of approval and blunt compliments and half-muttered pleas for leniency. Only two persons neither exclaimed nor moved. Helga stood in the rigid tearless silence she had promised, her eyes pouring into her lover's eyes all the courage and loyalty and love of her brave soul. And the chief sat gazing at the rebel brought back to life, without so much as a wink of surprise, without any expression whatever upon his inscrutable face.

After a moment Alwin went on steadily, "I hid myself under this disguise because I believed that luck might grant me the chance to render you some service which should outweigh my offence. Because I was a short-sighted fool, I did not see that the better the Norman succeeded, the worse became the Saxon's deceit. My mind changed when your own lips told me what would be the fate of the man who should deceive you."

The chief's face was as impassive as stone, but he nodded slightly.

"A man of my age does not take it well to be fooled by boys," he said. "It is a poor compliment to his intelligence, when they have the opinion that they can mould him between their fingers. Though he had rendered me the greatest service in the world, the man who should deceive me should die."

Silence fell like a shroud upon the scattered groups. With a queer little smile upon her drawn lips, Helga softly unsheathed her dagger and ran her fingers along its edge. Alwin, earl's son, drew a long breath, and the muscles of his white face twitched a little; then he pulled himself together resolutely. With one hand he plucked the knife from his belt and cast it into the chief's lap; with the other, he tore his tunic open from neck to belt.

"I have asked no mercy," he said, proudly.

Leif made no motion to pick up the weapon. Instead, a glint of something like dry humor touched his keen eyes.

"No," he said, quietly. "You have asked nothing of what you should have asked. You have even failed to ask whether or not you have deceived me."

With her dagger half drawn, Helga paused to stare at him.

"You—knew—?" she gasped.

Leif smiled a dry fine smile. "I have known since the day on which Tyrker was lost," he said. "And I had suspected the truth since the night of the day upon which we sailed from Greenland."

He made a gesture toward the shield—maiden that was half mocking and half stern. "You showed little honor to my judgment, kinswoman, when you took it for granted I should not know that love alone could cause a woman to behave as you have done. Or did you think I had not heard to whom your heart had been given? That my ears only had been dead to the love tale which every servant—maid in Brattahlid rolled like honey on her tongue? Or did you imagine that I knew you so little as to think you capable of loving one man in the winter and another in the spring? Even had the Norman borne no resemblance to the Englishman, still would I—"

"But..." Helga stammered, "but—I thought that you thought—Rolf said that Sigurd—"

For perhaps the first time in his life, Rolf's cheeks burned with mortification as a derisive snap of the chief's fingers fell upon his ear.

"Sigurd! Your playmate! With whom you have quarrelled and made up since there were teeth in your head! By Peter, if it were not that the joke appears to lie wholly on my side, I could find it in my heart to punish the four of you without mercy, for no other crime than your opinion of my intelligence!"

211

Alwin took a hesitating step forward. He had been standing where his first defiance had left him, a light of comprehension dawning in his face; and also a spark of resentment kindling in his eyes.

Now he said slowly, "It is not your anger which appears strange to us, chief. It is the slowness of your justice. That knowing all this time of our deceit, you have yet remained quiet. That you have allowed us to live in dreams, and led us on to behave ourselves like fools! We have been no better than mice under the cat's paw." He glanced at Helga's thin cheeks and the pain–lines around her mouth, and the full force of his indignation rang out in his voice. "To us it meant life or death, heaven or hell,—was it worthy of a man like you to find amusement in our suffering?"

Though it was as faint as the rustling of leaves, unmistakable applause swept around. Rolf dared to clap his hands softly.

The chief replied by a direct question, as he leaned back against the maple and eyed his young rebel piercingly. "Befooling and bejuggling were the drinks you prepared for me; was it not just that you should learn from experience how sour a taste they leave in the mouth?"

Though moment after moment dragged by, Alwin did not answer that. His eyes fell to the ground, and he stood with bent head and clenched hands.

The chief went on. "You who could so easily fathom the workings of my mind, should have no need to ask my motives. It may be that I found entertainment in playing you like a fish on a line. Or it may be that I was not altogether sure of my ground, and waited to be certain before I stepped. Or perhaps I was curious to see what you would do next, and felt able to gratify my curiosity since I knew that, through all your antics, I held you securely in the hollow of my hand. Or perhaps—" Leif hesitated for an instant, and there crept into his voice a note so unusual that all stared at him,—"or perhaps, in becoming sure of my ground, I became uncertain of the honor of the man whom I wished to place highest in my friendship, and so deemed it wisest to remain under cover until he should reveal all the hidden parts of his nature. It may have been for any or all of these reasons. You, who have come nearer to me than any man alive, should have no difficulty in selecting the true one."

The Thrall of Leif the Lucky

Was it possible that reproach rang in those last words? It sounded so strangely like it, that Tyrker involuntarily curved his hand around his ear to amend some flaw in his hearing.

Alwin's face underwent a great change. Suddenly he flung his arms apart in a gesture of utter surrender.

"I will strive against you no longer!" he cried, passionately. "You are as much superior to me as the King to his link–boy. Do as you like with me. I submit to you in everything." He fell upon his knee and hid his face in his hands.

Then the tone of Leif's voice became so frankly friendly that Helga's beautiful head was raised as a drooping flower's by the soft spring rain.

"Already you have heard your sentence. The fair words I spoke to Robert the Norman I spoke also to Alwin of England. When I promised wealth and friendship and honor to Robert Sans–Peur, I promised them also to you. Take the freedom and dignity which befit a man of your accomplishments and—with one exception —ask of me anything else you choose."

With one exception! Helga sprang forward and caught Leif's hand imploringly in hers. And Alwin, still upon his knee, reached out and grasped the chief's mantle.

"Lord," he cried, "you have been better to me, a hundredfold better, than I deserve! Yet, would you be kinder still... Lord, grant me this one boon, and take back all else that you have promised."

The chief's brawny hand touched Helga's face caressingly.

"Do you still believe that I would rub salt on your wounds, if it were in my power to relieve you?" he reproached them. "But one man in the world has the right to say where Helga shall be given in marriage; he is her father, Gilli of Trondhjem. Already I have done him a wrong in permitting, by my carelessness, that one of thrall–estate should steal his daughter's love. In honor, I can do no less than guard the maiden safely until the time when he can dispose of her as pleases him. I do not say that I will not use with him what influence I possess; yet I advise you against expecting anything favorable from the result. I think you both know his mercy."

CHAPTER XXX. FROM OVER THE SEA

```
At night is joyful
He who is sure of travelling entertainment;
A ship's yards are short;
Variable is an autumn night;
Many are the weather's changes
In five days,
But more in a month.
     Ha'vama'l
```

It developed, however, that the lovers' chances for happiness did not hang upon so frail a thread as the mercy of Gilli of Trondhjem. While the exploring vessel was still at sea, with the icy headlands of Greenland only just beginning to stand out clearly before her bow, unexpected tidings reached those on board.

Watching the chief, who stood by the steering oar, erect as the mast, his eyes piercing the distance ahead, Sigurd put an idle question.

"Can you tell anything yet concerning the drift–ice, foster–father? And why do you steer the ship so close to the wind?"

Without turning his head, Leif answered shortly, "I am attending to my steering, foster–son."

But as the jarl's son was turning away, with a shrug of his shoulders for the rebuff, the chief added in the quick, curt tone that with him betrayed unwonted interest, "And I am looking at something else. Where are your eyes that you cannot see anything remarkable? Is that a rock or a ship which I see straight ahead?"

Sigurd's aimless curiosity promptly found an object; yet after all the craning of his neck and squinting under his hand, he was obliged to confess that he saw nothing more remarkable than a rock.

Leif gave a short harsh laugh.

The Thrall of Leif the Lucky

"See what it is to have young eyes," he said. "Not only can I see that it is a rock, but I can make out that there are men moving around upon it."

"Men!" cried Sigurd.

Excitement spread like fire from stern to bow, until even Helga of the Broken Heart arose from her cushions on the fore–deck and stood listlessly watching the approach.

Eyvind the Icelander muttered that any creatures in human shape that dwelt on those rocks, must be either another race of dwarfs, or such fiends as inhabit the ice wastes with which Greenland is cursed; but an old Greenland sailor silenced him contemptuously.

"Landlubber! Has it never been given you to hear of shipwrecks? When Eric the Red came to Greenland with thirty–five ships following his lead, no less than four of them went to pieces on that rock. It is the influence of Leif's luck which has caused a shipwreck so that the chief can get still more honor in rescuing the distressed ones."

The Icelander grunted. "Then is Leif's luck very much like the sword that becomes one man's bane in becoming another man's pride," he retorted.

While he threw all his strength against the great oar, the chief signalled to Valbrand with his head.

"Drop anchor and get the boat ready to lower," he commanded. "I want to keep close to the wind so that we may get to them. We must give them help if they need it. If they are not peaceful, they are in our power, but we are not in theirs."

As the boat bounded away on its errand of mercy, every man and boy remaining crowded forward to watch its course. In some way it happened that Alwin of England was pushed even so far forward as the very bow of the boat, and the side of the shield–maiden.

The sun rose in her glooming face when she turned and saw him beside her.

"I have hoped all day that you would come," she whispered; "so I could tell you an expedient I have bethought myself of. Dear one, from the way you have sat all the day with your chin on your hand and your eyes on the sea, I have known that you needed comfort even more than I; and my heart has ached over you till once the tears came into my eyes."

Her lover gazed at her hungrily. "Gladly would I give every gift that Leif has lavished on me, if I might take you in my arms and kiss away the smart of those drops."

A fierce gleam narrowed Helga's starry eyes. "Before we part," she said between her teeth, "you shall kiss my eyes once for every tear they have shed; and you shall kiss my mouth three times for farewell,—though every man in Greenland should wish to prevent it."

Suddenly she hid her face against his shoulder with a little cry of despair.

"But you must never come near me after I am married!" she breathed. "The moment after my eyes had fallen upon your face, I should turn upon my husband and kill him."

"If it had not happened that I had already slain him," Alwin murmured. Then he said, more steadily, "This is useless talk, sweetheart. Tell me the thought which comforted you. At least it will be a joy to me to cherish in my heart what you have treasured in your brain."

Helga looked out over the tumbling water with eyes grown wide and thoughtful.

"I will not be so hopeful as to call it a comfort yet," she said, "too vague is its shape for that. It is a faint plan which I have built on my knowledge of Gilli's nature. As well as I, you know that he cares for nothing but what is gainful for him. Now if I could manage to make myself so ugly that no chief would care to make offers for me... is it not likely that my father would cease to value me and be even glad to get rid of me, to you? I would disfigure myself in no such way that the ugliness would be lasting," she reassured him, hastily. "But if I should weep my eyes red and my cheeks pale, and cut off my hair... It would all come right in time; you would not mind the waiting?"

Alwin looked at her with a touch of wonder.

"And you would go ugly for me?" he asked. "Hide your beauty and become a jest where you have always been a queen, for no other reason than to sink so low that I might reach up and pluck you? Would you think it worth while to do that for me?"

But his meaning was lost on Helga's simplicity. She gathered only that he thought the scheme possible, and hope bloomed like roses in her cheeks.

"Oh, comrade, do you indeed think favorably of the plan?" she whispered, eagerly. "I had not the heart to hope much from it; everything has failed us so. If you think it in the least likely to succeed, I will cut off my hair this instant."

In spite of his misery, Alwin laughed a little.

"Do you then imagine that the gold of your hair and the red of your cheeks is all that makes you fair?" he asked. "No, dear one, I think it would be easier to make Gilli generous than you ugly. No man who had eyes to look into your eyes, and ears to hear your voice, could be otherwise than eager to lay down his life to possess you. Trust to no such rootless trees, comrade. And do not raise your face toward me like that either; for, in honor, I may not kiss you, and and you are not ugly yet, sweetheart."

Shouts from those around them recalled the lovers to themselves. The returning boat was almost upon them; and from among her burly crew the wan faces of several strangers looked up, while a swooning woman was seen to lie in the bow. Her face, though pinched and pallid, was also fair and lovable, and Helga momentarily forgot disappointment in pity.

"Bring her here and lay her upon my cushions," she said to the men who carried the woman on board. Wrapping the limp form in her own cloak, the shield—maiden pulled off such of the sodden garments as she could, poured wine down the stranger's throat, and strove energetically to chafe some returning warmth into the benumbed limbs.

While the boat hastened back to bring off the rest of the unfortunates, those of the first load whom wine and hope had sufficiently revived, explained the disaster.

The wrecked ship belonged to Thorir of Trondhjem; and that merchant and his wife Gudrid and fourteen sailors made up her company. On the voyage from Nidaros to Greenland with a cargo of timber, their vessel had gone to pieces on a submerged reef, and they had been just able to reach that most inhospitable of rocks and cling there like

217

flies, frozen, wind–battered, and drenched. The waves, in a moment of repentance, had thrown a little of their timber back to them, and this had been their only shelter; and their only food some coarse lichens and a few sea–birds' eggs.

It was little wonder that when Leif had brought the last load on board, and drowned their past woes in present comforts, the starved creatures were almost ready to embrace his knees with thankfulness.

"It seems to me that we should be called 'the Lucky,' and you 'the Good,'" Thorir said, as the two chiefs stood on the forecastle, watching the anchor and the sail both rising with joyful alacrity. "Without your aid, we could not have lived a day longer."

And Gudrid, opening her eyes to see Helga's fair face bending over her to put a wine cup to her lips, murmured faintly, "A Valkyria could not look more beautiful to me than you do. Tell me what you are called, that I may know what name to love you by."

"I am called Helga, Gilli's daughter," the shield–maiden answered, with just an edge of bitterness on the last words.

Gudrid's gentle eyes opened wide with wonder and alarm.

"Not Helga the Fair of Trondhjem," she gasped, "who fled from Gilli to his kinsfolk in Greenland? Alas, my unfortunate child!"

In the eagerness in which she clasped her hands, the wine–cup fell clanging from Helga's hold. "Is he dead?" she cried, imploringly. "Only tell me that, and I will serve you all the rest of my life! Is Gilli dead?"

But Gudrid had sunk back in another faint. She lay with her eyes closed, moaning and murmuring to herself.

Leif, biting sharply at his thick mustache, as he was wont to do when excited, turned sharply on Thorir.

"What is the reason of this?" he demanded. "What are these tidings concerning my kinswoman, which your wife hesitates to speak? Is Gilli of Trondhjem dead?"

218

The Thrall of Leif the Lucky

Thorir answered with great haste and politeness, "No, no; naught so bad as that. Naught but what I expect can be easily remedied. But it appears that when Gilli attempted to follow his daughter to Greenland, last fall, he suffered a shipwreck and the loss of much valuable property, barely escaping with his life. From this he drew the rash conclusion that his daughter had become a misfortune to him, as some foreknowing woman had once said she would. And he declared that since the maiden preferred her poorer kinsfolk in Greenland, she might stay with them; and—"

The words burst rapturously from Helga's lips: "And he disowned me?"

Thorir stared at her in astonishment. "Yes," he said, pityingly.

It was just as well that he had not attempted a longer answer, for he never would have finished it. Madness seemed suddenly to fall upon the ship. In the face of her disinheritance, the shield–maiden was radiant. Down in the waist of the ship, two youths who had caught the words threw up their hats with cheers. Leif Ericsson himself laughed loudly, and snapped his fingers in derision.

"A mighty revenge!" he said. "My kinswoman could have received no greater kindness at the churl's hands. Could she have accomplished it by a dagger–thrust, I doubt not that she would have let his base blood run from her veins long ere this."

He turned to where Helga stood watching him, her heart in her eyes, and pulled her toward him and kissed her.

"You chose between honor and riches, kinswoman," he said, "but while there is a ring in my pouch you shall never lack property; you have behaved like a true Norse maiden, and I am free now to say that I honor you for it. Go the way your heart desires, without further hindrance."

Helga stayed to press his hand to her cheek; then, before them all, without a thought of shame, she went the way that ended in her lover's arms.

They stood side by side in the gilded prow, and he kissed her eyes twice for every tear they had shed; and he kissed her mouth thrice three times, and not a man in the whole world rose up to prevent him. Side by side, they stood in the flying bow, a divinely

219

modelled figure–head, gilded by the light of love.

CONCLUSION

As the sun's last beams were fading from the mountain tops, the exploring vessel dropped anchor before Eric's ship–sheds and the eager groups that had gathered on the shore at the first signal. Not only idlers made up the throng, but the Red One himself was there, and Thorwald and every soul from Brattahlid; and with them half the high–born men of Greenland, who had lived for the last month as Eric's guests, that they might be on hand for this occasion. They shoved and jostled each other like schoolboys, as they crowded down to meet the first boat–load.

The ten sailors who stepped ashore were a prosperous looking band. Their arms were full of queer pets; their pouches were stuffed with samples of wood and samples of wheat, and with nuts and with raisins. All were sleek and fat with a year's good living, and all jubilant with happiness and a sense of their own importance. Even while their arms were clasping their sweethearts' necks, they began to hint at their brave adventures and to boast of the grain and the timber and the wine. The home–keepers heard just enough to set their curiosity leaping and dancing with eagerness for more. And each succeeding boat–load of burly heroes worked their enthusiasm to a higher pitch.

Then, gradually, the song ran into a minor key, as Thorir's pitiful crew landed upon the sand. Haggard and worn and almost too weak to walk, they clung to the brawny arms of their rescuers; and the horrors of their privations were written in pitiless letters on Gudrid's fair white face. The rejoicing and laughter sank into wondering questions and pitiful murmuring.

While Thorir told the Red One briefly of their sufferings, the throng listened as to their favorite ballad, and shuddered and suffered with him. Then, in words that still rang with joy and gratitude, Thorir told of their rescue by Leif Ericsson.

Strongly speeding arrows need only aim to make them reach their target. Flights of wildest enthusiasm had been going up on every side. Now Thorir gave these a mark and an aim. Curiosity and triumph, pity and rejoicing, all merged into one great impulse and rose in a passion of hero–worship. Toward the boat that was bringing the Lucky One to land, they turned, face and heart, and laid their homage at his feet. Never had Greenland glaciers heard such a tumult of acclaim as when the throng cheered and stamped and clashed their weapons.

It was a supreme moment. Leif's bronzed face was white, as he stood waiting for the noise to subside that he might answer them. Yet never had his bearing been statelier than when at last he stepped forward and faced them.

"I give you many thanks for your favor, friends," he said, courteously. "It is more than I could have expected, and I give you many thanks for it. But I think it right to remind you that I am not one of those men who trust in their own strength alone. What I have done I have been able to do by the help of my God whom you reject. To Him I give the thanks and the glory."

In that humility which is higher than pride, he raised the silver crucifix from his breast and bent his head before it. Out of the hush that followed, a man's voice rang strongly,—the voice of one of Greenland's foremost chiefs.

"Hail to the God. of Leif Ericsson! The God that helped him must be all–powerful. Henceforth I will believe that He and no one else is the only God. Hail to the Cross!"

Before he had finished, another voice had taken up the cry—and another—and another; until there were not ten men who were not shouting it over and over, in a delirium of excitement. Eric turned his face away and made over his breast the hammer sign of Thor, but there was only pride in his look when he turned back.

Leif stood motionless amid the tumult; looking upward with that strange absent look, as though his eyes would pierce the clouds that veiled Valhalla's walls and search for one beloved face among the warriors upon the benches.

Under his breath he said to his English squire, "I pray God that Olaf Trygvasson hears this now, and knows that I have been as faithful to him in his death as I was in his life."

He did not feel it when Alwin bent and touched the scarlet cloak–hem with his lips, nor did he hear the fervent murmur, "So faithful will I be to you hereafter."

THE END

9 781419 185168